THE BLESSING OF BURNTISLAND

THE BLESSING OF BURNTISLAND

Jenny Stanton

KARNAC

First published in 2011 by
Karnac Books Ltd
118 Finchley Road
London NW3 5HT

Copyright © 2011 by Jenny Stanton

Cover illustration: painting by M. K. Čiurlionis, *Jūros Sonata* (Sonata of the Sea) (Andante, 1908), by permission of The M. K. Čiurlionis National Museum of Art, Kaunas, Lithuania. Photographed by Arūnas Baltėnas.

The lines from "Diving into the Wreck". Copyright © 2002 by Adrienne Rich. Copyright © 1973 by W. W. Norton & Company, Inc., from *The Fact of a Doorframe: Selected Poems 1950–2001* by Adrienne Rich. Used by permission of the author and W. W. Norton & Company, Inc.

The right of Jenny Stanton to be identified as the author of this work has been asserted in accordance with §§ 77 and 78 of the Copyright Design and Patents Act 1988.

All rights reserved. No part of this publication may be reproduced, stored in a retrieval system, or transmitted, in any form or by any means, electronic, mechanical, photocopying, recording, or otherwise, without the prior written permission of the publisher.

British Library Cataloguing in Publication Data

A C.I.P. for this book is available from the British Library

ISBN-13: 978-1-85575-732-5

Typeset by Vikatan Publishing Solutions (P) Ltd., Chennai, India

Printed in Great Britain

www.karnacbooks.com

To Katy and Rebecca Beinart
artists and daughters

AUTHOR'S NOTE

This story grew from a news cutting about a dowser working with wreck seekers and naval archaeologists to locate *The Blessing of Burntisland*, but all the characters and events in this novel are products of the author's imagination, as can be guessed from Joe Fairlie's visions of the two seventeenth-century survivors. Passages in the past use occasional unfamiliar words, such as "chimestrie" (a forerunner of our "chemistry"), where these help to convey a slightly different usage; in the manuscript sections, a far freer spelling is allowed, as there was no standardized spelling at that time.

For reading and offering feedback on various drafts, I am indebted to Anne Church Bigelow, John Marzillier, Katy Darby, Tony Richardson, Peter and Lesley Adamson, Julie Greenwood, Fiona Richardson, and Gabrielle Townsend. I am grateful to Michael Pushkin for notes on the view of Burntisland from the train; to Ben Hebbert of the Bate Collection of musical instruments in Oxford for information on early modern trumpets; and to the Jupiter Trust for a dowsing expedition to the Rollright Stones which gave me a flavour of what I was writing about. Thanks to Maggie Pelling for guidance about Munk's Roll and fevers—but all errors and inventions relating to the history of medicine, as with the rest, are my own work.

For further information about dowsing in the UK, visit www.britishdowsers.org.

Readers interested in the Digger movement are strongly recommended to seek out Gerrard Winstanley's writings, which inspired Thomas Newbolt in this story. For Thomas's partner Susan's involvement in the women's march to Parliament, complete with sea-green ribbons, I'm indebted to H. N. Brailsford, *The Levellers and the English Revolution* (first published 1961, ed. Christopher Hill, Spokesman, Nottingham, 1983, pp. 316–317).

The M. K. Čiurlionis National Museum of Art, Kaunas, Lithuania, kindly provided a reproduction of the painting by M. K. Čiurlionis, *Jūros Sonata* (Sonata of the Sea) (Andante, 1908), photographed by Arūnas Baltėnas, for the front cover. I am grateful to Adrienne Rich and to W. W. Norton of New York for permission to reproduce the five lines from "Diving into the Wreck" which appear at the beginning of this book.

I'd like to thank Oliver Rathbone at Karnac Books for opening an opportunity for works of fiction, among Karnac's mainly non-fiction list on psychology—in this case not entirely unrelated, as Joe, my fictional dowser, might say.

I came to explore the wreck.
The words are purposes.
The words are maps.
I came to see the damage that was done
and the treasures that prevail.

> —"Diving into the Wreck" by Adrienne Rich

CHAPTER ONE

As the launch puttered and bobbed across the open waters of the Firth of Forth, I focused my inner eye on my mental image of the wreck. There was *The Blessing of Burntisland* herself, a barge like a small sailing ship; there were King Charles's tapestries, silver plate, and paraphernalia; and there was the small matter of thirty unlucky crew and servants who had gone down with the boat. Only two survivors, identities unknown; perhaps surprising that there were any. No life-jackets in those days. Along with the half-dozen salvage crew, I was kitted out with a bulgy yellow number that I found very reassuring.

If I felt a twinge of unease, I pushed it to one side. Concentration was crucial.

My outer eyes were fixed on my pendulum, a honey-glazed ceramic bead the size of a large cherry, dangling from my fingers on a piece of nylon twine. Perched on the bench near the stern, I had developed a sitting sea-jig, my body moving with the boat, my arm and hand increasingly steady. My knuckles were raw from the sea breeze blowing up the firth from the east, but I scarcely noticed the cold.

The moment came: my bead was no longer swaying with the boat's motion, but starting to circle. My hair, buffeted across my forehead, stung my eyes. Waves slapped the launch. I leaned forward, holding the string, the backdrop to the bead veering from grey-green choppy water, to varnished rail, to cream-painted bulwark. The bead's circling, small and tentative at first, grew into a definite orbit. To me, that dance of recognition is always a dance of delight, like opening your hands and releasing a moth that spirals round rather than flying off. The men gathered near me to witness it, apart from one who had taken over the helm and was busy keeping the launch in one place.

"She's right here, under this spot," I yelled into the wind.

It was not such a great revelation. I had been through the whole process before, on paper. My bread-and-butter skill is treasure dowsing on whatever site I'm called to, using my rods and pendulum, but my special skill is map dowsing, which I do in the privacy of my own room—in this case, a boarding-house room, for they had insisted I come up to Edinburgh to consult. I'd given Healey and McKee the co-ordinates and suggested that would be the end of my role, but they insisted I should confirm my finding with on-the-spot dowsing this time. Fair enough; my first offering had been a dud, too far off the presumed route of *The Blessing of Burntisland*. I had been reluctant to join them out on the firth, because dowsing on water is always a tricky business. Worse than that, I objected to the smack of mascot or hired performer. But they were paying well, and they needed my definite confirmation.

McKee was broaching a bottle of single malt to celebrate. Bit premature, before the dive and further checks, but I wasn't going to quibble. The circling of my pendulum was proof enough for me—and for them—that we had indeed found the wreck. For a brief moment, I shared the elation of the wreck seekers.

Before I could stow my pendulum and reach out for my share of whisky, everything suddenly dimmed. My head felt squeezed, and there was an intolerable pressure behind my eyes. And then, it was momentarily as though I were under the waves, another person, in another time.

Wrap your legs around my waist, boy. I have to think the instruction and hope you hear me without speech. Your arms around my neck do not feel security enough for your salvation, as I struggle to beat upwards in this evil element.

Strange, that sliver of shining stuff that slices gently towards us. It cannot be—yes, as it touches your outstretched foot and glances off, in another downward slide, I sense it is indeed one of the great salvers. How it remained above us whilst all else was carried below I cannot tell. Unless one of the chests lingered awhile then burst open. As mine will surely do, any moment.

"Here, you've dropped it," said McKee, bending down to reclaim my pendulum from the deck. His face darkened and I could feel him thinking, "Ill omen." He handed me my tot in a small steel beaker. "Get that down your neck, Fairlie," he insisted. "You look like you could do wi' it. Sea's getting to you now, eh?"

I nodded, dumb, pocketed the pendulum and knocked back the whisky.

It was not seasickness. It was another, stranger queasiness. There was no temptation to tell my companions what had just happened. It had felt as though I were in the freezing water, desperately struggling to hold my breath. Yet, it was not I myself down there.

The others were whooping with excitement, making reckless predictions of how the world's socks would be knocked off when the wreck was raised. I shook my head, which reacted with a jarring pain as if it would crack in two.

"Don't be so sure," I said.

They turned and stared at me as one man, swaying and open-mouthed.

"You said this was the spot," growled Healey, who was usually most amicable. He sounded like an Alsatian whose bone you had tried to grab.

"It is, I'm sure of that. But there's no guarantee the wreck can be raised. And maybe she's best left in peace. You know—ghosts and curses of the long dead."

What I had just experienced might have been a strange fit, but the shock felt so real I could not ignore it. If it meant anything at all, it must be a warning, since it left me with such an overpowering sense of dread.

Momentarily, as I woke in the dark of the night in my narrow Edinburgh guest-house bed, I sensed that elation of the find, which is more appropriate to my land work, where the treasure is quickly exhumed to confirm my dowsing. "The cock-a-hoop feeling," my Dad used to call it, and I'd imagine my older sister Jeannie's green hula-hoop, hanging from a beam in the shed, with a cockerel standing inside it crowing. Within seconds, tonight's cock-a-hoop was knocked off its perch by a scaly monster that landed on my back and dug its talons in and squeezed me till dawn. My guts went into coils, my heart beat fifteen to the dozen, my breath refused to go deeper into my chest than about my collarbones. I christened my tormentor: The Dread.

The long drive home to Bishop's Stortford calmed me down. Things always seemed worse in the night, I told myself; there was nothing to be afraid of. My underwater vision of the two survivors was vivid, but not as real as it felt, and the physical sensations had been a side-effect of seasickness.

Sure enough, everything felt normal at home. I settled back into the humdrum of odd dowsing jobs. I had on my books a woman who had lost track of the mains water stopcock in her front yard—that would take me all of ten minutes, but she lived out at Thaxted, so I'd been putting her off—and a retired vicar who was convinced there was a crosier buried in the crumbling graveyard of the old church where he used to serve, down in Kent. In the weeks before Christmas there tends to be a lull. Between these excitements, I paid visits to my local pub to mull over the world's ills, and sat for soothing hours at the bench in my shed, working on my long-term project.

It seemed that the only aftermath of my expedition to Scotland was the cheque, which arrived a fortnight later, accompanied by a terse note. Healey's writing was incomprehensible, so I took the note down the pub to get it deciphered by Jack, who was helping me celebrate the cheque. Jack is a plasterer by trade, but he has a special interest in handwriting. Not calligraphy. The one where you read people's characters from their writing. Graphology. He told me Bernie Healey was dogged, optimistic, warm-hearted, and had a touch of the visionary about him. I told him he was right, although I had the same characteristics and my writing is a damn sight more legible, and did he mind getting on with the job or my warm-heartedness might evaporate. So he translated:

> Dear Fairlie,
>
> We sent down a diver three days after our outing. Why did you rush off like a blue-arsed fly? You should have been there when the lad touched wood. Payment encl.
>
> Yrs, Bernard Healey.

"What the hell does he mean, 'touched wood', do you suppose?" Jack asked when he'd worked out all of the wording. He'd come straight from work and his hair was soused with pinkish-white powder. It made him look twice his age, till you saw the smoothness of his face. He's actually thirty-seven, five years less than me, but when he's cleaned up people take him for even younger.

Touch wood. The feebleness of our attempts to ward off nemesis. I thought of The Dread, of bad luck conjured by tampering with what's dead and buried beneath the sea and the silt of centuries. With an effort and a swig of bitter, I pushed those thoughts aside. "What he means is, the diver touched a bit of the wreck."

Jack gave a low whistle. "So that means you were proved right? And now they can haul her up and polish up the king's silver. Will they give you a cut?"

"Yes and no. I was right, but it will take months for them to double-check. I told you, Healey's lot are in with the Navy in the search? The Navy got stuck, that's why they called me in. But now the naval archaeologists will want to use all their scientific gear to explore the spot, so as not to rely on the word of a weirdo like me. When they do confirm that the wreck is *The Blessing of Burntisland*, they may have difficulty raising her. And I won't get a cut anyway, this cheque is it. I've told you before, it doesn't work if I dowse for treasure for myself."

"So why were you so chuffed about finding the wreck?"

"The glory."

Whether Jack understood that concept or not, he shut up when I offered to refill his glass.

Healey called me up just a week into the new year.

"Joe," he said, after we'd exchanged good wishes, "you've got to come up to Scotland again."

My stomach clenched. "What's up?"

"We're holding a press conference in Fife. It'd be great to have you there."

I was bemused. "A press conference. What for?"

"To announce we've found *The Blessing of Burntisland*, of course."

"It's as definite as that?"

"I told you in my letter. We sent down a diver."

"Yes, and he found timber. But that doesn't prove the identity of the wreck."

"C'mon Joe, what's this nonsense? You set out to locate her, you've found her, why so sceptical all of a sudden?"

It was a tribute, them wanting me there. Often, customers don't want to know you, once you have found them what they are after.

This was by far the biggest find of my entire life. Yet I declined, as politely as I could. I thought if I stayed at home, I could evade The Dread. Not that it was entirely working, so far. I still awoke, from nightmares in the dark, or in the morning, choking in the grip of a scaly monster, my heart hammering away, and my mouth dry with fear. But it eased off quicker than it had in the Edinburgh guesthouse.

The press conference—which I took no notice of—was on a Friday. Next morning, I was digging my vegetable plot in a nice effortful rhythm, musing on my strange experience over the wreck, when the question occurred: Who was he, the person whose head I seemed to occupy in that vision? A bout of queasiness hit me, making me drop the spade. At the same time, the garden turned misty and the light faded. Part of my mind hoped there was an eclipse starting, which I had failed to hear about because I don't follow the news much. I glanced up towards the sun; it was shrouded by thin cirrus. I gave an involuntary shudder, and then for the second time I was seized.

Through the eye-holes in my leather mask I gaze out above the crowd. The faces seem like wavelets on the sea, and the deep tolling of the bell like the tolling of a ship's bell. I must rally. Now, on the scaffold, beside the block; there is something I have to do presently. The guards escort the King out from the Banqueting Hall where the lords and ladies are gathered, out through the embrasure where they have removed the window, and I am struck by how small he seems. Our eyes meet, though thank God he cannot properly see mine. Only once before have I seen that look in the King's eyes—when was it, and where? He is speaking now but I do not follow his words, which are but a praise of his own righteousness.

The lapping of waves confuses my senses, the platform beneath my feet is the deck of the King's ship, the Dreadnought, *soon after the* Blessing *went down, and I stand shivering with the message I have to bring him.*

With a start, I shake myself into the present. No, it is not yet my turn; the priest hovers close, the final prayer is muttered. A traitor-priest, in Charles's eyes, and I the traitor-physician, did he but know. The executioner at least is no traitor, merely performing his given function. The King kneels. High swings the axe, high in the grey sky. Down with a juicy thud, just such as you hear every day at the butcher's block. Thank God, no need for a second stroke.

It's amazing how much, how fast it flows, as if a mere man contained a river, an ocean of the stuff. Having me check the body for signs that all vital force has left is mere farce, and I perform the task in the most perfunctory fashion. My role would have been larger had the executioner bungled his part. Now the worst: I hold up the gory head by its locks, for the crowd to see. The myriad faces, that seemed a moment ago like the dancing waves, are still. There is an awed hush.

CHAPTER TWO

I did consider consulting a doctor, or even a psychiatrist. But what could I say that would not sound crazy? Perhaps I could have saved others and myself a deal of trouble by seeking a cure at that early stage. But later, there was proof these were not mere brainstorms. So, who knows?

I consulted Emma, instead. It was no good turning to my sister Jeannie, Emma's mum; she was always, unreservedly, on my side, but she called my hunches "superstitious nonsense". I had inherited my dowsing skills from Dad, as well as some of the insight, or second sight, from Gran, but Jeannie had missed out on both, poor thing. Emma, like her mum, lacked the special abilities, but she had more time for my dowsing and other stories. Plus, she had a degree in history of art and worked in the museum services, in London. Because I'd helped out with baby-sitting when she was a toddler, we had a special uncle-niece relationship.

I phoned Emma the day after my vision of the execution. Early, before she went out to play squash. Where she lives, there are no decent places to go for walks, so she has to throw herself about indoors to keep fit.

"Hello darling, how are you?"

"I'm good, Uncle Joe. Yourself?"

"Funny you should ask. You know that wreck I found, they announced it to the press on Friday."

"That's great, isn't it? Sorry I didn't get the paper."

"Don't worry, it'll only be a small item at the moment, till it's raised. Trouble is, I've got a strong hunch it shouldn't be."

Emma had grown up with my stories. She knew that my hunches generally turned out to be right. Like the time Mrs O'Leary didn't come out of her house all day, nothing at all unusual about that—she was a recluse—but I went and knocked on her door and when there was no reply, I rang the social services. They fetched the police and sure enough she was dead. Well, not much help to her, but if I hadn't been on the case she might have lain there for days or weeks, and the relatives would have felt awful. Or when the Robertsons lost their dog, a big black retriever, and I told them to look in Gordon Higgs's shed on the allotments. It wasn't Gordon's fault, he hadn't even been up there. The dog had knocked the door shut with that great wagging tail, but nobody would believe me if I told them that. How could I know? Just a hunch.

Emma asked what was up. I didn't want to tell anyone, even her, about my strange visions. "I've a real bad feeling about *The Blessing of Burntisland*, some vibes I picked up when we were out in the Firth of Forth. Reckon someone could get hurt. I thought you might have an idea how to ask the authorities to reconsider the salvage."

"Reconsider?"

"I mean, not go ahead with raising the wreck. Let sleeping dogs lie."

"But—I mean, I thought they still had to authenticate it."

"I don't think that will be a problem. The thing is, once they've done that, there'll be no holding back. We need to put the brakes on right now. At least till I can get my head round what actually is wrong."

"What sort of thing do you think it is, Uncle Joe?" She sounded intrigued, not worried.

"That's the trouble, it's not exact, just a really strong gut feeling about something horrible happening. I need more time, like I say." The word suddenly came to me. "A moratorium."

"I don't actually deal with that side of things in my job. Let me have a think and get back to you."

She called me later that same day, saying the exercise had loosened up her brain muscles. That expression was a hangover from her childhood days when she used to make us laugh with her sayings. "I know who you should talk to. My friend Alison. Do you remember, I told you about the older student who got into the Department of the Environment?"

"No."

"Come on, Joe, I'm sure I told you—she was fast-tracked and she's three grades above me."

Those grades mean nothing to me, but I could well appreciate it was a piece of luck, Emma knowing someone in the right line of work. They make all sorts of contacts at university. Must be half the reason for going.

There was no end of fuss to get in to see Alison, despite my letter of appointment that had taken the best part of a fortnight to arrange. It was little consolation to know they did this to all visitors, all the more since the various London bombings. Everything short of fingerprinting. I'd dressed respectably and trimmed and combed my beard, but the security guard made me feel like a criminal suspect. Eventually he passed me on to a man with a withered arm, seated behind an enormous bare desk, who painstakingly issued me with a pass valid for all of two hours. A lift lined with mirrors like a conjurer's device whisked me up to a sterile corridor, and a moment later I was in a small, airless office across the desk from Alison James.

I never like offices, and this one was making my chest feel uncomfortable. To distract myself I observed Alison while she introduced herself. Light brown hair on the verge of escaping from its neatly cut bob and making a halo. A fullish figure, in a silky abstract-patterned blouse, soft grey matching her eyes. There was a tilt to the corners of those eyes, and a glint to them. She struck me as someone pretending to be very controlled and a bit boring, but actually quick to anger and quick to laughter. Age uncertain, probably mid-thirties. When she went to fetch me coffee, her tailored dark grey skirt emphasized her slim waist and broad hips, the hem swinging as she moved like a dancer in disguise. She spoke with the gravelly texture of an ex-smoker, and a slight London accent I could not pinpoint. Me, I carry the stamp of the Fens around in my voice.

"You're older than I expected," was her unflattering opening move, as she set the mug in front of me and sat down.

I forgot my carefully prepared statement. "Why, what did Emma say?"

"One night we were all telling our first memories, and hers was Uncle Joe with seaweed on his head. Somehow I had you down as a bit of a lad."

I laughed. "I was a lad back then. It was about twenty-five years ago, she was two or three and she got these phobias. We were on holiday at Great Yarmouth. She refused point blank to put her feet on the beach because of the seaweed. A whole lot had been washed up in a storm. I can tell you Jeannie—that's my sister—was getting exhausted from carrying her around the whole time. So I piled some seaweed on my head and pulled funny faces, and for some reason that cured her."

Alison allowed a small smile, then looked at me appraisingly, her grey eyes steady. "You came about this wreck." A file lay open on her desk, next to a flatscreen computer. I could not see the display, but presumed it was about the search.

I told her that raising *The Blessing of Burntisland* was a risky business, not for the usual technical reasons only, but also something disturbing I had picked up at the site. If it were within the powers of her department to do so, it would be as well to delay the procedure.

She glanced down at the file.

"The only trouble I can foresee is some argument over whether to show the treasure here or in Scotland. A bit like the argument over keeping the Staffordshire Hoard in the Midlands, but this still has to be unearthed." She paused, probably realizing "unearthed" was the wrong term for underwater treasure. "As you know, the wreck's under a protection order from the Scottish Office. There's been excitement about it in this department, too. The archaeologists say they'll learn a great deal, and the public will be thrilled to see King Charles's treasure. It will be the biggest royal find since King Tutankhamen."

Foolishly, I took up that last remark. "Remember the curse of Tutankhamen. Didn't Lord Carnarvon die straight after opening his tomb?"

If you could shrink two sizes from someone's look, Alison's look would have done that to me. "I doubt if modern archaeologists are going to be swayed by superstition. Excuse me, I realize you use unconventional methods, but you do rely on more than a hunch don't you, when you're divining. Is that the right term?"

"It'll do."

"Emma asked me to see you because she thought you'd come up with something important. I wondered if you'd decided the location wasn't quite where you'd indicated. It says here you did have another set of co-ordinates originally." Her forehead furrowed as she gazed at the screen. "Before you went out? I don't understand."

I really did not want to explain to her about map dowsing. The wreck seekers had accepted it, but the Navy people were sceptical, to say the least. It was funny who did and did not want that part of me. Best leave it alone for the time being.

"Yes, a preliminary estimate, but that was quickly corrected. Then they took me out over the site. I know when my instruments respond, as well as the Navy does." She blinked at that. "And now they've actually seen her timbers. But *The Blessing of Burntisland* does not want to be disturbed, I know it. There is something wrong. I felt it in my bones as soon as we confirmed the site."

I spoke with heat, thinking of The Dread, thinking of the awful visions. Perhaps it was my desperation, knowing that I had no logical means of convincing her, that made her take notice. Somewhat to my surprise, she agreed to meet me again, in a pub this time thank heavens. I would have a few days to come up with something more than a hunch to persuade her, buy a little more time, and try to hold up the permit for the excavation.

I went down in the mirrored lift and saw about sixty-four of myself, repeated smaller and smaller into the corners until they all but disappeared. Each one dour-faced and lumpy. My beard had gone disordered again. Put me in a navy jersey instead of this shapeless grey jacket and I'd pass for a sea-dog.

I should not have thought of the sea. It brought to mind that last vision, and the man's memory of being on the *Dreadnought* shortly after the wreck. Before I could tell myself not to wonder what was happening there, I was gone.

The King appears to be gazing past me, across the waves that dance so innocently, compared to their monstrous regiments during the fateful storm. I notice his nose is a little red, but his eyes are not watering. Still, there is a terrible look in those brown eyes as he focuses on me.

"Yes, Dr Newbolt? What news of Robbie?"

None of the poor devils could swim. Thirty lost their lives. Naturally everyone believes the King is distraught about the treasure, and he is so, but he cares somewhat for the hapless creatures that went down with it. And he cares more than a little for Robbie, or at least for his flashes of insight that illumine the King's dark moods. He has had strong belief in his powers, ever since the day he touched the lad after he came out of a fit, and a boil on the regal jaw disappeared within the hour.

If I had not been on the barge, Robbie would have drowned with the men. He could swim no more than could many of his station. Yet I can expect no thanks from the King for saving him.

"The fever has returned, sire. I tend him as best I may." That was not what I came to tell him. Robbie is urgent that I convey the words that he spoke on the heath that day. "Sire, there is a warning, the boy says. This disaster makes the first part of it."

"If this be the first, we have no desire to hear the rest." With a small gesture of his fingers he dismisses me.

Unwise, to refuse my counsel. Almost it seems he blames me for the near-drowning of his wonderful boy. As if I had not pleaded for us to travel closer to the King. Rather he should blame Soames and Cawley who poisoned his ears against us.

Haltingly and in reverse, I descend the steep stairs to the lower deck where the child lies, the magical boy whose secrets I have been instructed to study. That was why I travelled with Robbie—that, and his fits, which have to be treated lest he succumb like his mother before him. I could have asked the King: whose fault was it that we voyaged on the barge with the common men, despite the boy's forebodings and my most earnest entreaties? He has been consistent in this, his refusal to pay heed to me. Being monarch, he must be right, always.

I shook myself as I came to, leaning against one of the mirrors. There was a sense of urgency in this vision, connected with the boy, but I could not focus on it. At least the identities were clearer now: the man and boy in my first vision were the two who survived the wreck; they must have been picked up by the king's boat. The man was a doctor, "Dr Newbolt", guarding the "magical boy" Robbie. The same doctor who much later found himself at the king's execution. I emerged blinking into the foyer, one hand to my aching head. The security guard asked if I was okay and I nodded, hurrying out into the street, my mouth dry with fear.

My footsteps took me towards the river. On the approach to the Embankment I found myself muttering, as I always did near the river in London, a snatch of Blake:

> I wander through each chartered street
> Near where the chartered Thames does flow
> And mark in every face I meet
> Marks of weakness, marks of woe.

Today the weakness and woe were mine, all mine.

I burrowed into the streets and alleys down near the river, until I found a café that was uncrowded. It was called Kofer's. The waiter told me the owner was from the Lebanon. "Like me, my name is Abed, born in Lebanon, but my father born in Egypt." He wiped the table a second time, and added, "My father professor of ancient languages." I nodded as though this information was exactly what I needed, and sipped at the surprisingly decent, bitter black coffee he had brought me. People who had higher hopes of life, like this young man, maybe want to tell sympathetic types they were not meant to be stuck in menial jobs.

Was I a sympathetic type? Mostly, at that moment, I was deeply shaken.

It was not that the waking dream had been particularly fearsome in itself, this time. It was the realization that these seizures could spring upon me at any moment. I had slumped in the lift. Presumably, if it had carried on much longer I could have collapsed, and then they would have fetched an ambulance and I'd have ended up in hospital. Dreadful to be trapped in hospital. Like in prison. Like Todd.

Gran had asked me round, a command rather than an invitation. This was doubly unusual at the weekend when she would assume I wanted to be with Marjory. Not that Marjory wanted to spend her time with me so much, those days.

"Todd's not come home last night."

"What's unusual in that? He's a young man."

My cousin was the tearaway of the family, outstripping me in the reckless speed with which he ripped apart the local lanes, even in my heyday. The day I met Marjory, a crowd of us eyeing up the talent on the beach at Great Yarmouth, I thought his James Dean image would attract her—not that either Todd or Marjory knew who James Dean was. I could hardly believe my luck when this cheeky, sleek creature with improbable sunstreaks in her hair singled me out. My 250 cc Honda was not usually any competition for Todd's 750 cc Norton. Lying on my jacket behind a rock, Marjory stripped down to her bikini, then ordered me to rub oil on her belly. It was a taut belly with hollows near the hips. The bikini slipped off ever so easily.

Great having her snuggled up behind me on my bike, her arms tight around my middle as we roared into the dusk. What she introduced me to, lying on the beach, we repeated astride my bike, parked not very far into the woods. As I was to learn, Marjory was always more turned on that way. Riding the beast, she called it.

Marjory had chosen me over Todd Vartin because my face had been in the papers for locating the kidnapped girl. I was briefly famous all over East Anglia, and Marjory could boast to her girlfriends about catching me. Fifteen minutes of fame—trouble was, it never lasted. Six years of marriage had dulled her appetite for me. Our outings on my bike were less and less frequent. Marjory had taken to suggesting I should get a proper job. No matter that she earned less as a travel agent's receptionist than I did with my dowsing and carpentry and oddments. Her job was proper.

"I have a bad feeling," Gran said. She had lost her second sight when Dad disappeared, but she occasionally felt the ghost of it. Like amputees with their phantom limbs. Just as painful, to judge by the way she screwed up her face.

"Todd's fine, Gran," I said, and went to make a pot of tea in her antique scullery. Her tiny house—two up, two down—had not seen the impact of the seventies or eighties, let alone the nineties.

When I returned to the parlour, she was replacing her clunky phone in its cradle. I hadn't heard it through the kettle's whistling.

"That was your Auntie May. Todd's been let out. The police had him in overnight. There's been an accident. He isn't hurt bad. The other fellow—if he dies, Todd will be up for manslaughter."

The fellow did die. For Marjory, our family's disgrace meant it was time to move on.

CHAPTER THREE

As I approached the King's Arms through the darkening crowded street, I thanked goodness it wasn't the King's Head. My sleep had recently been troubled by glimpses of the execution, alternating with the suffocating experience of struggling under water. The most recent vision, in that glassy lift, had told me that the person through whose eyes I saw these wretched snippets of the past was Dr Newbolt. In some sleeping dreams (as opposed to those accursed waking dreams), I was wrestling with him, trying to see the "magical boy" Robbie. In others, as the silver plate slipped through the water, a severed head slid off, trailing a cloud of blood. Each time I awoke with The Dread on me, I became more determined to keep *The Blessing of Burntisland* where she was.

My plan for the evening's encounter was not well-formulated, despite hours lying awake wondering what to say. If Alison seemed receptive, I would be as open with her as possible, even risking a hint about my visions or waking dreams. If not, I might resort to making up a scare story about the human remains—an unknown plague—or simply point out that a sunken boat full of bodies was a burial site, not lightly to be disturbed.

I ducked into the bar. Alison was there before me, settled in a corner seat, nursing a cup of coffee and reading a paper. The trio of artificial candles on a sconce above her head imparted a red-gold glow to her hair. I bought a pint and joined her.

"What exactly are you worried about? Is it that curse of Tutankhamen thing?" Alison's voice sounded different from when I'd met her at work, huskier.

"No, it's bigger. What happened before. War, turmoil." I surprised myself with this; it bubbled up from my subconscious.

"What do you mean, happened before?"

She might well look puzzled.

"What if losing the treasure in that wreck was an omen? Maybe it led indirectly to the Civil War, and to King Charles losing his head."

Even as I spoke, I had a momentary vision of one of the silver platters sinking towards the bottom of the sea, swinging back and forth as it went down. Myself, with the boy clinging on to me, pushing with all my might towards the surface. I grasped the edge of the table as the pub rippled slightly around me. I must block out those thoughts.

Alison was speaking: "... though of course I don't agree with capital punishment. But the divine right of kings, honestly! I'd have been a Parliamentarian, you know." With an effort I focused on her. She looked quite fine and glowing, and I could picture her on a horse taking a swipe at the opposition.

"Well, I'd have been a Royalist, so there you are," I replied, making myself part of the opposition. Not for the first time, I wondered what Dr Newbolt thought of the execution. He was clearly in the king's service at the time of the wreck, and yet he was assistant executioner sixteen years later. I took a deep draught of my London Pride, then regretted it, as the beer rushed to my head, and I felt myself slipping.

The captain leads me away down the back corridors as though I were the criminal, as indeed I am in the eyes of many of the crowd. I still shake, and not only from the sight of the gory head. Yes, for my own safety I must be smuggled out. Out of London altogether, anywhere that will take a fugitive stained with unnameable blood.

Not only for my own sake, I do not like this business. The man had not committed murder, not directly at any rate. He was wilful, misguided, but I believe he was sincere. In my view his death is wrong, but expedient. To allow him to live would be to allow the royalist parties to rally their forces, and sooner or later they would stage a counter-revolution.

It ill behoves me to argue thus; with whom am I to discourse on the matter? None must know, if I value my life.

Who would care in any sort whether my life is preserved or not? Yet perhaps there is one. The last I heard of Susan, she was taken with one of our more earthly sects. By their nature, they are well hidden.

I think I know where I shall go.

Alison was regarding me quizzically with her tilty eyes narrowed. I found I was clutching my pint mug to my chest. Perhaps, despite my beard, she could make out that my jaws were clenched. I took a few deep breaths.

"Are you okay, Joe?"

"Sorry, I had one of those headache spasms, you know. What were you saying?" The pain was more than a spasm, it was pressing behind my eyes and I had trouble concentrating as Alison continued. That vision had answered my internal question about Newbolt's views. I made a mental note to jot it down when I had the opportunity.

I had evidently missed a few sentences. "So, as Emma probably told you, I took advantage of Geoff's earning power to get my degree, a bit later than usual."

"Geoff's your husband?"

"Was. Is. Was."

"Sorry, Emma didn't mention …"

"Oh, don't worry, I don't care who knows. Seduced by some high-flier in loss adjustment. He's an accountant," she added, as if that explained everything.

"My brother-in-law, Norman, is an accountant. In a bank."

"Different sort. Geoff works in the City. Who's Norman—wife's brother?"

"No, no, sister's husband. Emma's father." What was this, an anthropology class? To reciprocate her confession, I added, "I used to be married, but it ended in tears."

"You left?"

"She left me. For a wanker with a bigger wallet."

"Are you still sore?"

"Oh no, it was years ago."

Alison leaned forward. I could see the beginnings of her cleavage down her blouse. Just as I was tensing up, expecting more probing about my marriage or revelations about hers, she asked about my trade. Did I always use a dowsing rod and pendulum for finding treasure; how do they work; can anyone do it? Not that she wanted to try it herself, just wondered. Before my involvement in *The Blessing of Burntisland*, she had thought dowsers only sought water beneath the earth.

This felt safer than talking about our marriages.

"I use the rods and pendulum for treasure, yes. But I could use them for water. My rods are metal, a compound that is a family secret. You've heard of dowsers seeking water with hazel rods?"

"Yes, forked ones."

"With them, you hold the two prongs of the fork and the main stalk gives a vibration when you're near water, then it twists strongly, up or down. With the rods—they're L-shaped, and you can use one or two—they swivel inwards as you approach the object. If you're using two, the tips cross over. In my case, when I'm right above water, I can feel a kind of thrum, hard to describe but when you've done it you know the exact feeling."

"You practise water divining as well, then?"

She'd used the word "divining" for dowsing before. It echoed in my head with "divine right of kings". That was Charles I's claim; seemed quaint now.

"I've done water, yes, only as a sideline. Where I came from, near Ely, there wasn't much call for that sort of thing—enough water and to spare. I reckon way back my ancestors were ordinary water dowsers, then they moved to the Fens for some reason—a marriage most likely—and they had to develop other skills. My father taught me the trade, he used the same tools I have now. Have you seen the Ixworth Cross?"

"Yes, of course, in the Ashmolean in Oxford. You've been there?"

"Didn't need to. Saw it just after they unearthed it. My dad helped, not officially mind you, but he was in on the find." I remembered him pointing out to me the exquisite cut of the garnets set in gold, fitting the flared arms of the cross, the curved ends.

"Your dad? He must be quite a pro."

"He was. Not been around for thirty years." This certainly wasn't the time to talk about all that. I hurried on: "Of course in my father's time they didn't have metal-detectors as rivals. Rather successful rivals, at times, I have to admit." I smiled ruefully, thinking of the riches of the Staffordshire find, stuff like the Ixworth Cross by the bucketful. "But we can still go deeper, find things they'd never trace. Not only metal either."

I explained that some dowsers have a theory about energy waves given off by water, by ancient stones, or by buried treasure, that the instruments pick up. There has to be an interaction between the instruments and the person holding them, that much is clear, because not everyone can do it. Since it's been handed down the generations in my family, I tend to think it runs in families. Not everyone holds with that. One of my friends up in Cumbria runs classes in dowsing, in between ones in dry-stone walling. I can't believe there's a call for either but he assures me he has plenty of custom.

"What sort of energy waves?" prompted Alison.

"Oh, this isn't regular physics. I don't know how much it's been investigated by the scientists, although they can't be entirely sceptical or they wouldn't have come looking for me would they?" I remembered entertaining those two from the university in my living room, for I would not step onto their territory, when they contacted me about *The Blessing of Burntisland*. I had imagined they would turn up in white coats. In the event, they were wearing ordinary clothes, not especially smart. They had notebooks, like reporters.

"So do they have a theory about how it works?"

"No more than we dowsers do ourselves, is my impression." Her face fell and I continued, "I'll tell you what I think. There's an axis: the target, the seeker, and the instrument between. Look, can I have that?" I leaned over, and took her spoon to represent the rod. She had a musky smell, overlaid with lemon. I slipped the saucer out from under her coffee cup, and set it down to represent the target, with my beer mug as the seeker. "Now anyone can hold that rod, or pendulum or twig, but it only responds if the seeker, the dowser, has some sort of charge that corresponds to the energies given off by the thing he's seeking."

Using the bottom of the beer mug, I pushed down on the bowl of the spoon, then released it so the other end clattered on the edge of the saucer.

Alison frowned slightly. "Would you say that your instruments are like lightning conductors, transmitting the energies—the charge, or whatever—between you and the target?"

A neat formulation. I considered it for a moment. "Yes and no. It's not sudden like lightning, and you don't feel a discharge so much as a connection. And with me, it doesn't always need the rod. Emma told you about Mrs O'Leary and all that?"

"Sort of second sight?"

That was my opening. Now or never, Joe, I told myself.

I took a deep breath, and said: "This is going to sound crazy, but the real reason I'm worried about the wreck is because I've got sort of entangled with one of the survivors."

That certainly grabbed her full attention. She reared back, and I thought I'd lost her sympathy.

"What do you mean, one of the survivors? It was three or four hundred years ago."

"Yes, a doctor from the seventeenth century. Name of Newbolt."

I briefly recounted my waking dreams—using that expression rather than "visions" to make them sound less crazy.

"They feel to me like a terrible warning. But I dare say you think I'm cracked?" I ended.

"I knew someone, once ..." Alison gazed past me, her eyes distant and troubled. I nodded, to prompt her to continue. "A boyfriend. He was into witchcraft. White magic, nothing harmful. He—well, there was a group of them—used to dance around stone circles when the moon was full."

"Sounds loony," I said, not sure if that was a pun. For a second, I wondered if they danced naked. "Did you join in?"

"Only once, just out of curiosity. Anyway, the point is, he used to claim he saw things, visions. He was in touch with a master from the past. What was his name?"

"You think I'm making up my visions, like him?"

"Marazion. That was it. I played along because I was a bit hooked on him. Then I found out the name was a village in Cornwall—honestly, you'd think he could have come up with something more original."

"What did you do?"

"Left him. Met Geoff and got married. End of my flirtation with the supernatural."

"So you're saying—you've been here before, and it's a fraud?"

She looked at me then, looked me level in the eyes. "On the contrary. Your account is more plausible. No drugs, no magic, just the odd seizure in the pub."

So the last fit had been that obvious. Embarrassment heated my face.

"Maybe I should be getting home."

"Joe, don't be so touchy. Just let me ask the obvious question, and don't be offended. Could these contacts with the past be wishful thinking, an elaboration of what you've heard about *The Blessing of Burntisland* and maybe bits you've read?"

I shuddered. "You wouldn't call it wishful thinking if you had one. They're awful. If only I could show you. I seem to come in at the worst moments of his life."

"Yes?" She was willing me to say more.

"This doctor—Newbolt—he thinks in a completely different way from me. Not only the doctoring business, or the time he's living in, though God knows those are foreign enough to me. But I am sure he knows things I don't. I couldn't have dreamed him up."

"But he was definitely one of the survivors?"

"No, they don't have the survivors' names."

"Well, there's an easy enough way to check if such a person really existed, though not whether he was on the boat."

It was my turn to be surprised. "How?"

"Look him up in the registers at the Royal College of Physicians."

"You think they have records going that far back?"

"Certainly. Especially if he was physician to the king, he'll be there. Tell you what, I can see this isn't your cup of tea, I'll do it myself, in my lunch hour. It'll be a bit of light distraction."

I was so obsessed with my own fears, with The Dread, that it was only when the train was clanking into Bishop's Stortford with a grinding of brakes that it struck me what Alison wanted distraction from. The break-up of her marriage, of course. Amazing that I had forgotten that pain.

Marjory left me one fine May afternoon. She came home from work, I offered her a bunch of garden flowers to perk her up, mostly marguerites, and she yelled at me for not buying her proper flowers from the florist's shop, like Marvin gave Janie. I threw the flowers at her. "You should have taken them out the vase first," Marvin told me later. Of course they weren't in a vase, but that burst of temper from me was her pretext to walk out. It took a few days of enquiries to learn that Marjory had gone off with a customer who took a fancy to her while he was booking a holiday in Tenerife. It must have been going on for a while.

Racked with jealousy, I took to spying on her coming out of work, till I found out where he lived—where my wife now lived with him. One evening, when they drove out into the country, I tailed them on my motorbike. That was foolish. I was out of practice, and came off on a sharp bend. Lucky to get away with a gash to my chin; the bike was in much worse shape. They never even came back to see whether I was dead or alive. I grew a beard to cover the scar, and sold the bike for scrap.

That summer, I formed a habit of hauling my sleepless carcass out of bed as the dawn was on its way, and walking for an hour or two or three, as long as it might take for physical tiredness to quell my racing mind. I'd walk out of town along the Royston road, till semis gave way to bungalows then mere hedgerows as the land began to rise, and I'd turn across the fields of young barley or wheat, or the rape not yet showing its shrill yellow in the grey dawn. Always at some point I would pull a switch from a likely bush, to lash at the long grass in the meadows or the sprouting corn. The dawn chorus, which I detested now that its liquid sweetness seemed a mockery, would break down into inane chirruping as the sun rose—not that I cared whether it rose or not, that summer. As the last tufts of mist slunk away into the hedgerows, I'd return home, my boots soaked with dew, cobwebs and slug-slime on my trouser turn-ups, my eyes red from insomnia and fury, but somewhat soothed. Somewhat soothed.

One suffocating August night, while it was still dark, I walked the other way, into town, across to his district, as if tugged by a string of elastic with one end wound around my guts, the tangle of it growing tighter the closer I reached his complacent little Edwardian terrace. There was no light on in the house; the nearest street lamp was twenty yards away, barely giving enough light to see the cherry tree in the ever-so-tidy front garden. My mind's eye could see clearly, though, the two of them asprawl in his bed, naked, asleep as you only sleep after a good bout of sex. The whole tight tangle rose to my throat, choking me. I may have made a noise then, I don't know.

At that moment, I spotted his car across the road, his smug green Volkswagen Golf (looking grey like everything else), and I wondered if she'd lain across the bonnet like she used to lie across my bike. I ran and jumped onto the bonnet and battered on it, then on the roof, with my booted feet, yelling: "Come out you cowardly runt, come out and fight!"

He didn't come out to face me, the craven bastard, but he wasn't afraid to pick up the phone and drop me in deep shit. All too soon, before I'd more than slightly dented the precious bloody car, a police siren sounded and I was whisked away. Made me cool my heels all day because I was chary about giving them my name and address; told me later I was lucky to get off with being bound over, and prohibited from going within a mile radius of that Sodom and Gomorrah of a house. Who'd want to anyhow? I'd made my protest, just so they didn't think I'd forgotten and forgiven.

I might have carried on with my night walking right through the winter, not much caring if I was frozen through, but I had that order hanging over me and wasn't about to give them any excuse to pick me up again. And then I developed a cough that seemed to wrack the very veins in my legs, it went so deep, so it was all that I could manage to keep going on my daytime jobs. My night-time television watching started about that time, for a funny reason.

I was doing a fence for Mrs Thring in October, and hanging a gate for her and working in the garden. But I refuse to believe it was her suggestion, though the stuck-up cow was forever offering me hot drinks so she could pinion me in her Aga-cosy kitchen and lecture me on how to improve myself.

"Young man," she always used to begin, though she wasn't all that old herself, about forty but well-preserved as the rich tend to be. "Young man, have you ever thought of going to college to do your A levels? Oh, you haven't got enough GCSEs, I see. Well, how about starting with a few more of those, and then a vocational course. Here, do try one of these asparagus puffs, you must build yourself up. Landscape gardening, the coming thing you know, I'm sure you'd have a gift for that, you were quite right about where I should put my azaleas." I mentally told her where she could shove her azaleas. I was always angry in those days, as if the whole world had colluded with Marjory in betraying me.

One evening, as I was knocking off work late, washing my hands in the kitchen sink, she came clopping in to see me off her premises with a few words of wisdom as usual, but this time she was in high-heeled shoes and a short black dress and a daft shawl, all made up, nice pair of legs showing, and her hair done in style instead of its usual dishevelled state. I said "You look nice," before I could help it. The last thing I wanted was to pay a compliment.

She said "Thank you, Joe," with a smile but a bit distant, like she was a film star and I was a fan who might be bothering her for an autograph. Still that was okay, till she spoiled the effect with, "I think you may need to buy another tin of Cuprinol, I really don't think the two will stretch. Could you be a sweetie and pick one up on your way in tomorrow? I shan't mind if you start a little late."

Since I normally started about eight o'clock and the store, as she well knew, didn't open till nine, I'd be losing over an hour of the morning's work—just so she could have a lie-in after her dinner party or wherever she was going. She would never give me a key. I could have let myself in otherwise, round the side of the house; never would have disturbed her. I'd asked her before, more than once, but oh no, she had to check up and give her orders for the day, so I had to knock on the front door every single morning I worked there.

Well, that night I dreamed—it wasn't exactly a dream, more of a fantasy—of Mrs Thring with her legs wrapped round me, her spiky heels high in the air, her little cocktail dress splitting up the seams. I actually felt a bit guilty when she answered the door next morning, still in her dressing gown, holding a mug of steaming hot chocolate. I refused when she offered me some even though it smelt really tempting. I couldn't look her in the eyes.

"Had a good time, last night, then?" I muttered.

"Yes, lovely thank you, how about you?"—as if I'd been to a party too.

"Yes thanks, some very good telly," I answered, hiding behind a cough as the image of her I'd created last night hovered in my mind. I could see the staircase with its salmon pink carpet and brass runners, and felt myself flushing.

"Oh, what do you like watching?"

I guessed she was hung over and making conversation to avoid facing the day.

"Open University." I'd never seen a single programme, but I wanted to shut her up.

"But that's in the middle of the night," she squawked.

"Yep. No problem for me, I'm a night bird," and at that I managed to lift my eyes and look at her. "So you weren't the only one up and about in the wee small hours, Mrs Thring," I said, and I must have looked weird, because she backed off a step or two. She put her cocoa down on the hall-stand, without her usual search for a coaster; her hands were shaking. There was a thick silence, and for half a heartbeat I knew I could reach out and grab those quaking hands, and if one of us dragged the other upstairs it might as easily be her as me. But then it passed.

"I must get dressed," she said. "Nigel wanted me to do some errands this morning. Have you got the wood treatment? Good, I won't hold you up any longer."

That night I really did switch on to the learning channel, something about trilobites. I love fossils, so that was a good start. Usually I could follow, whatever the topic, without too much difficulty—they go out of their way to make it all accessible and interesting. The only really impossible ones to follow without the course book are the languages, but I'd even watch them sometimes just to get away from my own thoughts. Maths too, that was another tricky one. In time my burning brain cooled down and even, after a couple of years, there'd be the odd night when I wouldn't wake up at all: no dawn chorus, no small hours hearing about the export products of Romania or how the violin got its shape.

I became a risky asset on the pub quiz team—once I'd emerged into society again—stuffed with odd bits and pieces of knowledge, able to answer the most unlikely questions one time and totally stuck another. It never joined up, either. I never followed any one course through; I didn't want to give the Things of this world the satisfaction of seeing me acquire any qualifications.

I was cooking my breakfast when the phone rang. The sausages were sizzling under the grill, and I'd just broken two eggs into the frying pan, alongside the partly-cooked mushrooms. With a curse, I ran into the front room and picked up. Once there I was stuck as I hadn't got around to changing to a cordless phone.

"Kevin Dooley of the *Ouse News*." I recognized the title: the local rag for the area I come from. "I understand you're having second thoughts about the treasure you found up in Scotland. We think this will make great copy. Local dowser finds treasure then forecasts disaster. I've got the headline. 'King Charles's treasure: Boon or Doom?' Now I just need you to fill in a few details."

I told him to fill in his own details and returned to my cooking. Had Alison leaked, or Emma? It could have been one of the Scottish crew.

Luckily I had eaten half my breakfast when the phone rang again, otherwise Alison might have caught the sharp edge of my tongue. She seemed very excited. She had found Dr Newbolt's name in *Munk's Roll*, whatever that was—she had to spell it out so I didn't think it was monks as in monasteries—and the dates were right. To her this was evidence that my waking dreams weren't a load of codswallop. To me it was evidence that these records were reliable.

We now had his first name: Thomas.

"But Joe, there's more. It's mysterious. His death date isn't there like it is for all the others. He just disappears from the record."

That shook me a bit. "Does it give the date when he stopped being physician to the king?"

"Yes, he last appears in 1635." Two years after the boat sank.

Apparently he was only a minor figure, and it didn't say where he went after leaving the royal household.

"But he was still alive at Charles's execution," I said. "That was 1649. Does it say when he was born?"

"When do you think?" She was testing me.

"I have a hunch he was in his late twenties when the boat went down, and forty-four or forty-five at the time of the execution—I'd say he was born about 1605."

"Spot on."

"So now you have proof I'm onto something, will you put a stopping order on the raising of the wreck?"

"It's not that simple." Her tone changed. "I'll try speaking to my boss. But like I said, this is a big find. There's potentially some conflict with the Scottish department, of course. If I interfere, there could be more trouble."

"But you'll try?"

"I already am, aren't I?"

I was not sure what she meant, just the *Munk's Roll* business or something else, but sensed there was no point pressing further. I thanked her with real warmth, and returned to my cooling eggs and sausages.

Alison's find gave me a momentary sense of power, as if our identifying Newbolt in the records would free me from the waking dreams and The Dread. Riding the short-lived surge of relief, I tried not to wonder what happened to the doctor after he left the king's service, nor what he was doing on the doomed boat in the first place.

CHAPTER FOUR

In my shed, I selected a piece of birch, set my lathe going—a foot-operated model I'd built myself—and let my chisel bite in, shaping the cylindrical chunk into a white pawn. I'd been manufacturing the chess set intermittently over many years, the most enduring of a series of projects to turn to for solace when I needed to rest my mind. With wood-shavings curling up and back across my hand, I mulled over my conversations with Alison James. Since I'd talked with her in the pub, the nightmares had become less frequent, The Dread easier to dispel. Knowing that Thomas Newbolt was on the historical record did not explain my waking dreams, but it appeared to reassure Alison, and now she seemed more disposed to help me.

I stopped my treadling, and the whirl of the spindle slowed to silence. Among all the details Healey and his crew had provided about the wrecking of *The Blessing of Burntisland*, there had been no information about the survivors. Their names, their identities, had not been recorded. I wanted to know more about that boy. The doctor I could do without. I hated the way I was pulled right inside his mind, aware of his fears, sweating with him on the scaffold, suffocating with him in the deep water. He was arrogant, I could tell that, and worse—a traitor: he'd said so himself. If he'd left the king's service in 1635, it was likely he'd been on the other side in the Civil

War. But I didn't want to think about Newbolt. The lad was another matter; I felt powerfully drawn to him. I started to turn again.

These pieces I was turning, even the pawns, were each individual, that's why it took so long to make them. No two pawns had the same grooves around their neck and base; I made the pattern differ subtly, like bar codes. The pawns were as tall as my middle finger, and the kings and queens twice that height. The board hung on the wall, in a corner to avoid direct sunlight, a polished chequer of the red of yew and white of ash, limed for extra pallor. Between the squares ran fine lines of ebony, and at every intersection I'd inserted a brass pin, and around the edges diamond shapes of mother-of-pearl inlaid in the ebony. Inlays in inlays. Well, that had taken me the best part of four years, on and off; more off than on.

I glanced up to rest my eyes from the close work, gazing out of the shed window at the garden. Damp and cold; hard to believe spring was around the corner. The view before me dissolved.

"Keep your head down," a voice hisses from my right. I think it's Harburton. The men are spread around the arc of the ridge, hidden from the Royalists below as each takes advantage of the slightest dip or cranny in the heath. Obediently, I pull my head down. I've seen what I want: John Lambert's standard over to the right, below us, emerging from the wood. With Lambert leading, and the element of surprise, and the pincer movement, we may prevail against the more numerous enemy in the mead across the stream.

I wish I could say "God willing" but my faith went the way of my loyalty to the King. I'm not a fanatic like the men I fight with, and that makes it the harder for me. The waiting is the worst. I know when it starts I will find the courage, and when it's over I will be—if I still live—called on to ply my other trade. I'll be among the last to leave the field. Unless we're defeated—but better not think on that. If that happens I will not be among the prisoners, I have precautions about my person.

The fan-like disposition of our men across the moor is just such as I recall near Otterburn, that day I accompanied the King on a deer hunt. He had been amused by my objections that I knew nothing of the chase, that I had little taste for such pastimes. "You shall ride with our party, Dr Newbolt, and extend your education that has been so sorely straitened."

It was a grim blustery day but amid the squalls of rain, the sun's rays would peep out between the low racing clouds and illuminate one corner then another of the valley. It was steeper land than this battlefield, further north. Beams of light struck the raindrops caught in last year's brown ferns and in the heather. Beaters crept forward stealthily, then roused up and ran, with fearsome wails echoed by the deep baying of the hounds, to drive the stag across the King's line of vision. He lifted his weapon, then lowered it.

"Come my lords, come Dr Newbolt, let us pursue our quarry," and he put his spurs to his horse's flanks. We followed.

The beaters were in a ragged line now and out of breath. We overtook them and rode uphill after the russet beast that leaped as though it were scarce bound to the earth as mortal creatures are. Its branched horns gleamed with a velveteen glow, suddenly obliterated as the next shower descended.

Despite my scepticism, I could not help the thrill rising in my breast. We lost sight of the stag as it crested the hill, then spurring our horses cruelly, we came up over the rise ourselves, and there it was below, stock still for the instant, looking back toward us through the drizzle. It had forded a stream and the hounds ran thither and back along the near bank, whimpering, loath to wet their paws.

"Now!" shouted the King as he laid his gun to his shoulder, and the others did likewise but I held my reins and watched as the deer leaped away, before even the crack of the first shot rang out.

A scream from below. Not the cry of a wounded animal, but a human scream. Charles Stuart turned to me, his gun still smoking. Mingled with the usual haughty air there was puzzlement. All was not as it should be in his kingdom.

We rode down the glen and there in a hollow by the brook, we found the boy, a bullet in his shoulder. So Robbie was introduced to the King in the company of nobles, and he comported himself remarkably for one so young and so insignificant.

"Beg pardon your lordship," he said, "I wasna trespassing as such. It's but the quickest way from here to there."

The King laughed, actually laughed, and ordered me to staunch the bleeding and sent for two of the beaters to carry the boy back to the castle where I could extract the bullet. One of the gillies, a local man with ruddy hair the colour of the stag's coat, told us the boy's name. He had lost his mother in the past winter and fended for himself, with help from neighbours, for his father had not been seen for many a year. The boy's pale hair was matted to his brow with the rain, and he must have been in pain, but his greenish eyes gleamed with delight as the men carried him after the King.

A loud cry wrenches me back to the present.

"Now!" shouts the colonel, and I find myself among the foot-soldiers, rising up from the heath and scrub, running down the hill with the brackish taste of fear dissolving in my mouth. Memories of Robbie fly away behind me. There is only the noise of battle cries, the rush of air past my ears, the *weight of the matchlock hampering me. This is my punishment for bringing doubt upon myself, their doubt about my probity. So be it.*

My pawn was ruined, there was blood on my hand, and my head was pounding. But I threw my chisel down and ran into the house, feeling a surge of excitement. This time my waking dream had brought me more of Robbie. Not directly; more a memory of Newbolt's at some later stage, just before a battle. My knowledge of the Civil War was sketchy, but I guessed it might have been Marston Moor. I added the latest waking dream to my notebook, still in a trance. The doctor was a dowsing rod, maybe, a channel for me to make contact with the boy.

Alison's curiosity about my trade was strong enough to provide an excuse for an excursion. I offered to take her out on a necessary but non-urgent trip to examine a couple of sites on behalf of the Bury St Edmunds amateur archaeology group. It was unpaid, so I'd been putting it off, and they were probably despairing of their chances of ever getting on *Time Team*. Alison agreed to make the trip with me the next Saturday.

She must have risen early to reach me by ten in the morning. I was glad to let her drive, in case I had one of my turns. There was no way for me to know how long I was "out". Even if each waking dream only lasted a few seconds, it was still risky to be behind the wheel. I began to relax as we drove along the northbound M11.

"Where exactly are we heading?" she asked.

"The area around Ixworth. They've mapped out a dozen or so possible burials sites."

"Don't they have a clear idea of which is likely to be most productive?"

"Well no, the group look at pointers in terms of landscape features, signs of settlement and so on. There's a load of sites where there might be graves. The couple I'm looking at today are the ones I've identified as worth further investigation." In other words, though I didn't say, these are the ones my map dowsing pinpointed as most likely to be fruitful. In the case of such ancient sites, with lots of little bits and bobs, there was nothing to beat actual on-site dowsing.

Alison told me she had done a bit of googling since our pub meeting, and found out that bona fide archaeologists were investigating the use of a dowser to help select which sites to excavate, in a part of the Middle East where ancient remains were widely scattered and buried in the desert. "If their pilot survey produces verifiable results, you dowsers might find yourself in great demand."

"I already am, in case you hadn't noticed."

I understood that Alison, like a lot of people who are initially sceptical, was finding her own way to convince herself there might be something valid in what I do.

"Why did this lot call you in?"

"They had tried digging up the easier sites, but they found no grave goods. Either poor people were buried there, without goods, or they'd been robbed—like most of the Sutton Hoo barrows. Miss Elvet said those were robbed in the sixteenth century. Luckily they missed one."

"Who's Miss Elvet?"

"Our upper primary teacher."

Alison laughed. "You lived round that area then?"

"Not at all, no. But Sutton Hoo was much more spectacular than anything up our way. Miss Elvet relished the story. She made Basil Brown the hero."

"Basil Brown?"

"He was the local man, worked at the Ipswich Museum. Specialized in digging the sandy East Anglian soils. He was the one Mrs Pretty called in to open up her barrows; she had several on her land. This was just before the war." Miss Elvet had capitalized it: The War. "He put trenches through three of the barrows in the summer of '38: found them all ransacked long ago. Next summer, '39, Basil Brown opens the largest barrow, the one overlooking the Deben estuary, and finds the boat."

"He was the first to see it?"

"Except it wasn't there."

"What do you mean, wasn't there? Everyone knows there was a boat in the Sutton Hoo barrow." She sounded indignant.

"It was only the outline, the ghost, of a long boat whose timbers had vanished. Nothing to go on except a trace of discolouration on the sand, together with rows of rusty rivets."

We had been riveted, Miss Elvet's class. I had truly believed she had seen it with her own eyes, perhaps alongside the two holiday-making ladies, Miss Mercie Lack and Miss Barbara Wagstaff, who'd happened upon the excavation and were retained as photographers. They took thousands of photographs, Miss Elvet said, and we kids knew they were heroines, like Basil Brown was the hero.

And halfway through, what happened? When Basil Brown (and Miss Elvet) came to the most exciting bit, the burial chamber and its odd-shaped lumps signifying treasure, a chap from Cambridge came along and took over, with other top chaps from other universities, and the Office of Works in charge. All they had to do was brush off the sand and lift those amazing treasures—very carefully, granted—and pack them off to London where they spent The War in a side tunnel of the Underground. I'd been to the British Museum later, to see the sword-jewels of inlaid gold, and the silver bowls and the rest. According to the official account, which was probably all that Alison knew, the heroes were the chaps who went on to become professors of archaeology around the country. What became of humble Basil Brown? He remained humble, evidently. He'd dipped into the ground, and shown them the beautiful lines of that boat, and where the treasure was, and they took it all and afterwards they didn't even bother to fill it in. So when the rains fell, the ghost-boat disintegrated. Miss Elvet was very cross about that. Even The War was no excuse.

Alison was looking at me sharply out of the corners of her eyes. It gave her a slightly crazy squint, like a cat that's thinking of pouncing.

"The trusty trivets—what comes after that? They found the treasure, didn't they?"

"Yes they found the treasure." I didn't want to go into the whole sad story, the demise of the ghost-boat. I wanted her to keep her eyes on the road.

"This is it," I said, and Alison pulled up beside a field gate. Beyond the hawthorn hedge there was rough pasture, covering the top of a low rise that we'd just ascended. A light drizzle that had been smudging the windscreen had stopped. Once in the field, I turned with a raised eyebrow, wondering if she would want to walk by my side, but she gave a tiny shake of her head.

"Carry on as if I wasn't here."

Of course it was impossible to forget her presence. With my rods in my hands, I walked to the corner of the field nearest the gate and started up and down, like I was threading the warps of a loom. By the time I was half done, I could tell where the burial was, more from a slight change in the texture of the ground beneath the turf than from the rods' response, but I did the weft as well to be on the safe side.

"Right, it's here," I said, indicating an area about the size of a double bed.

Now I had my pendulum in my hand it was essential to concentrate and ignore her completely. I took a few slow deep breaths, then three quick ones that I snorted out of my nostrils like a dragon trying to make smoke signals. That was my trademark, but she wouldn't know that. Don't think of her, I told myself again, looking back at the ground. I did the breathing routine once more, held the pendulum out in front and, narrowing my eyes, looked at a tuft of grass at the near edge of the circular area I'd mentally marked out. Very slowly I walked towards it, shifted my gaze smoothly ahead to another tuft, moved on, across the zone of the burial chamber. If that was what it was. Not a twitch. I walked back and forth, but after the first traverse I knew I wouldn't get a signal.

"No bite," I said, dropping my hand, standing still and releasing the tension that builds up in my shoulders as I work. "What we probably have here is an older burial, could be Bronze Age, there may be pottery goods. Or it could have been a small storage pit, holding grain or whatever; not a trace would be left."

"You only detect metal?"

"Metal, glass, precious stones, but not regular stones—otherwise I'd be making finds every two inches on a field like this."

"Not even bones?"

"Ah, bones now, that's a moot point. I could maybe detect a skeleton in good order, but these soils tend to eat away at bones till there's nothing much left after a thousand years or more."

"So do you get a different response to each type of material, or is it just one kind of response, and you only know when they dig it up?"

I considered this, looking at my hands. "It's different. But there will be a dominant one, usually the metal if there's any there; that'll be the one I sense, and anything less definite like glass will be like a whiff of another scent that you can't quite place. I can tell the depth by lengthening or shortening the string."

We moved on to another nearby site, on the same hilltop but in another field. I knew from the definite twitch of the rods that there was more than just disturbed earth below the flat surface. I cast back and forth again with the rods, thinking gold, silver, bronze, then worked the pendulum. "Just here," I told Alison, "five or six feet down, between two large stones, there's a cache of metal, I'm not sure what, but I suspect iron and bronze."

"I thought you didn't find stones."

"Did I say that? Ordinary ones, no. But these must be sacred ones, quite large, I can feel those."

That cock-a-hoop feeling again. I grinned at her.

It was about fifteen minutes' drive to the other site, north of Ixworth. Here, on a rise between a stream and a hazel coppice, there was a substantial mound, with a stone entrance on the south side. I whistled. Even though it's not far from Thetford where I grew up—and where Jeannie still lives—and even though I'm interested in these things, I hadn't seen it before. Alison sensed my excitement.

"It wasn't like this till a preliminary excavation five years ago," I explained. "Evidently the entrance had become completely covered in earth and then overgrown with turf and brush, like the rest of the mound. This was as far as they got, clearing the overgrowth. It's an obvious candidate for a dig. But then there are so many."

"How old is this—older than Sutton Hoo?"

"By a millennium. But the Anglo-Saxons sometimes used these older mounds for their own burials." I dived into the low entrance where two pillar-stones supported a large flat capstone.

I thought she would follow me because it was obviously an exciting site, but she lingered outside. Some people find these passage graves claustrophobic—as, to some extent, I do, but my professional purpose overrides my fear.

Two paces further in there was a slightly wider area, still very low, so that I was crouched over, as I fumbled to hold my pendulum. The weight of earth all around seemed to compress the air. My own body blocked out most of the light, although I wasn't more than a few feet into the mound. Ahead was blank stone. Beneath my feet, damp soil.

A loud knock on my chamber door. I open it to discover the red-haired gillie, Hamish, on my threshold. The royal entourage acquired him in North Humber Land and he has come all the way with us to Falkland Castle.

"You're to attend on the King," he says, peremptory with delegated royal authority, but without any of the heightened excitement that attends a summons for retribution.

It falls into my mind, as I follow the man along the castle corridors, that a gillie is an unusual choice of herald. "Do you know anything of the purpose of this audience?" I ask. Irregular proceedings allow some latitude of intercourse, I feel, but to cover any suggestion of anxiety—or attribute to myself another kind of anxiety—I add, "I was at my books, and fear I'm ink-stained and lacking fresh linen that I would have donned to visit His Majesty."

"It's about Robbie," answers Hamish, as though sweeping aside the sartorial question. "That's all I ken."

It is enough.

Within the King's outer chambers, we come upon a knot of whispering gentlemen, but ourselves continue to the anteroom to the royal bedchamber, a dark panelled room whose three high windows are obscured by dark blue velvet drapes embroidered with faded golden fleurs-de-lis. These are part of the appurtenances that travel everywhere with the royal household; as is the wardrobe with its cover open showing several silken jackets. In this nearly innermost sanctum, the King stands beside a writing stand, with the Reverend Cawley bowing and scraping beside him. To my relief, he dismisses the rogue before turning to me. There is no one else with us, excepting the valet who approaches to comb the royal locks in this interlude, and Hamish whom the King motions to stand aside. The man waits like a statue in an embrasure between two windows.

"Your Majesty called for me?"

"I wish you to attend the boy Robbie. We have supposed the fits to be connected with his healing powers, and with his fortune telling."

I have heard of that, certainly, as evinced by the King's success in hunting the royal eagle. And more. That the boy entertains the King, singing for him strange songs in another tongue, till the lad is near to keeling over with fatigue, long after the feasting has finished—feasting he does not share, of course. And that some among the nobles disdain this common entertainment, but dare not say so, yet.

The King continues, "However that may be, I fear him coming to some harm through too severe an attack. I wish you to meliorate their effects as far as may be possible, and also to note their timing so that we may establish whether the connection be close or, perhaps, imaginary." He waves the valet away and raises his eyebrows, to indicate I should respond.

"But Dr Soames ..."

"Was undertaking this task, yes, but the boy has expressed so strong a dread of Dr Soames and his clysters and phlebotomies that I think it wisest to change the physician, rather than merely the physic."

"By changing the physician, Your Majesty, you most certainly do change the treatment. In place of those Galenic remedies I shall follow the system of Theophrastus von Hohenheim." The King's eyes flicker, and I wonder if he knows this is the alias of Paracelsus, whose name I dare not utter within these walls. I hurry on, "I have but recently read his treatise on the falling sickness, which advocates gentle treatment, observation, mild botanicals, and chemicals."

"You shall have all you need, Newbolt. Merely ask my chief steward."

The royal visage is relaxed and I wonder, as I leave his presence—walking backwards and nearly treading on Hamish's toes—whether I imagined that flicker of concern. How much does the King know of Paracelsus and his teachings that reach beyond treatment regimes? Some appear even in the text I unwisely mentioned in his presence, and more have been handed down from his lectures and writings— many unpublished but read by his pupils— over the past hundred years. His scorn of bombastic money-grubbing, patron-pleasing physicians (just such an one is Dr Soames) makes Paracelsus anathema to the established men, and a hero to such as myself. The more so, for his general scorn of authority based on birth.

Hamish leads me to the lower quarters and leaves me where Robbie is housed in a species of kennel, that he must share at night with three other lads. I begin to question him about his fits: how often does he have them; does he remember when first they began? But his bright face grows dull; he turns his head away and will not answer.

"What is it, Robbie? Do not be afraid to tell me. I will not put you under strict discipline as did Dr Soames, you know that." I sense that he does know, that he not only dismissed Dr Soames, as it were, but appointed me in his place. And I am obscurely pleased, not only for the progress this makes in my security with the King. That, after all, may depend on my success in curing the boy, while preserving his powers—a delicate task. No, rather, I feel favoured by something benign.

"I want to run outside, sir," he says, looking me full in the face for the first time since I entered his room, which is indeed close shuttered. "I want to be in the open air."

I found myself on hands and knees, feeling giddy. So there was no escape from my waking dreams, even here. I gave myself a little shake, half turning before realizing it would be easier to reverse out.

"Anything of interest?" Alison asked, a tremor in her voice. I wondered how long I had been; it had felt like a half hour in the world of Dr Newbolt. "That was the longest five minutes. I thought I'd lost you in there," she added.

"I have a feeling about this barrow. Grave goods rather than body would have been my hunch. But the pendulum never picked anything up."

"Wasn't it too dark to tell?" She pushed past me and stuck her head in the entrance. "Goodness, you'd need a torch surely?"

She was definitely spooked by this place. In her layperson's way, she was picking up on the same vibes I'd felt. The ones that belonged here, not the Newbolt ones.

"No," I said. "Believe me, if the pendulum responds, I know it. Now, if you'll excuse me, I need to make a few notes."

I wrote as she drove, feeling car-sick or vision-sick, my scrawl atrocious. Alison hinted strongly that she would like to read my dowsing notes, but I told her they were strictly for my own use.

The White Hart at Ixworth was an original, not a chain pub, with dark woodwork of an indeterminate period between the two Elizabeths, and a grimy stone floor that wouldn't notice the mud on our boots.

"I'll ring my sister," I said, "once I've got the drinks in." We weren't far from Thetford, and I was hoping to cadge an invitation to take Alison over.

"I'll buy them."

"Oh no you won't. Call me a chauvinist if you want, but I can't let a woman go up to the bar for me." This was not a strict rule, but depended on my mood and who I was with. Emma, for example, would never let me get away with it.

Alison pulled a face then grinned. "Better make it a low-alcohol lager," she said. "Here, you can use my mobile."

"No way, those things fry your brain."

Alison cradled her drink, while I wrestled with small change in the corner by the phone.

Jeannie sounded flustered. "Good to hear from you Joe, but I can't talk long. Emma just rang me from London"—as if I didn't know where my niece lived—"and she said you're seeing a friend of hers. I'm the last to know, you go weeks without ringing."

That was untrue. One of the few family duties I tended to stick to was the weekly check-in with Jeannie. The first few years after my ill-fated adventure with Marjory, she always asked why I didn't move back to Thetford. Gradually she accepted that however unsatisfactory my life and my ex-council house in Bishop's Stortford might appear to her and Norman, I wasn't going to shift. I was stranded there where Marjory had left me, like a cuttlefish washed up by the tide.

There was something distracted about the way Jeannie wittered on that made me wonder if she had problems of her own. She didn't grill me in her usual sisterly fashion about my "seeing" Alison, so I didn't get a chance to assure her it was not a romantic involvement. It clearly was not a good time for a visit.

Alison and I ate meat pies, home-made and lush with gravy, and warmed our toes near the fire. Half my attention was on Alison's questions about dowsing and about my family background, and half was on the scene I'd been drawn into in that barrow. I hadn't been struck down with a headache this time, but I'd been left with an internal quiver, a tremolo. Not excitement, but apprehension, a modified version of The Dread, I supposed. I thought of telling Alison about it, but I was building my hope of contacting Robbie, and did not want to share that with her.

We maintained what I hoped was a companionable silence, as we drove into the red-streaked dusk.

CHAPTER FIVE

I had a very strong hunch as to what Alison wanted; but I was curious about the circumstances. She was ringing me midweek, a few days after our jaunt.

"You'd like to go with me up to Scotland, to see the site of *The Blessing of Burntisland*, wouldn't you?" I asked her straight off. I was gratified to hear the little inrush of her breath.

"Joe, if I didn't know you better, I'd say you were psychic," she said in her husky mate-in-the-pub voice.

"You don't know me better," I reminded her. "Now tell me the why and the wherefore, because you're asking a lot here."

"I know I am. But so are you, Joe, with your speculation about troubles in the kingdom if they raise the treasure."

Alison filled me in on her crisis situation, for that's what it was, though she sounded remarkably calm. When she'd made a move to delay the permit for the excavation, as they called it, she hit trouble because it was already in the pipeline. Not following these Civil Service bureaucratic twists and turns, I pictured an underground pipe, with flotillas of documents like those paper boats you make at school when you're bored. I saw Alison's hand reaching down through a manhole to pluck one of them out of the stream. Next thing, she got her knuckles rapped. Her boss—not her immediate boss, but a bigger cheese, two notches above him—called her in to his office to suggest she take some paid leave. It was an order, she said, not a proposal. In actual fact, they were suspending her with immediate effect.

Suspension: that sounded serious all right.

"Don't you see, Joe? They wouldn't react like this if it were just a question of delaying a permit for a perfectly innocent excavation. Either there's something fishy about *The Blessing of Burntisland* itself, and they think I've rumbled it, or they're using the excavation as cover." She'd lost me there, but she refused to explain further over the phone.

I was afraid of going near *The Blessing of Burntisland* after what happened last time; paradoxically, it was for that very reason that I agreed to the trip. Staying away hadn't worked. Revisiting the site could give me a chance to investigate what I had accidentally tapped into that time. A hunch told me it was my best chance to exorcise the waking dreams, and with them, The Dread.

Just so Alison wouldn't feel too cocky, I told her that for a rational bureaucrat she was behaving like a crazy woman. She laughed and said she'd be with me in a couple of hours.

"What is it, Robbie? What are you trying to say?" The boy is shaking still, but he has come out of his seizure.

Throughout the fit, while I kept my kerchief between his teeth that he might not bite his own tongue, his arms were convulsively clutching to his body the trumpet that has become his pet. Why he brought the instrument on our walk out into the wild heath I cannot tell. Was he intending to summon spirits with his ill-trained notes? Master Lanier's generous gift cannot be in recognition of the boy's accomplishment; the fairest interpretation would be that the King's trumpeter divined a spark of promise in the boy. For sure Robbie loves to hear the stately music in banquet hall or chapel, almost more than I do myself. Once at a masque, he called it "angel's voices" there in front of His Majesty. On a nod from the King, Lanier asked the boy to say more about this music that was evidently still so fresh to his ears. In his artless fashion he replied how marvellous it must be for the King, to be so great a lord as to converse with Heaven itself, in its own tongue. The King was undoubtedly much delighted with this speech.

In my opinion, Robbie really thinks that music is another language, along with the almost-foreign English, the French, and Latin that he hears at court, the chanting of the clergy, and the melodies of the ladies as they sit and spin.

There on the spot, Lanier presented the boy with the little trumpet. A less charitable view of this action would be that he sought the King's favour, which indeed he receives in sufficient measure for his glorious compositions. Thereafter, he has found little enough time to instruct Robbie, with the result that the boy's musical progress has been painfully slow. He has made more headway in the alchemical arts under my tuition.

"His kingdom" he says now, through cracked lips. His whole aspect is so ghastly, I regret pressing him to speak. And yet I could not bear to leave him silent, in fear that his soul had slipped too far away for recall.

"Hush, now, Robbie, all is well. See, I am with you," I say, stroking his clammy brow.

"His kingdom come—come undone—on earth as it is in heaven." He stares past me, up at the clouds. "And his mother, what his mother ..."

"Soft now, there's no need to speak."

"And where his mother lost, so shall he. And what his grandmother lost, so shall he."

I am trembling now, more than the boy. I know I shall write all this down presently, back in my room, along with my other records of Robbie's falling fits and strange sayings. But no words will capture the sense of dread that accompanies my hearing him speak thus. What he means, if indeed it is more than nonsense, I do not know. And yet I feel he sees another realm, one I do not want to believe exists.

His eyes return, thank goodness, to a natural focus on his surroundings, and presently I help him to his feet.

"Are you strong enough to walk back, Robbie?" I ask him. He glances down, and so do I, at the little trumpet in his arms. In his unconscious frenzy, possessed of strength beyond normal limits, he has crushed it so that its flanged end is no longer a round "O" but dented inwards at two opposite sides, so that it resembles an open shouting mouth.

When I came to myself, I was sitting by my fireside with a book on *Birds of Scotland* open on my knee. I knew I had been waiting for something, but could not remember what. I urgently wanted to write down that scene, and the boy's words, and stumbled upstairs to my so-called study, to find my notebook. I felt woozy, like after an anaesthetic at the dentist's.

Robbie is afflicted, I thought, he really suffers with his gift. If only I could reach out to him. I remembered that night when the sky fell in on our family, after I had helped find Dad. Gran Vartin had held my head in her arms, put a poultice on my forehead—a cloth full of hot clay mixed with herbs, always herbs with her. I didn't know which herbs; my skills didn't lie that way.

When the doorbell rang I half-expected to see Robbie or my grandmother. Alison dumped a large portmanteau down on the doorstep. She looked sharply around when I showed her into my front room.

"How long have you lived here, Joe?" she said, as though the furnishings and décor could be excused if they belonged to the previous occupant. I had bought the ex-council semi when Marjory and I married and moved down here. A 1950s fireplace surrounded by fawn tiles dominated the sitting room. The textured wallpaper, Paisley pattern on a yellow ground, had been Marjory's choice. I'd never got around to redecorating; I'd always felt I was camping out in that house. So I led Alison out to my shed, to give her an idea of my own taste.

Alison's eyes widened with pleasure when she saw my woodworking tools arrayed along one wall, and the chessboard hanging among them.

"Joe, that's marvellous," she said. "Did you do that?"

I nodded. The pieces were tucked away in a box, and I hesitated to bring them out. Instead I switched on the light boxes, to show off the bottles gleaming in their many hues around the other two walls. As well as electricity, I'd installed a tap for washing the bottles. I explained to Alison that the water system inside the house was wrongly aligned for working purposes, though it was just about passable for domestic use. Blue glass, brown, clear, opalescent; mainly Victorian, some older and some newer—they were bottles that had been used for drinks and medicine and cosmetics.

"Joe, why don't you have these on show in your house?" Alison asked. "They'd look fantastic."

"It's funny, I know, but Marjory took against them, and I never ..." I trailed off, and led her back toward the kitchen, embarrassed because it seemed silly to be shy of talking about my long-ago marriage. But when my throat clammed up, there was nothing I could do about it.

Alison stumbled on the threshold. Grasping her elbow to steady her, I sensed that she had been hiding her exhaustion. She was more shaken by her suspension than she'd admitted. I sent her through to the sitting room while I concocted a nightcap of cocoa. When I took the mugs in, she was nodding in the easy chair. She had her legs tucked up under her, and her little stockinged feet nestled in her right hand.

"I've made up a bed for you in the spare room, but there's something I want to ask you before you go up," I said. Alison's tired eyes snapped wide open. Did she think I was about to make a pass? I hurried on. "When you looked up Thomas Newbolt in those records, was there any mention of a special task he'd been given in the king's household, looking after a boy who had fits?"

"No, they don't go into details." The clicking of her weary brain was almost audible. "Was this the one you mentioned, the second survivor?"

"Yes, Robbie."

"Remind me, what was he doing in the king's household?"

"Quite random, they picked him up on their way north. But he had a gift of prediction, and I think he foresaw something terrible, though I can't tell what. He was some kind of soothsayer."

"Like you, Joe?" she replied, and vouchsafed me a tired smile.

"No, I reckon he'd have a thing or two to teach me."

I was preparing to shave with my safety razor, when I noticed how ghastly I looked. I'd been wrestling with The Dread for at least two hours in the night. It was like a boa constrictor trying to squeeze the breath out of me, and I had tossed and sweated, only sinking into an uneasy sleep with the dawn. Leaning in closer to the mirror, I pulled down my eyelid: it was dull red rather than a healthy pink, and red veins were crawling across my eyeballs. The grey bags under my eyes were nearly as dark as my stubble. God, what a disgusting sight. If I were a woman seeing me, I'd run a mile.

A nauseous sensation rushed over me, but I clenched my teeth and lathered up. The ritual of shaving, even the limited bits around the beard, was a comfort in times of distress. Thank goodness the water was hot. With easy, regular strokes, I swathed away stubble and foam, rinsing the blade after every couple of passes.

He looks so conscious of his importance, standing very upright, holding the barber bowl as though it were a chalice, I have difficulty restraining a smile. With utmost care, to match Robbie's solemnity, I test with my thumb the blade I have stropped on my riding belt, and apply it to my cheek above the beard.

"Thus, with the blade angled toward the direction of the stroke," I say. I am turning my mouth sideways, but even so, the act of speech disrupts the very movement I attempt to demonstrate, so I hold the razor aside. "Watch now, how I pull the skin forward to make taut the hollow before the ear."

So attentive an apprentice, this boy! As with the chimestrie now also with the shaving, as though it were of equal import. Well, he will be an expert in barber work when and if the time comes for him to shave.

What am I thinking—"if"? A chill sweeps across my back.

Robbie, standing behind me, studying me in the mirror, gives a start and a strange high shriek, and lets drop the bowl. His eyes are grown so wide they are almost circles. No, they are not looking at me after all, but past me.

The bowl clatters on the floor, splashing water over Robbie's feet and mine.

"Careless boy!" I chide him.

My good pewter bowl with the scooped rim, that doubles for bleeding patients, ceases to rock on the stone flags and settles askew, an ugly dent marring its base. Hot with choler I reach for my belt, that is hanging over the rail of the bed-end. Robbie shrinks back, but his outstretched hand is not toward me, not fending off my proffered correction. He gestures with splayed fingers as though to push away something to one side of me.

"Do you not see it?" he gurgles.

I drop the belt on the floor and grasp the boy's shoulders. Very gently I shake him, and pull his face around to look at mine. I am afraid suddenly, afraid he will sink into one of his fits. But he continues with his chatter.

"That man, or devil, staring at us ..."

Though I have seen him frightened before, it was never in this manner. Some peculiar force seems to crackle in his golden hair. It is ghastly, repulsive. I nearly leave go; only my love for the strange youth overcomes my abhorrence.

"There is nobody here, Robbie, save you and myself, you can see that," and I attempt to turn him around.

"Not in the chamber, in the mirror."

His second sight, it must be. Heaven forfend he has access to the world of evil spirits. Yet, it need not be evil, his vision. His fear may be only from the awe. I risk a question that reveals my half-credulity.

"This creature, did it speak?" If so, this might be the source of his prophecies.

"No, though I felt it would. It faded as I cried out."

What does it betide, this spectre I cannot see? How earnestly I wish that I were endowed with Robbie's powers.

I felt very chilly. Light flickered from the fluorescent strip over the basin. Must fix that, get a new tube. I stood there staring at my face in the mirror, while a thin trickle of blood ran down my cheek, from a nick in front of my right ear. The red stain met a bulge of shaving foam and diffused around its edges. I felt as if I'd never move, I'd watch each bubble of foam burst, I'd watch the blood congeal. I could see my right hand holding the safety razor in mid-air. I was alone.

Godammit! I threw the razor in the basinful of water, gripped the edge of the basin, and spat at that bloody mirror. The other mirror, the one in Thomas Newbolt's room, had been quite different, softer, silvery. He hadn't seen me, but the boy had, I was sure. For somewhere behind that waking dream, like a figure in a concerto unnoticed as you concentrate on the main melody, was my sense of seeing him with my own Joe Fairlie eyes. Yes, he'd looked terrified; his blue-green eyes open wide, his whole face a picture of startlement.

Next time, I wouldn't be covered in shaving foam, I wouldn't look such a fright. And maybe if I could get him used to me, and maybe if I could get him on my own without Thomas Newbolt, I could talk to him.

Driving north that day, Alison expanded on her notion that there was something sinister going on behind the excavation of *The Blessing of Burntisland*. For example, she said, there had been a long drawn-out battle between the Navy and fishermen whose nets got snarled in the propellers of nuclear submarines on secret manoeuvres, in Scottish coastal waters. Some had lost boats, some even their lives, yet for years the Navy denied all responsibility. Then there were reports of Russian subs, before and after the end of the Cold War, patrolling these waters.

"Suppose something like that's been going on here," she said, "and they want to investigate without arousing the suspicions of the public or the media. What better way than to bring in a lot of Navy boats to help with the raising of *The Blessing of Burntisland*? While everyone's attention is fixed on the treasure, a few divers can be checking up on the poor little haddock fishing boat that's buried down there."

I stared at her profile as she rattled on, her eyes fixed ahead, talking as if she was addressing a trade union meeting or a Quaker gathering. She was declaiming, not holding a conversation. She was full of certainty: "They" were up to something.

What was it that jarred on me? My skull felt like it needed to expand to contain all the contradictions and complexities.

"Alison, hang on. Announcing they've found *The Blessing of Burntisland* is hardly the way to hide whatever else they might be doing. Pretty soon the world and his aunt will be there gawping and snapping away. Stop right there ..." She glanced at me, startled, and the car swerved a little. "No, keep your eyes on the road, woman. I mean stop and think what you're saying. About the media." What was amazing was that it had only just occurred, or recurred, to me.

"What about the media?"

"Who told Kevin Dooley about me?"

"Oh, fair cop, Joe. Yes, the *Ouse News*." Dammit, she sounded amused.

"It's not funny. I am not, repeat not, media friendly at the best of times. They always get it wrong. And this—you know this is difficult stuff, Alison. What on earth were you thinking of?"

"Joe, I decided to help you, okay? You came to me, in my dusty dead-end niche in the Department offices, because you didn't know where else to turn. You were desperate. You were so desperate, and it wasn't just because you're Emma's uncle, it was something about your whole air, I felt you were genuine even though what you told me made no kind of sense. I decided to help."

"Very kind, I'm sure."

"Joe, no need to be ungracious."

"All right, let me try again. We wouldn't be here if I wasn't one hundred per cent convinced I have to do something about this blasted treasure, and if I hadn't managed to make you ninety-nine per cent convinced too. But why, why on earth Kevin Dooley, Alison?"

"Not ninety-nine per cent. More like sixty-five per cent. But I decided if I was going to help, I had to work on more than one front—we had to. I was going to tell you, but I forgot. One way to test the waters was to alert the media, in a small way to start with—a minuscule way, really. You couldn't call the *Ouse News* more than a pinprick to the Department."

"Well, I didn't give him a story."

"He wrote one anyway. Look in the glove compartment."

That gave me a jolt. I looked, and there was a copy of the *Ouse News*. On page five was a column headed "Boon or doom?" Beneath, in smaller bold print it read: "Local treasure-seeker voices fears if Scottish treasure raised." Two mistakes already. I'm not a treasure-seeker, I'm a dowser. And the treasure belonged to King Charles the First so it's national, not Scottish, if that still means anything. The king took it along on his first visit to Scotland, to tour those bleak

Scottish castles, but it mostly belonged in England. Including Henry the Eighth's 200-plus piece silver dinner service, worth an absolute fortune. I scanned the article.

"It doesn't say anything."

"No, not much. And it's on an inside page of a totally obscure provincial paper. So why do you think it put the wind up my bosses at the Department?"

"Pass. You tell me."

"They wouldn't have found this article. I was planning ahead, aiming for the story to build locally, then break through to the nationals in a few weeks. Sooner, if necessary, with a little prompting." I whistled a sliding note of admiration, though not approval. Alison nodded in acknowledgement. "What I hadn't counted on was this Dooley, after you sent him off with a flea in his ear, trying to get hold of me and by some god-awful mistake being put through to my boss. Who apparently didn't do anything about the call until the next day, when I tried to hold up the permit—my second stratagem. The two things chimed, you see, and an alarm bell started ringing."

"So they suspend you."

"Yes, they suspend me, and right now I dare say they're looking at my files and trying to figure out how much I know."

"Which is in fact almost zilch."

"Well, yes. I'm trying to remember what I did with the note about your visit to me, that day you came to my office."

"Alison, don't you see—if they find that, end of problem! Those Whitehall mandarins are hardly going to take any notice of my ramblings, are they? They'll just think you're crazy to have listened to me."

"Unless they see, or fear, that I've stumbled onto their game, by accident, through the agency of your strange foreboding. Like the Navy using you to find the treasure—the right result for the wrong reasons. Or, at least, inexplicable reasons."

I was silent, watching the hedgerows flick past. Still almost barren, but a hint of green bud here and there. Another part of the swirl in my head crystallized.

"Maybe what I picked up wasn't *The Blessing of Burntisland* at all, but a submarine, or a fishing vessel." Even as I spoke, I knew this was dodgy. Whatever else I may do badly, I know my dowsing, and I know the feel of what I am seeking.

"Look," she said, "they've already sent divers down, haven't they, and confirmed the barge is there? My theory is that there's something else nearby. Fortuitously, for them."

"But if you're right, they'll be watching out. You'll get a pretty hot reception."

"That depends. They might be watching my movements or they might not. Perhaps I'm totally barking up the wrong tree. But if they do make a move up there, it'll confirm my suspicions. It could be Kevin Dooley's biggest scoop ever."

She laughed, but I was feeling a bit sick.

Almost, I cannot contain my bile. It will come spilling out, in words if not in actions, should I confront that toad Cawley. But I must be politic, I must remain silent, or I shall confirm the very accusations they make against me. That perfidious Dr Soames, I am certain, has instructed Cawley to whisper to the King: Dr Newbolt is not to be trusted, Dr Newbolt is of a Puritanical persuasion, he is a false servant to the King. Next they will imply I am not to be trusted with the boy. They hate Robbie almost as they hate me, yet Soames I dare say would have him back in his clutches if he could.

The King refuses an audience, and I must steady my hand before I write a note, pleading that Robbie and I be permitted to travel with His Majesty on the Dreadnought. *Surely he would have relented, could he have seen the terror in the boy's eyes this morning when we stood beside the slipway, overlooking* The Blessing of Burntisland *as the loading was begun. I fear it is too late now, but I must try.*

I blinked, bemused for a moment, with the now-familiar throb settling behind my eyes. Alison was turning off onto a side road at a sign for a service station. Fumbling in my bag for my notebook, I wondered if I'd lost the thread of conversation. But it didn't matter. This was more important, surely: a sign that the problem was related to the wreck, as I had sensed from the first vision. It would be all too easy to be distracted by the red herring that Alison had dangled under my nose.

"Alison, you know this is all about *The Blessing of Burntisland* for me. I thought you were going to help me stop the raising of the treasure."

She glanced at me sideways, not a feline glance this time, more commanding.

"I'll help you, and you'll help me."

"So what do you want me to do 'up there' as you keep calling it? Find the sub for you, or what?"

"Or what, Joe. I don't know. I'm more like you than you realize—I also operate on hunches. Let's play it by ear."

She pulled up at the petrol station. I got out to grab the hose, and she grinned at me rather wearily. "Fill her up. We might make Newcastle by nightfall, do you reckon?"

CHAPTER SIX

As I pushed through the door from the residents' quarters into the saloon bar I tried to spot Alison, but the crowd obscured the view. The bar was all dark wood and grimy posters on the walls—hard to tell if it was genuinely dilapidated, or a fake-aged job. Still, I sensed a genuine cheerfulness in the dense air, and some sort of expectancy. It seemed to radiate from, or converge towards, a bunch of characters around a corner table. There were five of them in varied shapes and sizes, with plenty of grey in their hair and beards. They were drinking out of pewter jugs, a couple of them had colourful embroidered waistcoats over their baggy shirts, and it didn't need the collection of peculiar-shaped boxes spilling out from under their table to tell me they were musicians.

"Hi Joe," Alison called over from further down the room. "I saved you a place." I struggled through the crowd. She was sharing a table with two strangers. The others were a young man with bushy black hair, and a honey-coloured girl.

We'd selected the Rose and Crown for its proximity to Jesmond where Alison's mates used to "hang out", as she put it, during her university days. We somehow hadn't spotted the sign "Live music in the bar tonight", till after we'd booked in. An unlooked-for bonus, or minus: we'd see. Still, we reckoned we were lucky to find an inn with two rooms to spare at such short notice, though we'd had to pay a premium for occupying doubles singly.

"I've got a problem with my room," I began, starting quietly so only Alison would hear, but I had to repeat it louder because of all the clatter. "The lie of the water. Wondered if you'd mind exchanging with me?"

I'd been shown to a first-floor room at the back, and for some reason I assumed Alison's room was at the front of the building, around the turn of the corridor. But it turned out she was next door but one. That meant the same alignment. In a big building like this, it could have been a large mains pipe, but my hunch was that more likely it was an underground culvert. I was going to have an awful night with the flow tugging away at me, whatever way I lay in bed. I'd been testing it, which was why I was later down at the bar than Alison.

"Sorry about that Joe."

"Not your fault. D'you want another?"

Alison shook her head. For a moment, I caught the eye of the young fellow across the table. What was he looking at me for? We didn't know them from a bar of soap, and there was no reason I should offer a drink to a perfect stranger. It was unsettling, though, that direct, enquiring stare. Bit of a gypsy look about him.

As I stood at the bar waiting my turn, weighing up Newky Brown against the regular Vaux bitter, out of the corner of my eye I spied Alison talking to the two at our table.

"Joe, these kind people have a solution," Alison announced when I returned and settled down with my pint of bitter.

The young chap leaned forward. "Your friend's explained the situation, and we'd be happy to swap rooms. Ours is at the front, which we gather you wanted."

It was not clear to me if they knew why I needed to shift. A flush of embarrassment crept up from my collarbones to my jaw. Not because it's wrong to be sensitive to water flows and suchlike, but because to the generality of people it must seem peculiar, like being psychic. Or, I thought suddenly, like being autistic, except you couldn't hide that. I'd seen *Rainman* and everybody said Dustin Hoffman caught the essence brilliantly. Though the autistic guy was shy, there was no way he could pretend to be anything other than what he was. Whereas most of us do have the choice, and tend to exercise it in favour of appearing "normal", a position I suppose we calculate by looking at people around us. Which poses problems too.

"No need to bother, thanks," I said with the scrap of grace I could muster, and took a dip into my beer. There was comfort there in the hoppiness and maltiness, a good balanced brew.

"It's not a bother." The girl spoke up now, and there was a pleasant lilt of some foreign accent I couldn't place, some kind of Scandinavian maybe. "We haven't started to unpack our things."

"In fact, you'd be doing us the favour," her compadre chipped in, "because we'd be away from the noise of the road, and Irma is really sensitive to noise." His dark eyes slid over her with pride. Some people actually talk about being sensitive. And why not, after all? If I were in his shoes, I'd be proud of her too, and whatever little quirks she displayed would seem endearing. Pity Marjory never felt like that about me.

"That's settled then," said Alison. I stared into my beer, aware I should be grateful. Then we were caught up in procuring our meals, and very welcome they were, pie and chips in my case, and after that I bought a round, to cover up my unease.

The young man's name was Zemon—he spelled it out, and then added: "like demon with a Z". That got up my nose for some reason. I deliberately mis-remembered and pronounced it to rhyme with "lemon" instead. I kept asking things like, "Tell us, where are you from, Zemon?" and "So, Zemon, what do you do for a living?" He was from Nuneaton, near Leicester, a freelance musician and acrobat and a friend of the old guys playing here tonight. He and Irma were living in a commune in Cardington, near Wenlock Edge. I knew that was in Shropshire, as well as in a poem, but I'd never been there. Not a place for demons nor lemons.

After he bought us a round, I quit this silly game and simply tried to avoid using his name.

Irma was a different kettle of fish altogether. Dutch, "one quarter East Indian" she told us; I asked "Which quarter?" and pretended to look under the table and she giggled. She had come over to improve her English with a view to becoming a teacher back home, became swept up in some "green" movement, met this guy, and hung around. Whenever she spoke, it was as if the flame were turned up inside a lamp so that a calm, contained sort of light suffused her face.

"Look, they're tuning up," said Alison.

Sure enough, the bunch of musicians had pushed their chairs back and taken their instruments out of the boxes, there was the odd run of squeezebox or fiddle notes, one plucked his guitar, and they all leaned towards the note. The pub chatter quietened as people turned to watch, then grew again to a hubbub, which was abruptly swallowed when the first song began. By heaven, they had powerful hands and lungs, those guys—it was all acoustic, but once they got going there wasn't much chance of more chat. One of them had the flat Irish drum, the bodhran, and I could feel its vibrations right in my solar plexus. The two fiddles vied with one another or joined forces, as suited the lines of the song, searing and soaring by turns. The main vocalist was a red-faced, flat-nosed guy who looked as if he'd stepped out of the boxing ring—and acquired a few extra years and a beard by the way—but his baritone flowed effortlessly around his urgent guitar melody. All were melded, underpinned, by the surges of accordion. During the purely musical interlude before the finale of the song, the crescendo was like being in the sea when a great rolling breaker crashes over your head and whirls you around. This was a song about a sailor lost to his true love, as far as I could tell—the words tended to blur in the overall sound. They proceeded on to *Matty Grove*, which the less inhibited joined in with, then a few I didn't know, followed by a set of jigs.

Luckily I quite like that folksy stuff. Alison looked relaxed, so I guessed she was enjoying it too. I found my mood had mellowed, and I was aware of a sense of bonhomie towards everyone in the place. Even Zemon.

There were limits though, and I firmly refused to dance when a tiny space was cleared. The other three tried badgering me, but they got the message and left me to guard the drinks. I watched semi-amused for a while, then inevitably I had to go to the toilet. I edged around the crowd. Alison waved at me. When I came back in, I leaned against the wall for a minute, for a different angle. The drink that had percolated through my system must have been stronger than usual; there was an unsteadiness in my head and knees. I grasped at a cornice, and shut my eyes for a moment, to blank out the eager bodies in motion.

Thanks be that those jackanapes have ceased their cavorting, and the cacophony that accompanied it. These were imported through Harwich especially for this glittering court. Why the Queen favours such inept tumblers, over the polished declaimers of English verse, is a mystery. Some would place it at the foot of her foreign extraction, but I blame her light mind that seeks ever-newer sensations for its stimulation. Truly how apt that this crew carry as mascot a little antic monkey, complete with yellowish whiskers, for their capers were as graceless as the monkey's. (And, dare I think it, the little creature resembled somewhat in its person their royal patroness.)

There struts Dr Soames black-garbed as a priest, smoothing with oleaginous smirk his progress among the throng—and his progress into the royal confidence. But will he dance now the proper musicians are come? That would indeed be a most comic spectacle, for he has all the grace of a crow. It will be more entertaining than the monkey-actors.

But here comes my lady Woolaton, with the most composed of smiles. Will she dance with me? Later, perhaps. And under the cover of our circlings and lifts, will she whisper to me whether and where to meet this night? Oh, how exquisite the ripple of light along the grey silk of her gown, and how the coral trimmings show off the fabric, and those knowing lips, so cunningly.

Five years ago. Can it be so long? In secrecy, in defiance of her birth and breeding, she bestowed on me her most personal favours—and then as if in reward, raised me up to the notice of the King's almoner and thence into his direct service. I used to torment my brain for long after: was I so marvellous a lover, or had she placed me as her agent? Or should I believe her protestations that she would see merit rather than birth as the grounds for promotion? Now more than ever, I must guard my counsel with her, I warn myself as she approaches close by my side for the gavotte.

She glides light on my arm as a goshawk, and her scent that I recall from that time shakes my senses as I reel with her.

"Amelia, your beauty is more intoxicating than ever," I venture. If she objects to my familiarity I shall withdraw and make no further assault. But she tilts her head and raises her brows, then laughs.

"The doctor has not forgotten his skills with ladies' hearts," she answers.

All around us the hall is aswirl with silk and lace and velvet in movement. The King, ever uxorious, is dancing with his Queen. Soames has not made himself ridiculous by joining the press but whispers in a corner with his cronies. I do not recall having seen Woolaton since I returned to court.

Her ribbons are coral, her lips dusky roses, but I want to see if the tips of her breasts are still the rosebuds they once were. Martha told me that my lady had a child with Woolaton, but there is little sign of it in her elastic figure. She must have left it at their estate.

I blinked. The lights in the bar brightened then dimmed, darker than before. What was going on between Newbolt and this noblewoman, I wondered. By the prickle on my neck and the quickening of my pulse I registered an excitement corresponding to Newbolt's own, though at a quieter level thank goodness. I was intrigued, too, that the royal court was in my part of the country, in this vision.

Just as I was about to thrust through the crowd again, Irma appeared in front of me and, with a firm hand that would brook no denial, took my arm for the slow number that the musicians were striking up. Irma! But what about Zemon? Then I saw, over the heads of a shorter couple, him and Alison squashed together and shuffling around. Honestly, was there no limit to that young puppy's cheek? I made a point of doing my best to dance with Irma like a stranger helping out when there was one partner short—which was about the measure of it anyway—not clutching at her or leaning into her. She did feel nice and lissom on my arm. What she thought of me with my bear-like dancing gait I didn't like to picture.

At the end of the song, I bowed to Irma and lumbered back to the table. No more of that nonsense for me. I listened to their spirited rendition of *Jack Orion*, noticing more than usual the sexual allusion of the cock crowing in the lady's chamber. I'd finish up here, and go to bed, the sooner the better. Annoying that I had to ask Zemon to show me the room and to extract his and Irma's stuff so I could move in, but it was necessary.

"Where are you off to in the morning?" he asked, as we headed up the stairs. When I said Edinburgh, he remarked he and Irma were heading up that way too. I didn't want to pursue this coincidence.

It was true they hadn't unpacked. The only item laid out on the bed was a brightly woven web inside a circle of willow twigs.

"Irma's dream-catcher," Zemon explained. He hooked it over his little finger, and grabbed the luggage, leaving me alone to settle into the traffic and music sounds, the distant flow of the culvert, the light leaking in from the street lamp.

Despite the tingle of Irma's fingers on my arm I was coming to the perilous realization that I would rather have danced with Alison.

"Here. In here," comes her voice from behind the arras. There is a tiny alcove and once I have joined her, my lady and myself so completely fill it there seems no possibility that we might move. Although this reach of the palace is deserted at so late an hour, I feel less than secure. Yet it is certain she knows how to enhance the air of intrigue such that her suitor cannot tell if his breathlessness is more desire or fear.

Swiftly with her kisses, and caresses given as well as taken, she inflames my ardour to the pitch where I care nothing if an entire armed watch should trample past our hide-out. I have raised her skirts and petticoats with one hand while the other plays with the breast released from her half-unlaced bodice, when she whispers, "Ah dear Thomas, it is not enough to meet thus. You have another place where you meet your friends, is not that so?"

At this I freeze, for an instant. Dangerous talk. What does she know and how? "Which friends, my lady?"

"Soft my dear, do not think I aim to trip you. For all my finery I am more in sympathy with the cause you espouse than you would think possible. So has it always been. Do you think I would thus freely give myself, were it otherwise? In my station a woman may not choose whom she marries, but there are those few who choose how they study and where they direct their patronage. And in my case my affection."

I am willing to believe this, for she accompanies it with another kiss of such melting ardour that despite the cramped quarters, soon our compacted bodies shudder in the dance of love. Silken skinned lady, sweet of breath, sharp of nails as she digs into my neck.

My heart was thudding so loud it drowned out the music reverberating from below. I was in my room, lying awake in bed, but spilling as with a wet dream. The nausea that accompanied several of the previous spells bubbled up but I fought it, as I fumbled in the semi-dark for the paper hankies in my jacket pocket. Then I turned onto my belly and tried to absorb the import of the last two visions. Not their content; to take my mind away from that, I concentrated on the puzzle as to when they were taking place in Newbolt's life. He was at the queen's court, temporarily in Suffolk or Norfolk, not in Scotland. And if the fine lady had helped him into the king's service—where he was a relative newcomer, I sensed, during the Scottish tour—then this must be somewhat later. Not more than a couple of years, for I remembered Alison had found out that he had left the court in 1635.

The continuity of the two episodes—for they certainly seemed to be taking place on the same night—was a new twist. Had I called the second one to me, fired up by the erotic charge of the first? Or had I, this time, really been dreaming, dredging up what I wanted from my own subconscious, not dipping into Newbolt's after all?

"Oh for pity's sake, wake up," sings a voice close to me, and a hand is shaking my arm. I sit up straight away, my heart bounding in my breast. But it is a female tone. Yes, I know that one: it is Martha.

She has a covered lantern and lets a little light fall on my clothes. As I dress, she tells me that I endangered myself, by consorting with my lady this night. How she knew of our actions, she does not say, but I have before noticed that little is truly hid from servants. Later, after her mistress dismissed her, she lingered in an anteroom where she could overhear without being seen, for she saw a certain gentleman enter the bedchamber and feared for me. This gentleman asked my lady if she could confirm the rumours of Dr Newbolt's treason, which my lady readily did. At which he said, I was to be arrested at first light, or before if he had his way, and arraigned and then I would receive my just deserts like the poison viper.

Martha is weeping now. I have but a moment to place my arm around her shoulder. "Be brave, my friend, and may we meet in better times." Then I flee.

I have long since known that one day—or night, as it happens—my chancy business would bring me to this pass. But I would not have predicted the black terror gripping my intestines as I tread along the corridors, fearing at every turn to meet a guard. Am I then a coward? Oh to be out of this place and away. I shall have to go on foot, no hope of securing a mount at this hour and in my distress.

If I can only escape intact ...

I was shaking, sweating, crouched between the dressing table and the door of my room. Dull illumination from the street showed the position of window and bed. What was I doing out of bed? My stomach was heaving. Damn that man and his idiotic adventures!

I stood up and checked what I was wearing. Pyjamas, good. Straight out into the corridor. There was a bar of light seeping under the bathroom door, and I heard the toilet flush. I stepped back a bit so as not to bump into the person coming out, but I was caught in the light when the door opened. There stood Alison in a shiny dark red dressing gown.

"Joe," she said in a husky whisper, "are you all right?"

As I shook my head, then tried to nod, a wave of nausea overwhelmed me. I pushed past to collapse on my knees in front of the toilet, and let nature take its course. What a bloody rotten sensation, throwing up in the middle of the night. In a strange place, to make matters worse.

Alison was beside me, holding my head. Next thing she was wiping my mouth with some toilet roll. I felt too awful to mind.

"Must be that pie," was all I could say.

When it was over, she left me alone to clean up, then supported me back to my room. Sitting on the edge of my bed, she rubbed my hands, which had gone cold.

"It's a shame, after we had such a good time."

"Doesn't matter." I'd had both a much better time, and a much worse one, than Alison knew.

"Good night then," she said, and glided out. I watched her leave with a pang of regret.

CHAPTER SEVEN

"You didn't think to ask me first, before inviting them along?"
"They did swap rooms with you, Joe."
"Fat lot of good that did me."

Alison eyed me quizzically as I chomped through my fried bread and bacon. I'd come down late, no longer queasy, but the bear with the proverbial sore head after my night's adventures. The others were packing already. There was no point arguing, but it annoyed me the way Alison kept making decisions for me.

I felt better about it when everyone agreed that Zemon and Alison would take turns driving, and I slid into the back seat with Irma.

It was another grey day, and cold too. With Alison driving and Zemon navigating, we took one wrong turn after another. Soon we were lost in a housing estate with high-rise blocks that channelled the wind. Rubbish whirled along the pavements. We passed a row of boarded-up shops. The graffiti was worse than in London.

Letting them get lost was partly revenge for Alison unilaterally taking the others on board. But partly, it was my usual fascination that anyone can fail to read something as simple as a two-dimensional road map. I can read into and beyond such maps; I can tell the location of what's not marked. For me, the most complex ordinary map is like a child's crayon drawing compared with what it could be, if we made real maps with all the layers or dimensions.

Eventually we untangled ourselves from Newcastle and rolled out along the A1, as they thought, north to Edinburgh via Berwick. Only the road we were on wasn't the A1, but the A69 due west—which of course I could have told them, but I wanted to see how long it would take that fancy young man to figure it out. It was a childish sort of entertainment, but harmless enough. Meanwhile I was having a pleasant conversation where Irma kept asking things like: "How long you have been a dowser, Joe?" or "What are these flashbacks Alison says you are getting?" I was weary, and sore-headed, but I wasn't in a bad mood altogether. I kept answering Irma with anecdotes from my past career, together with minimal information about this *Blessing of Burntisland* business.

"And what did you say your mission is, going up to Edinburgh?" I asked her, when I felt she was getting too pressing about my recent experiences.

"We have some more friends of Zemon's to see, in the music business, only younger than those guys last night I think. And then we're to travel on to another place where there is this sort of commune, only it isn't one really."

From what I'd seen so far I could picture the sort of thing Zemon would be involved in: crusty vegetarians with rings through various parts of their bodies, and dogs on strings, protesting about something that the locals thought was irrelevant. Getting up everyone else's noses, while thinking themselves the purest of the pure. Roads or trees or nuclear power, could be any or all of them.

"Hang on, this isn't the right road," said Alison, slowing abruptly so the car behind nearly rammed us. I thought I could hear the driver swearing, we were that close. Irma had banged her wrist rather sharpish on the back of Zemon's seat, and I rubbed it better for her.

"Anyone fancy some Roman ruins?" I asked.

We were near the remains of the Wall fort known as Housesteads. Once they had overcome their indignation that I'd known where we were heading all along, there was general enthusiasm for a quick visit to Hadrian's Wall.

I stood on the bluff, atop the Roman ramparts, looking out north across the steep valley that was still rusty with last year's bracken. The others were inspecting the remains of the communal lavatories, which I'd directed them towards as we entered the Housesteads site. I knew they'd find it amusing to imagine how the soldiers used to sit around together, playing games or singing while they relieved themselves, then wiping their bums with sponges on sticks. Very hygienic those Romans—nobody came near their standards for another two thousand years.

My main concern was to be alone for a few minutes. I had no desire to read the educational signs, to be told what to make of these grey stones; I'd been here before, knew it all. I wanted to look out, as the sentries did when the Wall was functional, and to imagine myself back in those times. The scenery probably hadn't changed a huge amount, though perhaps there had been more woodland then, same as further south.

Standing atop the Wall, I reflected on what it had meant during the Roman occupation, how it had remained as a steady reminder of their power and their decline for all the centuries since. I wondered what someone who knew nothing of its history would make of that barrier of stone, snaking up and down the hills in this inhospitable part of the country. Pretty much what I would make of the Great Wall of China, presumably: amazement that people had once thought to solve their incompatibilities that way. At such expense of muscle power. Better than battering each other's brains out, though doubtless plenty of that went on too. I'd heard somewhere that the peasants living in this area had lost loads of their land, confiscated by the Romans for this massive project. They were probably press-ganged into helping to build it too.

Even more than the past, there was something else I wanted to access: a connection with the innocent elements around. This need had come upon me as we drove across the increasingly open landscapes of the north, and had been reinforced by the peculiar sensations of last night.

Taking slow, deep breaths of the spotless air, I slid my mind out of gear and let it float down the sheer wall of man-built stone and natural rock and turf. Down it drifted, down through tufts of fern and crouching rowan branches, resting a moment on the dense curled moss coating wet boulders in the stream. And then I was in the water, a glint of light dancing on the surface, a streak of bubble curving around a stone. Freezing cold water with a tint of brown. I am the water and the water is me.

"Guess who." Lemon-scented hands across my closed eyes, warm breath in my ear. I started, tilted, felt I was about to fall headlong.

"Jesus, don't do that." I pulled the hands away, spinning round to face Alison.

"It was only a joke, for Christ's sake."

Jolted from my moment of serenity, I felt like a terrier settling its feet for a fight. I'd forgotten her concern for me in the night, and only remembered her dancing with Zemon. "Why aren't you with your new friends?"

Alison turned away. She strode off along the wall-top path, stumbled down the steps, and fairly ran across the sloping lawn towards a lower point, where two small figures wended arm in arm towards her.

Her hands across my eyes had been startlingly soft, as well as plain startling. Joe Fairlie, you're a right fool, I told myself.

In the thin light of evening—the first real sunlight of the day and already fading at five o'clock—Zemon and I walked along the riverbank into the centre of Edinburgh. Strange to shake out into his company, but the womenfolk had both insisted they wanted to bath and relax for a bit, and Zemon had been eager to accompany me in the hunt for a good pint. The others would join us later, at the Burns monument since everybody thought they could identify that.

Our path was bounded by railings, and overhung by scrawny urban foliage. I noticed the colour of the river was similar to the stream I'd almost seen at Housesteads. Thin, dappled light slanted through water the colour of light ale.

Zemon was telling me about his and Irma's plans for the next few days, but I was not paying much attention. I was reflecting on the episodes of Thomas Newbolt's life I had experienced the night before. Perhaps he had not escaped alive, in which case I suspected he would not plague me any more. But that would be a problem as well as a relief. So far, I had only seen the past through his eyes. Much as I wanted to contact the magical boy Robbie directly, I probably needed to approach him via Newbolt at first.

"This way," whispers a voice near to me in the darkness. I stagger as an invisible creature brushes my arm. For a moment my feet tread off the path, squelching in the spongy ground. But the keening wind in the reeds obliterates the noise I make—so I hope. As the unseen hand plucks again at my sleeve, I see a crack of reddish light, and abruptly I am inside some low abode. As I straighten, I realize I must have been running at a half-crouch since I left the flanks of the palace. I also realize I can barely stand upright without my hat brushing the roof. Only, I have no hat.

"I stand before you, uncovered," I say to my hosts. There is a man with a rough square beard that betokens cloddishness but whose canny eyes

suggest a more refined intellect; two others in the shadows; and a child of perhaps thirteen. To my surprise I find this child, Susan, was the scout guiding my last few steps. I could chide her with causing me nearly to fall into the bog, but there are more pressing matters.

They know who I am and intend to pass me on to other friends, but first there is a need for my doctoring skills. One of the fellows has a gash on his arm that will not stop leaking a dark, sluggish trickle of blood.

"What is your name?" I ask him as I examine the wound.

"Anthony," he replies, looking up at me under his brow. The way he glances, shy yet defiant, reminds me of the youth Robbie, but in my weariness I cannot pursue the thought. My legs are shaking and I call for a low stool, heated water, and leeches. They do not have these last, though there must be plenty in the leaking lands around. I shall have to rely on pressure and clean linen. If they do not bring me some beverage or gruel soon, I shall be the patient and not the doctor.

I came to myself, sitting on the tow-path, with Zemon propping me up against a fence.

"Seems I won't be needing too many pints to get into the spirit of things," I said, but the words didn't come out very clearly.

"Can you manage to stand up?" Zemon asked.

"I'm not a cripple." I scrambled to my feet and walked on at a quick pace. He practically had to run to catch up with me. Inside, though, I was still shaky.

"You do realize you nearly fell in the river back there?" he demanded.

"I suppose you're going to claim you saved me."

"Joe, what's the matter? Are you ill?"

I stopped, turned to face him, and let out a long breath. "No, I'm not ill, but there is something funny going on. Didn't Alison tell you, along with all her other precious interfering?"

"Something, yes. I didn't realize it involved passing out. She said you could do more than find treasure, you could get in touch with the past."

"Jesus, she doesn't believe in holding off, does she?"

"Is that what was happening there?"

"I don't want to talk about it."

"Joe, this could be incredibly important. Think what it could mean. You don't have the right to keep it to yourself."

"Who's to be the judge of that? Look, I may have stumbled on a kind of second sight that dips into the past, but it's worse than useless to me at the moment. It's screwing me up. I don't know what it's all about."

"Then you're in the same boat as most of us. Most people have hidden powers if they only knew it, talents of all sorts, but they don't know how to make use of them."

It struck me that Zemon was talking sense.

We found a pub on Grassmarket, one I gauged to be halfway between a local and a tourist outfit. It wasn't "themed", just plainish blue and cream paintwork and blue plastic seating. Several of the blokes propping up the bar looked and sounded as though they might come in here every night—perhaps on their way home from work as builders, postmen, the types who service the upper crust of Edinburgh society that can afford actually to live around the centre. There were also a few yuppie types, and a lanky bloke who fitted in neither category, a mature student judging by his specs and notebook. Some synthetic pap played quietly on the jukebox. We'd had a couple of pints and Zemon had wittered on about his scheme to move his commune, too vaguely for me to take much notice. We'd hit one of those lulls in conversation that are fine between friends but awkward with someone you hardly know.

Without so much as a by your leave, he got out his tin whistle, and played it right there in the bar. The burly bartender looked over as if he didn't believe his ears, finished pulling a pint for a man with hair striped like a badger, took the money, then stared over again. Most of the people around us had fallen silent. The lanky bloke was giggling.

"Zemon, you'd best leave it there," I muttered.

Next minute the bartender was looming over us. This was when I noticed tattoos of fanged snakes on his huge bare arms, set off to full view by his black T-shirt, under a leather waistcoat liberally sprinkled with studs.

"Would you mind to shut the fuck up with that racket," he said, or at least that was my best guess, not being accustomed to the accent.

Zemon paused in his playing, looked up all innocent like, and replied: "Free entertainment for your customers, mister. Unless you prefer canned Bono to live music?" Then he did another little tootle.

That was plain provocation. I was divided as to whether to stick by him, or run for it.

The bartender snatched the tin whistle out of Zemon's grasp, and I thought he was going to bend it in two, like a hairpin. But he merely said: "Now you can either leave, or shut the fuck up. I hate Bono but I hate this worse, and it's me that works here, not you."

"Okay, okay, cool it, no offence," and Zemon held out his hand palm up and the guy handed the instrument back, instead of whacking him with it as I expected, and watched while Zemon stowed it away in a pocket of his baggy trousers.

"You were playing with fire there," I said, after the man-mountain had departed to his lair behind the bar.

"Well, thank you, that's one of the more flattering things people have said about my playing," Zemon answered smartly, giving me a mock bow.

The way Zemon told the girls the story when we having supper in the Screaming Carrot, a decent enough though veggie café off William Street, made them laugh. It was the way he exaggerated that made it funny: Zemon and I cowering helpless before the barman's wrath as he rippled his snake-biceps, us being virtually thrown out, and so on. Of course I didn't like that, any more than the animal-tamer charm that Zemon had really seemed to exercise, probably because I was a little envious. But whichever way you dressed it, playing the tin whistle was not the accomplishment that Irma seemed to think. I've tried it myself and made as near a tune as he can. The fiddle now, if he could play that, it would surely have been more impressive.

"Joe, Zemon says he may be able to help us with the outing to the wreck site," Alison said.

The slim, long-skirted waitress cleared away our pudding bowls.

"Yip, I've got a mate who knows a guy with a motorized dinghy," confirmed Zemon.

"That could be useful," I said slowly. I'd got as far as realizing I could not ask the *Burntisland* team for help. Basically I wanted to understand better my desire to prevent them raising the wreck.

"I might be able to borrow a wet suit, too." Zemon could dive and I couldn't, and he offered to undertake some unofficial surveying.

"I am not sure it is good for Zemon to dive in these waters he does not know," said Irma.

"You cannot dive there, where the wreck lies, anyway," I said. "It's under restriction from the Scottish Office. You know that, Alison."

"Don't look at me like that, Joe," she replied.

"Like what?"

"As if I were a dog owner not properly controlling her dog."

Yes, I could see it: Zemon as a bouncy, over-eager retriever, tugging on his leash.

"Hey, cool it guys," Zemon said, frowning at Alison and me in turn.

Irma grabbed his hand and squeezed it. I wanted to do the same to Alison, but she was a prickly lady, and she might easily misinterpret such a gesture.

CHAPTER EIGHT

Mist kept clouding my eyes. Every few steps I had to wipe it away with the back of my hand. I imagined my eyebrows were dewed with droplets, like the scraggly heather growing in patches across the hillside. It was cold enough that at first I regretted leaving my gloves behind, but the gradient warmed me. This was in Edinburgh, but it felt like countryside.

Trudging up the well-worn path, I fell into the rhythm that quietens the mind and allows you to think more deeply. Or to cease thinking altogether if you're lucky. First I mused how is it that paths like these get so worn. Each single footfall leaves scarcely any imprint on grass, none at all on stone, yet the accumulation wears them away. Then I wondered if the hill that was Arthur's Seat was tamed or diminished in its soul, by having so many human feet, clad in synthetic-soled boots, tramping up and down its flanks.

But why should I think that a hill had a soul? I'd better watch out for Zemon's influence. What was it he'd said in the pub yesterday, when he was trying to persuade me to join an unnamed band of New Age types for an unspecified purpose? "Joe, you have a way of seeing into the land itself, through its skin, like an X-ray machine sees bones."

No, that wasn't it, forget Zemon.

For as long as I can remember I'd held the notion that since natural things—mountains, storm clouds, forests, even a bird in flight—can make you catch your breath, can touch *your* soul (if you let them), therefore in a sense *they* have some quality of soul themselves. "God speaks in mysterious ways," the preachers say; and I reckon that might be one of their meanings. Not that I'd been to church for years, preferring to keep that sort of thing to myself.

As I climbed, the mist thinned and the sun began to break through.

Alison was going to contact the archaeologists. I wanted to keep my return low profile, so I'd asked her to find out as much as she could about the timetable of the excavation. When they had made the public pronouncement of the find, nearly two months ago, they'd said they aimed to raise *The Blessing of Burntisland* in the summer.

I stopped still in my tracks. My first vision, or waking dream, had been over the wreck, but there had been no more for a couple of months. The awful second vision had followed the press release about *The Blessing of Burntisland*, timed to coincide with the anniversary of the execution—the very subject of my vision. Perhaps that publicity had filtered through to my subconscious. If that were so, then this feeling developing in me lately, that these were real people, that I was really entering inside Dr Newbolt's mind, that I really might one day actually speak to Robbie, was all a big delusion.

I walked on briskly. I should have been to see a psychiatrist, rather than Alison. It wasn't the wreck of *The Blessing of Burntisland* that I needed to stop them raising; it was deeply buried fears in my own mind.

The path curved up a steep shoulder at this point, and rounding the next bend, I spotted a little figure far below that reminded me of Alison at Housesteads, joining Zemon and Irma after I had snapped at her. Was that really only yesterday? I couldn't be sure it was Alison, and I didn't want to make an idiot of myself by waving at a stranger, so I carried on. Just shy of the top, seeing a family and a couple ahead of me, huddled round the trig point, I leaned against a rock to catch my breath and wait for the coast to clear.

"Where is the boy?" Soames snarls. Yes, you may well stare at me accusingly. It is a fair question, and I cannot answer it. But it is intolerable that you should intrude like this, and moreover position your odious person athwart my doorway so that I feel trapped in my own quarters.

"I am not a nursemaid, Dr Soames. My brief was to watch over Robbie in a general sense, not every hour of the day. It will take me but a few moments to find him now." I know I am in a weak position, which serves but to stoke my loathing of this self-important mule.

"When the King himself wishes to speak to his barber-surgeon, or should I say apothecary, and apprentice, I warrant he does not expect to be kept waiting. If you cannot attend with the boy on the stroke of noon, pray do not trouble yourself to come at all. I will relay the information that you were too busy writing learned commentaries to keep sight of your charge."

Through this little speech I bite my tongue; and still I say nothing as Soames casts a hungry glance at my table where indeed my notes are piling up. He turns and stalks out of my chamber, to my unutterable relief. Surely one more moment, or one more word, and I'd have run him through with my dissecting knife, or rather my dagger for surer effect.

The writing is apposite. I have told His Majesty that my observations are accumulating, but more will be needed to form a theorem. But I am not so sure of his interest as at first. He has called less often on Robbie to sing at his banquets of late, and only twice in the past month used Robbie's powers: once to interpret a dream and another time to help him make his decision over a dispute between two of the quarrelling Scottish lords.

Throwing my short cape around my shoulders I hasten down the stairs, along the echoing kitchen corridor, and across the great yard which stands empty at this hour but for a single groom walking a roan gelding across to the stables. I am running as I pass through the postern gate, over the bridge, and out through the home field onto the open heath under a watery sun.

The dream was a jest, to my mind. A veiled woman, carrying a porcelain vessel, snatches it out of Charles's way as he reaches to put his hand inside. He was anxious lest it meant there was an asp within the vessel that would have bit him, and where was this danger in his waking life? Robbie shut his eyes, swayed, and intoned in his broad burr that the woman was the Queen who was veiled because she was out of the King's sight, and the vessel was her purse that she did not wish the King to discover was empty, because of spending so much on new travelling players. A cruder interpretation occurred to my mind, involving the vessel as honey pot, but I kept quiet. Charles was well pleased with Robbie's tale, and who knows perhaps he does have second sight as I have begun to believe, for on the King's enquiring with great good humour in his next missive, within a fortnight he heard reply that it was indeed so, and Henrietta Maria had been afraid to tell him.

I run on across the heath, ignoring the stab of breathlessness in my side. I am almost certain Robbie has come out this way. Sure if he'd been with Hamish, or the kitchen boys, Soames would not have sought him with me. They prefer to circumvent me if possible. That was the way with the dispute. Afterwards, when Robbie returned ashen and exhausted, and fell in a fit, I was so angry that I sent word via Hamish that this was abuse of the child's powers. He could refuse the King nothing: but playing at justice was far beyond his strange soothsaying, and it trapped him into a world of politics he was too young to be party to.

Doubtless my outburst has benefited neither the boy nor myself. He has not been called since. I must learn to speak with more diplomacy. Today for example—perhaps this will be a chance to re-establish ourselves in the King's favour.

Now I spy him, walking at a fast pace, close by the little lake or loch whose shores we have trod on several occasions since that ill-fated first outing on the moor.

"Robbie, wait for me," I call. He turns at my voice, but then runs on.

He is at the brink. His arm twists back, then springs into the air as he flings something from him. Even at this distance I gauge from the brassy tint and the size, and an ounce of intuition, it is his trumpet. Quite slowly it seems to me, it describes an arc, up toward the sky and down over the water. I am still screaming "No!" as a tiny fountain announces its immersion. At almost the same instant I hear the sound of the splash.

I came to, and in a few strides sprang onto the rocks that crown Arthur's Seat, and stood there swaying slightly in a state almost of ecstasy, completely unaware now of any other people up there. I'd been vouchsafed a real humdinger of a vision this time, no mistake. I gazed out over the Firth of Forth, a serene-looking stretch of blue beyond the Toytown ranks of Edinburgh houses. To my left crouched the tawny folds of local hills. Across the other side of the firth, hazy with distance, I could make out the apparently lower, but in reality much higher, mass of the Ochills. On the edge of the firth, invisible from here, I knew there lurked the town of Burntisland.

A voice close behind made me turn. "Christ, Joe, why the hell don't you have a mobile?" It was Alison. Precisely so people like you don't bother me, I could have answered, but that seemed redundant now she was bothering me anyway. "And why the hell did you have to go off on your own, when it's you that wants this sorted?"

Alison was winded from the climb, but not too breathless to chide me. I almost laughed at her ruddy face, disordered hair, and indignant frown.

Instead I blurted what was on my mind. "You know what Zemon said last night, about friends in Eden Valley? I've been thinking, I'd like to take him up on the offer, go and scout around Falkland Palace. It's where the treasure was travelling from, after all. Might pick up some clues."

Alison stared as if I were a particularly unsatisfactory sample of lichen. "Joe, I didn't bust my gut clambering up here so's to listen to your latest maunderings. I managed to get hold of Dr Anderson, and he's willing to see us this afternoon. At two o'clock sharp. So we must get our skates on—if you still want to come."

Yes, I did want to talk to Dr Anderson, one of the Naval Archaeology bigwigs. This was a chance to extract information about progress on *The Blessing of Burntisland* from the horse's mouth. But I also urgently needed to go to Falkland. An idea was forming in my half-addled brain, that if I could devise some way of tracking that trumpet and recovering it from its watery grave, then I should know that my visions were for real. If not, perhaps I'd better ask for professional help to sort my head out.

Alison turned away, looking for the best path down from the summit. I watched for a moment. Whether "real" or delusions, my sorties into the past were certainly powerful stuff; I was still shaking a little from that latest one. The rocks here had been polished by such a concentration of feet, they were smooth and slippery as worn dark bronze. Indentations held puddles from overnight rain, littered with debris: chewing gum wrappers, crushed cans, polystyrene burger boxes. Why can't people walk with empty hands and mouths?

"Well, are you coming?"

Good old Alison, brisk and businesslike. That's what I needed, I realized, as much as the chance to ponder in solitude. Alison was effective at spurring things on, partly because she missed the tortuous complications of my relationship with the past. For her the question was simple and scientific: was there any hidden danger lurking in or nearabout *The Blessing of Burntisland?*

CHAPTER NINE

What I was proposing carried a high risk of discovery, but if it worked, it might reveal a lot more of the insiders' view than an open approach. It would rely on the fact that Dr Anderson had neither seen nor spoken to me. One of his minions, a research officer, had contacted the East Anglia University pair who recruited me. I was going to be one of these, Dave Berry, and Alison was acting herself, unsuspended.

I racked my brains for the Edinburgh research officer's name, while Alison sat drumming on her steering wheel with one hand, the other holding her mobile ready to dial. Roddy somebody. She had dressed for the occasion in a box-pleated skirt of chocolate coloured wool, and a three-quarters coat in camel, which hung open showing a soft jumper in pearly grey. Angora, that looked like.

A tiny knob of gristle from the pie I'd hastily munched for my lunch was jammed between two of my molars, distracting me from Alison's legs and my memory-search both. They make these funny pies up in Scotland, with the top much lower than the edges, filled with savoury mince, quite tasty and very cheap. This one, from a chippie on the way through Leith, only cost a pound. Alison had turned her nose up at my offer to buy her one, and marched on to a posh sandwich shop. We'd run short of time, after getting lost in the city centre, snarled up in one-way systems and stuck in jams, fuming as we crawled over one of the bridges above Prince's Gardens. The upshot was, we'd grabbed these snacks and then ate sitting in the car, right there in the car park behind the Naval Archaeology Department, discussing our strategy through over-large mouthfuls.

The Department was an odd conglomeration of buildings, mostly nineteenth-century brick, but with modern pre-fab extensions tacked on, sprawling across a site that might have been a rope-walk or any manner of boat-related space in the more expansive days of Leith harbour. On our way here I had noticed signs of demolition, rapid rebuilding, and adaptation of old for new all around. Hard against the eastern edge of this university area, just before we turned in for the car park, I'd seen a high fence with double-spiked railings painted in battleship grey, its gates adorned with notices both ferocious and indecipherable. Actually, anyone could decipher "MoD", also the picture of an Alsatian baring its fangs, but "Beware U.H.F. & U.S.W. DANGER" and "SCOROMASS" had me baffled. On a booth just beyond the gates another sign barked: "NO ENTRY WITHOUT SECURITY PASS. ALL VISITORS PLEASE REPORT HERE" though the booth was empty. Lucky there was no such paranoia at the Naval Archaeology Department. It felt like we were visiting the last free country before the Iron Curtain. An outdated term—like in an old spy novel—I said to myself. Even so, it crossed my mind that Alison and I, hunched in the car, might look like conspirators. If anyone was looking, which they weren't.

"Roddy Pearce, that's it," I said at last, and she pressed the keys, calling up the Department's number, the last one she'd dialled. A few moments later she had established that Roddy Pearce was out of town today.

"No, I'll call again tomorrow," she said, in answer to an offer to take a message, and switched off. She turned to me with a mad glint in her eye. "Okay Joe, you are now Dave Berry of East Anglia University. Think you can pull it off?"

"No idea. But I tell you what you can do to help."

"Don't tell me to shut up and let you do all the talking. I'll absolutely burst with frustration. In fact, I won't come with you."

"Hang on, let me finish. I was going to say, could you flirt with Anderson a bit?"

"What do you mean, flirt?"

"Nothing that will compromise your honour. Just a subtle play that he won't even be conscious of, but that will throw him off kilter so's he won't notice any gaffes I make."

"My god, Joe, you don't ask much, do you?"

"I ask nothing I think you are not eminently capable of, my dear young lady."

She shot me a filthy look. Filthy, but friendly. "And what if Anderson's gay?"

"Then I will have to do the flirting."

She couldn't keep a straight face at that suggestion. Whether it was the unlikelihood of me as gay, or as flirtatious, I didn't ask.

As we walked past the Portakabins towards the rear entrance, I rubbernecked to catch a glimpse of what went on inside these outliers. In one section a shaven-headed boy sat staring at a computer screen and rubbing his ear; in another a man and woman stood talking, the woman cradling a red mug. Behind her was a tall metal rod with glass tubing clamped onto it, just my idea of lab apparatus—but nobody seemed to be paying it any attention. We reached the back door of the main building, only to find it locked, with a number pad beside it, which you obviously needed a code to use. So they weren't so free and easy after all.

"Joe, that's normal for academic places as well as government buildings, what with computer theft and all. They must have specialist equipment here too. Now, are you sure you've got your story straight?"

I nodded, though I was feeling less confident the nearer we got.

Round the front, at a massive varnished wooden door, we rang the bell and were admitted by a smartly coiffured secretary wearing—as seemed apt—a navy blue suit. I couldn't help noticing how her clothes sat stiff and prim on her, while Alison's almost equally businesslike skirt swung from side to side as she walked, emphasizing the movement of her hips. Navy Suit guided us through a maze of corridors. We passed a door marked "Dr G. Anderson", another labelled "AV viewing room" and then were ushered into a long, well-lit area with a series of counters or benches, some bearing unfamiliar machinery. A barnacle-encrusted propeller, taller than a person, leant against the far wall, beside a doorway with those silhouette man and woman signs for toilets.

The secretary announced: "Your visitors, Dr Anderson," and withdrew. A tall, bespectacled, grey-haired man looked up from notes laid out on one of the benches and hurried across, hand outstretched.

I was aware of Alison adjusting her skirt, as if it had become a little twisted around, and in doing so revealing more than was strictly necessary of her thigh. Had Dr Anderson's eyes flicked down to notice, or was that my imagination?

"Ms James, Dr Berry, delighted, good of you to come," he said, as though he'd made the request for this appointment, not us. His hand pumping mine felt hot and dry. "Seems as though *The Blessing of Burntisland* is suddenly flavour of the month. Had that Tooley chap here this morning, couldn't quite follow his drift, so I thought I'd refresh my memory. Then you rang, Ms James—most fortuitous. You may be able to fill me in on progress."

While wondering what the heck he meant, I couldn't help but admire the way Anderson handled the pronunciation of that slippery "Ms". With me, it comes out as "Muzz" like the start of "muzzle", which is surely not PC.

"Actually," said Alison, "I was rather hoping you'd be able to fill us in. My sector has been following progress, of course, but we gathered you thought the coming summer might be an over-optimistic estimate for raising the boat?"

Anderson gave an odd hum or puff through his nose. "And then some. We cannot be one hundred per cent sure it is the wreck, although the sonar soundings have provided one rather promising profile, which I'll show you in a moment if you're interested." We both nodded. "My problem, as I'm sure you'll understand, is that this is only one of a dozen projects which I'm supervising, and quite honestly I'm sure you know more about it than I do." We both shook our heads. "Dr Berry ..."

"Call me Dave, everybody does."

"Well, Dave, you of course are in the enviable position of being able to concentrate on your own research. Which is? I'm afraid I've forgotten, old age creeping up. Though of course it was Roderick you dealt with, wasn't it?"

This was the moment I'd been dreading. Could I possibly bluff my way through? I called on the spirit of Basil Brown, as channelled through Miss Elvet.

"I do have my own research, yes, basically very routine stuff on the interface between undisturbed sandy soils and the infill material in grave sites." I was glad to see his eyes glaze over more or less instantaneously—this was clearly outside any of his fields of interest—so I ploughed on. I was also gratified to catch, out of the corner of my eye, an unfamiliar expression on Alison's face: admiration. "Mostly around central East Anglia, for obvious reasons, but we're hoping to extrapolate to Anatolia in a pilot project, combining with tests of dowsing."

Anderson looked alert again. "Ah yes, the dowsing investigation, now, that was Professor Heffenblum. Always liked playing left field, old Heffenblum." That odd harrumph again. Perhaps it was Anderson's version of a chuckle.

"Yes, it's his baby, but I'm involved in a small way, which was why Roddy contacted us when the salvage team up here decided they wanted a dowser. Actually, that's why I came along today."

"How do you mean?"

"Well, I'm up here for family reasons, but when Alison said she was calling on you at some point, I thought I'd take the opportunity to ask you, off record, what you think about the dowser's findings on *The Blessing of Burntisland*. I promised the Prof I'd sound out the more sceptical brethren."

"Well, I didn't actually meet Mr—what was his name?"

"Fairlie."

"Yes, yes. He came highly recommended, as such persons go, and of course the timing—you recall, no doubt, that the salvage team were drawing blanks and we were thinking of pulling out. Only exploratory at that stage, but we needed a solid hook if we were going to channel any grant money that way. I must admit I thought it was a counsel of despair to turn to the occult, but Roddy undertook to do it unofficially. And then of course this Fairlie chap came up, in the first instance, with the suspected bearings of the *Perseus*."

I felt Alison stiffen beside me, like a pointer dog that senses prey. For myself, I was near to choking over Anderson's use of "the occult". The nerve of the man! My work was no more occult than what he and his chums got up to; a good deal less, most probably. I controlled myself and said, "Yes, I remember." Alison, bless her, managed to nod too. I would have to check later whether she recalled that false cast I'd come up with at first. I had a feeling I'd brushed over it in our preliminary conversation.

"Well, I remained unconvinced," continued Anderson. "He could have heard about that from any number of sources. The story's probably sprung more leaks than the *Perseus* herself." And he gave a colder version of his strange laugh.

"Oh, I really don't think so," Alison said, with a note of indignation that I frankly thought was stretching a point. I jabbed her very gently and discreetly with my elbow. She dropped her challenging glare, and pretended to pick a piece of fluff off her jumper, from a point midway between her breasts. Which looked becomingly rounded and soft in that material.

Anderson pushed his glasses up his nose. "If nowhere else, he'd have likely heard it from McKee, who undoubtedly knew, and would scarcely be likely to restrain himself from telling the rest of the salvage crew over a pint, or five. The point is, when I told them to give this dowser chap the brush-off, he promptly came back with another set of co-ordinates. One of their divers confirmed there were beams of wood down there, said he'd even touched one, so we were on. Although the idiot failed to procure a sample so we still have no date." He turned to me. "Did you know they took this Farley chap out in a boat over the supposed site?"

"Fairlie," I corrected him. "I didn't know the exact methodology, no."

"If you could call it that. With map dowsing, as Roddy explained it to me, there didn't seem any call for the dowser to visit the site. What if he'd asked to check the other co-ordinates, the first set? It was vainglorious, pandering to the sensationalists in the media if you ask me. Photo-opportunity."

There had been one picture taken of me in the boat that day, not by the press—they weren't informed till much later—but by Bernard Healey of the salvage team; a blurred effort due to the sea spray on his camera lens.

"You're saying the dowser did find the wreck," Alison persisted.

"I'm saying the wreck has probably been found. The dowsing element was incidental, is my belief. I think these people pick up on all sorts of hints given off by others, and there were plenty of clues about this site for anyone who was listening."

That's the sort of thing people always say about dowsers' finds if they don't want to believe in our powers. How did Anderson think any amount of "clues" would have told me the exact spot where *The Blessing of Burntisland* lay fathoms deep, among all those square miles of water? I began to feel my usual response—the sharp desire to see the find brought to light, to prove I was right. But no, no, that was not what I wanted this time.

"Had you heard that that Fairlie's been voicing his own doubts recently?" I said.

"No." He sounded bored with the subject. "Would you like to follow me?" He made to move off.

"Yes, talks about threats if the wreck is raised, plague germs was it Alison?"

I heard Alison take a breath, for this was way outside the scenario we'd planned. But her voice was steady as she spoke. "And now he's got people behind him saying the human remains should be left *in situ* as a last resting place."

"Is that so," said Anderson reflectively, stopping and turning back to us. "You see, I knew you'd be able to enlighten me. This undoubtedly explains the presence of that Doolin chap this morning. He was angling for just that sort of thing. Didn't think he was genuine. But we can refute them immediately on the plague idea, can't we, Dr Berry?"

He had me stumped there. I noticed he hadn't called me "Dave". As he waited for my reply, I felt sweat break out on my forehead. What the heck was he driving at?

After what felt like ten minutes, he prompted me. "Well, the date."

"Yes," I said eagerly—at least this was something I knew. "1633."

"No plague outbreaks ten years either side, were there?"

Alison ran in to cover me. "That's what Dave told me when we were discussing this before. And anyway the spores wouldn't last that long, didn't you tell me?" I nodded, grateful, but there was a sting in the tail. "Apparently the daft dowser wouldn't listen, kept muttering dire warnings."

I ignored her smug smile. "I thought you were driving at something more subtle," I said to Anderson, hoping that was the sort of comment an academic might make.

"No, no subtlety in Naval Archaeology, I'm afraid, not like you mainlanders." He spoke with dry amusement, but was he fooled? "Unless we can count our latest all-seeing innovative technology. Come along, I'll show you the scans."

With that, he ushered us towards the door we'd entered by. Turning to Alison, he asked about her Minister's view on the Scotland versus England claim on the treasure. As the others passed through to the AV viewing room, I called out that I'd catch them up in a minute, and headed back to the Gents.

It was less a case of needing a pee, more that I was being driven absolutely crazy by that bit of gristle and needed to dislodge it, away from public view. I tore a corner off the business card I'd picked up at the B&B that morning, and used it as a makeshift toothpick. I had a pee for good measure, then emerged from the Gents and saw to my right another door, identical to the one from the lab. It would be an easy mistake to make. So I made it.

The wrong door put me in a short stretch of corridor at right angles to the bit with the toilets in. There were a couple of office doors across the way, with names listed on laminated strips stuck on with bulging blu-tac. One said "Roderick Pearce". It was a comfort to know he was not going to emerge any minute and reveal my identity. To my left was an anonymous door with a wired-glass panel, through which I caught a glimpse of heads and computer screens all in a row; I guessed that was a general office. To my right the corridor stretched past the many-labelled office doors, and then turned to the left, in the opposite direction from the lab. I headed that way. Around the corner, after about twenty paces, the corridor was blocked by a solid door, bearing a "HAZCHEM" notice, bright orange with large black letters, and a yellow and black sign with a triple-ray logo that I was fairly sure was a radiation warning. I tried the handle, expecting to find it locked. It was. Nearby on the wall was a finger pad with numbers, similar to the one by the back door to the main building. There was also a swipe mechanism at waist level, which was blinking a little red light at me. I didn't like it one bit.

Standing there at that locked door, I momentarily "saw" a line cutting through me, a line that was a continuation of the tall spiked fence outside. As much as if I had been out in the road, I was on the boundary between civilian and military—or at least naval—facilities. I was meddling with stuff I didn't understand. I turned and dashed back towards the cross corridor.

But was the Naval Archaeology unit purely civilian, or did it cross that boundary? I stopped and knocked on the office door with Pearce's name.

"Come in," said a youthful voice. I poked my head round the door. There was one empty desk, and another occupied by a dishevelled looking individual who only reluctantly pulled his gaze from his computer screen.

"Roddy Pearce about?" I asked.

"Nope. Gone to Aberdeen."

"I'm Dave Berry. East Anglia. He was going to take me through to the Navy yard. About the wreck—*The Blessing of Burntisland*. Must have forgotten."

He frowned. "They haven't brought up any bits, as far as I know. You sure he was taking you into the yard, or do you want the labs? You'd best speak to Dr Anderson."

"Oh, I said hello to him, but he seemed fixated on this *Perseus* business." The man looked blank. So that was not general knowledge. "Anyhow, I'll ask him now, thanks." I backed out of the office before he thought to question me.

Potentially, it seemed, *The Blessing of Burntisland* spanned both sides of the invisible line I had felt in the corridor.

I was almost running as I re-entered the lab, but I slowed my pace, and veered towards the bench where Anderson had been checking his notes when we came in. He'd left the file open, papers spilling out. In the state I was in, there was no way I could read any of the pages of scrawl and what I guessed were email printouts, but I riffled through with an eye open for any pictures or diagrams. There were three.

One, near the top, was a picture I'd seen before: a reproduction of a lengthways cross-section of *The Blessing of Burntisland*—not a contemporary engraving, though done in that style, but a reconstruction of what she may have looked like, with baggage wagons and horses loaded on board. The sea appeared as a series of neat curly waves. Added on in blue biro, there were illegible notes around the margins, and in the same ink, a line scored heavily across the whole page, way above the original artist's plimsoll line. At some point, this told me, Anderson or a minion had worked out that the boat had been seriously overloaded, which contributed to her taking water in the storm, and then sinking so rapidly.

Just below this in the pile was a less sophisticated version of what I took to be the same thing, a cross-section of the boat, but lacking several of the features I'd recognized on the first one. There was no water-line drawn in this time.

The other, deeper in the file, was a sub. Also a diagrammatic cross-section. It was a poor quality photocopy or printout, with capital letters scattered around, half of them blurred, so that the key made little sense. But I did not need a key to understand the triple-ray logos: one in what appeared to be her engine room and another in one of the storage bays. A nuclear-powered sub, possibly nuclear-armed too. When had she gone down? There was no date on the diagram. I glanced at the adjacent pages of notes but my head swam, and I knew I could not absorb anything.

I daren't linger. Anderson would come looking for me any moment. I hurried to join him and Alison in the AV room. They turned as I entered. A multi-coloured slide, about two feet wide, was clipped up on a light box behind them. Sure enough, Anderson cocked an eyebrow at me, and murmured something quaint about had I fallen down the pan. Then he begged Alison's pardon.

"So that's your sonar scan. Pretty impressive," I said, trying not to sound out of breath. Actually it looked like a psychedelic moonscape.

"Except it doesn't reveal date, or what else lies beneath the surface silt. This is obviously one rib or spar that happened to poke up. Now, if that diver had managed to grab us a sample, we'd have been in business, with the carbon dating. Gave excuses about terribly poor visibility, and currents. Incompetence more like."

"Just as a matter of interest," I ventured, "why didn't they send someone down again, on a better day?"

"Oh, we're going to, don't worry! Just as soon as the boys next door—as soon as we can slot it in, busy schedule you know. We're not leaving it to the salvage lot this time, in fact our Scottish Office has very kindly put an injunction on amateur divers within a radius of a hundred metres around the site."

I thought of McKee, Healey, the whole rumbustious crew. "Didn't the salvage boys kick up a fuss?"

"They may have done, I don't deal with that side of things. It's for their own good, though, as I'm sure they'll come to see in due course. They simply would not have the resources to carry through a job like this."

"But they're the ones who started the search, and found it."

"Yes, and we're grateful to them of course. But you know better than most, Dave, they could never have hoped to keep this on a private footing. Of course we had to take it on, under aegis of Government."

"Like Sutton Hoo," I muttered.

"Beg your pardon? Oh yes, like Sutton Hoo. And they came to us, don't forget that."

"One last question," said Alison. Anderson turned to her, with a courteous look of attention. "Do you have any scans of the other vessel? The *Perseus*?"

His face closed. "You aren't concerned—you will understand—that's another matter."

"Oh of course, I wasn't asking you to show them. Just wondered."

Dr Anderson offered to order us coffee. I had to admire his polished manners; this was clearly a closure rather than an extension of the meeting. We declined. It was time to go.

"Phew," said Alison once we were out in the fresh air. "What do you reckon to that? He was amazingly open with us, wasn't he? The real old-fashioned absent-minded prof type."

"Or else he put on a good act, like we did."

"What do you think the *Perseus* is? A nuclear sub?"

"Well done, lass, how did you know that?"

"Female intuition. And how do you know I'm right?"

I told her about the third diagram in Anderson's file. As we drove back to our lodgings, I mused on how this affected my sense of dread about the wreck. I wished it were that simple; a radioactive hazard lying beside *The Blessing of Burntisland*, or in the other location. Yet, despite the evidence we had just come across, I could not feel that this was my answer.

"There are dozens of wrecks in these shipping lanes," I said, leaning across Alison to help myself to some more wine. We were all gathered again in the Screaming Carrot, which had the advantage of allowing you to bring your own bottles, though you had to pay two quid for corkage. The remains of neep mash and nut roast lay around on our plates. "From what Anderson said, I gather they have no intention of going ahead till they have more evidence this is the right one."

Alison and I had discussed heatedly how much, if anything, to tell our hippy friends about our interview with Anderson. My instinct was to keep quiet; hers, to share all. Being as she was Miss Bossy, she won. Thank goodness, in my burblings on Arthur's Seat, I hadn't mentioned the trumpet, so she couldn't let them in on that. I'd simply told Zemon that it would be great to visit his friends near Falkland and he'd obligingly rung them. The plan now was to make our boat trip tomorrow, then proceed to Eden Valley. I wouldn't get to Falkland Palace till the next day, but I would have to contain my impatience.

"If they don't go ahead, it could be because they know it's a nuclear sub." This was Zemon, coming back to his favourite theme. We were all going round in circles, as the wine sank in.

"No, that would make them definitely want to raise it," said Alison. "Think of all they could find out about the Ruskies' weapons programmes."

I had told them the indistinct lettering had not been Cyrillic, but we all agreed that did not rule out it being a Russian sub, a diagram labelled by our lot.

"The Cold War is over," said Zemon, "and anyway the point is, it could just as well be a British sub."

"Oh come on, we'd have known if one of ours went down." Alison had a lot more faith in the system than the young ones, probably because she was a part of it, as Zemon had pointed out earlier. She had replied indignantly that she'd been suspended for challenging authority and she was here with us, so what was the problem?

Irma leaned forward. "Joe says you mustn't dive, Zemon. If there is a nuclear submarine ..."

I didn't like to interrupt Irma, but she was missing the point. "He mustn't dive because there's a ban on diving in the area. And I don't think the sub is there, it's way further up the estuary."

"How do you know?" Irma turned her wide-eyed look on me.

"One of those things dowsers do know." I'd been a tiny bit wary about that first location, though I was still rather shocked I could have got it that wrong. Now I realized it must have been the sub—though why I'd picked up on that, when I was trying for a seventeenth-century wreck, was a mystery. But there was no doubt that the location I'd actually visited was *The Blessing of Burntisland*. Our trip out on the Firth of Forth tomorrow to the same spot should allow me to pick up "vibes" as Zemon called them, to help identify the threat I'd felt from the wreck.

While the waitress cleared away our plates and brought the pudding menu, we revisited the various options. Plague. The boat as graveyard. Or perhaps a dispute over ownership, Scottish or English, that could become heated enough to break up the United Kingdom. That seemed particularly unlikely, but none of the theories chimed with my inner fears. The others would not understand that, not even Alison.

"I'll have the spotted dick," said Zemon.

We'd more or less ruled out the plague possibility, but I thought this was a tasteless choice.

CHAPTER TEN

The breeze tugged at my hair and beard as I stared down from the quay at the bright orange inflatable bobbing below, with room for maybe twelve people. It had probably as much capacity as the little launch that Healey had used, but sat much lower in the water. Scanlon, the skipper, was showing Zemon the ropes. Or in the case of this boat, the cord that would start the outboard. There was some tarp-wrapped gear lodged under one of the benches.

"What's that stuff?" I asked Alison, not stopping to wonder why she should know any more about it than me.

"Something Scanlon's smuggling across the firth?" she replied.

We two had arrived at Newhaven by taxi. The others had been collected a bit earlier by Scanlon in his salt-rusted Citroen. Alison looked rather fetching this morning, in her light grey parka, though not as fetching as Irma in dark green.

Irma brushed past us, and started to climb down the iron ladder to the boat, lugging a lumpy kitbag with her. Her black leggings strained over her knees and thighs as she descended.

"Can I help," I called, but too late—Zemon leaped gracefully to the foot of the ladder, making the boat rock. If I were the skipper, I'd have yelled at him.

I yelled anyway. "What have you got in there?"

"Some weather gear, in case it turns nasty," Zemon called up, and he and Irma rolled the bundle under one of the benches near the stern.

It bothered me only marginally that the skipper bore a resemblance to myself, in facial hair and in general physique. It reminded me of that fantasy of Joe as sea-dog I'd had in the mirrored lift, in Alison's office block, about half a lifetime ago—or could it really be only a fortnight? Neither Scanlon nor I was wearing my fantasy nautical jumper, though. He had on a dirty donkey jacket and I was sporting my decrepit cagoule.

What was really bothering me was the risk of us drawing attention to ourselves, in view of the ban on exploring the wreck area. If we were going to be sitting pretty out there for as long as I needed, I should have arranged to hire fishing rods. I hadn't thought of it, with my head full of my escapade as Dave Berry, and the whirl of questions in my brain—that and the flight of Robbie's trumpet.

I turned to Alison. "Four visitors hiring a boat at this time of the year, and not even pretending they're going fishing. Bit obvious, isn't it?"

"What isn't obvious, Joe, is why you're so grumpy. Revisiting the site was the main reason you wanted to come up here in the first place, wasn't it?"

"Yes, but I hadn't reckoned on it turning into a circus." I'd have preferred it was just her and me. But the others had insisted on coming along, and I could hardly refuse, since it was Zemon who set up the boat trip. Scanlon was asking a low price and no questions. Plus, Zemon could help handle the boat. Despite my enjoyment of boat outings as a lad, when we'd visited branches of the family that lived by the sea, I'd never mastered sailing. Motor bikes, cars, tractors even, I loved driving or taking to pieces and putting back together. The innards and the control equally fascinating. But boats were somebody else's territory. I always had a special awe of the sea; a rational fear of the irrational, or was it the other way around?

Alison was right; I was grumpy. I felt scratchy and wound up. Doubtless it was the combined tension of returning to the wreck site, plus the delay in getting to Falkland. I could not get that trumpet out of my mind. Plus, I was worried that I might have a strange turn, like last time, over the wreck.

Scanlon nipped nimbly up the ladder. Close up, I saw he had an ugly nose, mottled and bulbous. Not like me after all.

"You can board her now," he said, standing to one side. First he handed Alison down, then turned to me, but I wouldn't take his hand. He cast me a wry look as I fumbled with my foot for the first convenient rung.

Once we were all settled, with Scanlon taking the wheel amidships and the rest of us sitting around the stern area, Zemon gunned the outboard. We slipped out of the square little harbour, with its fish-gutting sheds given over to a heritage museum and a Harry Ramsden's. Best not think about fish and chips now. On the far point of the northern quay stood what looked like a large pepper pot—a small-scale lighthouse, gleaming white against the grey cloud behind. Wheeling gulls caught the stray beam of sunshine, and my spirits lifted.

Immediately outside the harbour, we passed a cluster of raw new buildings, including a Travel Inn. The water began to lift and drop us, a trotting horse rather than a bucking bronco, and I thought, "I've got my sea legs this time." To the west, the Victorian miracle of the Forth Bridge loomed, with the modern road bridge beside it. Eastwards, towards Leith on the near shore, the royal yacht *Britannia* hove into view. Generous of Her Maj to give it to the nation. Beyond that, massive cranes, immobile—the commercial dockyards, distinctly unbusy. Somewhere in that vicinity was the MoD establishment, and beside it the Naval Archaeology Department, but I could not make them out at this distance. Beyond that, the firth widened and widened to join invisibly with the open sea.

"Crawling with tourists, no doubt," said Zemon in dismissive tones. It took a second for me to twig that he was talking about the *Britannia*.

To my relief, there were plenty of other small boats chugging around, enough so's we would not be conspicuous. I realized I had pictured our bright orange vessel all alone on the miles-wide stretch of water.

Clouds passed fast, high overhead; every so often, watery sunshine came our way. Irma's dark honey hair blew around, till she pulled on a striped black-and-yellow woolly hat.

"Buzz, buzz," I said. She laughed rather flatly, and I wished I'd cracked a more original joke.

"What are those islands, Joe?" she asked.

"The Inches." I was gratified to see Irma's frown of puzzlement.

Alison, nose reddened from the wind, was holding her hair down with one hand and grasping the side of the boat with the other. She also gave me a querying look. Cue for Joe the tour guide.

I explained these four islands that poke up out of the firth were all called Inch-something. One had seals on it. You could land on Inchcolm where King Alexander the First had built an abbey in the twelfth century. I remembered thinking, when Healey was giving me this same run-down, that Alexanders were usually Greek or Russian kings, but I hadn't quizzed him because he was such a proud Scot, he might have been offended by my ignorance.

"Then there's Inchkeith, where poor folks with the plague were quarantined in 1497," I finished my lightning survey.

"Wasn't that when Columbus discovered America?" asked Alison.

"No, that was 1492," said Zemon, not turning from his scrutiny of the route ahead.

"The plague," echoed Irma.

"It couldn't have survived the centuries." Alison answered the unspoken thought. "Plague bacilli can lie dormant, but not for that long."

"You sure about that?" asked Zemon.

"Completely." She turned to look out towards the sea end of the firth.

"I would really like to see the seals," said Irma.

"If there's time on the way back, maybe," said Zemon.

Like day-trippers out on a jaunt, I thought, thrusting my cold hands in my pockets. But of course this was fun for them, whereas for me it felt portentous. I stared at the dancing glassy hillocks of grey water, chopped and swirling with foam in our wake.

"Here, can you check the position," Scanlon called out to Zemon.

"Somebody take the throttle," said Zemon.

Before I could extract my hands from my pockets, Irma slid her bum along the side bench and was reaching to take over the control from Zemon's grasp. He stepped up beside Scanlon and his long white fingers began doing complicated twiddles with an instrument that looked like a compass with knobs on—plenty of knobs.

"So, what happened last time?" Alison reclaimed my attention. "Did it freak you out right away?"

"No, I was okay to begin with, though a bit reluctant. I'd told them the co-ordinates from the map."

"You'll have to explain to me about map dowsing, how it works."

"Sure, another time. The point is, the only proof for the sceptics would be the dive, later on. But since they'd asked, I used my rods till we were near, and then my pendulum, and when it started to spin around, I said 'X marks the spot, lads', and there was a cheer, and McKee opened a bottle of whisky and we all took a swig. It fitted quite well with their calculations about the sea-way the barge would have taken, tides and so on, but they'd not been able to pin down any one spot because a lot depended on the force of the storm that had capsized her, and whether she'd been blown off course much, and the strength of any currents—the sorts of things they couldn't calculate from the contemporary descriptions."

"So when did you start …?"

"I thought I told you. Right there. It was like I was under the water. Struggling. The boy, he couldn't swim. Then back home, the other ones, I realized it was Newbolt I was tapping into each time. They hit me without any pattern, in my life or his." I shook my head.

"This is real for you, isn't it, Joe?" It was a statement more than a question, and for that I was grateful. The "for you" though was a bother. Alison's hand slipped into mine, squeezed it. I felt her sympathy and gave a little pressure back. Then she moved away, to help Irma.

After a while, the tossing motion and slapping of the waves against the boat, as we chugged steadily out across the firth, worked to soothe me. The chill wind blew sharply, but the chinks of almost-sun lit up the hills to the north, and the waves as I stared into them were a little less grey, more tinged with green.

I recalled the way the Forth had looked that day I'd come out with Healey and the others, back in November. They were joshing me for being a Sassenach, but in a thoroughly good-humoured way. The water was a different green then, with more dark blue in it, and their little motor launch cut through it faster; and I recalled staring at the wake as I was doing now, but from a greater height, and it having an almost hypnotic effect. As we had approached the spot, with Healey calling out to McKee, their voices meant no more to me than the squalling of the gulls that had followed us out from the harbour at Burntisland. That's why everything felt different this time, of course; we were approaching from the opposite side of the firth—from Newhaven. That and the season. Then, the last flicker of warmth before the winter; today perhaps the first flicker of spring.

We had crossed the deepest part of the channel. I called to Zemon and the skipper. "We must be near our target by now." I recalled it was a mile out from Burntisland, and about halfway between the Forth Bridge to the west and Inchkeith to the east.

Fiddling with his complicated compass, Zemon knitted his dark brows then nodded.

"Another five minutes, people," he announced, and came back to the stern to take Irma's place.

Once more I felt a tinge of excitement, almost like that trip to locate *The Blessing of Burntisland*. Then, though, it had been the certainty I'd hit the spot, that the crew of seekers would rejoice, and I'd feel that rightness, like a key fitting a lock. Now, it was an unknown.

"Here's a test for you lot. Do you know what that is, over there?" I pointed across the mile or so of water, north-east to shore, where you could barely make out the pale streak of the concrete sea-wall, the grey of the slate quarry, and a jumble of town lapping up a steep hill. Alison and the others looked blank.

"That, my friends, is Burntisland." I did a couple of bars of trumpet fanfare with my fists lined up in front of pursed lips.

"It doesn't look how I imagined it," said Irma.

They had expected a more romantic sight, no doubt, as I had the first time. It was the bracketing, in the ship's title, of "Blessing" with that strange name—"Burnt Island"—that made you picture either an island torched to its bones of stone, with a crackling of blackened heather, or else a rebuilt but still historic town, with battlements and turrets. Not this awkward, workaday conglomeration of nineteenth and twentieth century utility.

"I like it how it is," I countered, "just another firth town struggling to keep on its feet, what with the shipyards closing and all that."

I remembered the town's great extended green, its tousled grass intersected with paths leading to footbridges over the sea front railway line. I could picture the way it used to look in Thomas Newbolt's time, sand dunes fronting the flat land where peddlers put up their stalls with food and booze and talismans to tempt the travellers making the crossing over the firth, to and from Edinburgh. The wide, rutted dirt road down to the harbour, the lines of baggage wagons queuing for entry to the jetty and onto the barge …

No, I must not go down that route. It was asking for trouble. Last time I was here, the wreck had seemed so distant. Or rather, the living people aboard the boat had seemed unreachably distant. The wreck itself, of course, was close by.

And here I was again. But this time, the people might be closer.

"Here," I said, at the same instant as Zemon, looking at his instruments, cut the throttle.

"And now, what do we do?" said Alison in her businesslike way. "You going to dowse, Joe?"

"No point," I said. "I gave Zemon the co-ordinates; we're there, right, Zemon?"

"Check."

"So I'm not going to wave my rods around or twiddle my pendulum just for the sake of it. I'd just like to rest here quietly. Can you keep us in the same spot for a few minutes?" I addressed the skipper.

Scanlon cleared his throat loudly. "I'll have to keep her turning over. There's a fair spot of current running here."

"No problem. Mechanical noise is fine, background. But I want a few minutes with my eyes closed and I'd be grateful if we could all manage without talking. It might help if we remember we are directly over the grave of thirty men, women, and children." The others nodded solemn consent. Irma closed her eyes straight away.

"Another idea—just a suggestion," said Scanlon. "Joe, would you like to sit up front, the prow? I might need to ask your friend here for a spot of assistance."

That made sense. I moved gingerly around the housing in the centre of the boat, and lodged myself on the triangular piece of wood that fitted into the pointed prow area. Immediately I felt more relaxed, out of sight of the others.

I closed my eyes then, and took a couple of deep breaths. Petrol fumes, a faint whiff of fish. Cold, salty dampness. The irregular slapping of the waves on the boat's rounded sides. The regular chug-chug of the motor. The rocking of the boat, almost pleasant if you gave in and didn't fight it. The odd lurch, the wake from a passing boat or a bigger wave.

The cold wind. It had been cold that other day, back in November, but I had scarcely noticed, my hands and brain busy with the rods, then trying to compensate for the motion of the boat as I'd held my pendulum, my old battered bead on a string. How it had danced for me. But then the awful seizure, my first taste of Newbolt. Vision, or fit? Maybe I'd overdone my intake of McKee's whisky. No, that was afterwards.

Well anyway, I'm back here now, I thought. Let's see what …

There was definite lurch, and a loud splash. It sounded as if they had thrown a body into the water. Was that what was in those bundles, body parts that Scanlon had to dispose of, or some contraband to be collected later? Alison teasing me about him being a smuggler. This wasn't helping my concentration. I was tempted to open my eyes, or shout out to the others, but there were no more splashes and no commotion from the other end, in fact it was remarkably quiet. I took three deep, slow breaths. I must avoid paranoia.

The beat of the engine, thrumming on regardless, settled me again till I was in a sort of waking trance, enough to dip down below the surface.

Bubbles. How many bubbles of air, streaming past me, flying up to the surface. The pressure increasing, darkness closing in. The cold. It's gritty, this water. But it's as if I have dark-piercing eyes, can see through the dark and murk, and it's as if I were on a magnetic beam, between myself in the dinghy with my eyes shut, and that target down there. If only I can keep delving deeply, keep breathing steadily, keep going. At the top, they were like bubbles in grey glass, now like bubbles in mud.

I'm gripped by terror. What if Thomas Newbolt should seize me now, I'd be trapped underwater by him. I'm fighting off the possession. But perhaps that is what I came here for? Perhaps the only way to gain release is to give in? I'm writhing now, sick on my seat, on the verge of opening my eyes. Sweating despite the cold.

Deep, deep. Only a little push more. Scan the rucked silt, merged with muddy water, nothing solid. Yes. She's there, I can feel it, the bones and the bits of her, the ribs tickling the mud. Lodged beneath and between, oh my dears, nothing visible to the naked eye or even the goggled one of the ignorant diver, but there's the glorious treasure, yes for sure. And there among the human bones and the horse bones, the shattered shafts of the baggage wagons, the rusted bits and snaffles, in the shards of a perished saddle pack, not in the strongboxes, there is the strongest box of all. Safe beneath the silken silt.

He, the ignoramus, knowing nothing of this, reaches out his hand for a lump that might or might not be a timber jutting above the bottom, a hump of a lump, with its shadow flung on the flying silt behind it. Cast by the beam from his helmet light.

My eyes sprang open. I jumped up, making the boat rock, and clawed my way to the stern where Scanlon sat impassive beside the throttle and only two other pairs of wide eyes stared at me.

"What the fuck?" I bawled. Then: "Where's Zemon?"

But I knew already. I knew, before the guilty looks on the faces of Alison and Irma gave way to gabbling attempts to explain, that he'd stowed an aqualung in that bundle under the benches, the rest of the gear in Irma's awkward pack, had his wetsuit on under his clothes, and while poor old, stupid old Joe sat in the prow with eyes closed like a complete pansy, Zemon the Action Man had made his great dive. Against my express wishes, against our agreed deal, and against the law.

Irma in the end shut us all up. She was concerned about Zemon's safety, as if us quarrelling loudly up here would stop him getting back.

He bobbed up like an apple in a tub, about twenty yards to port, and Scanlon kicked her into gear and roared over, just missing him, and circled round to pick him up. As he floundered over the orange roll of the bulwark, and peeled off his mask, I was none too sorry to see his complexion was grey, and he was shivering violently.

Irma helped him wriggle out of his wetsuit and started rubbing him down with a big blue towel. I turned my back.

"Why, Joe, why are you so angry? He was only trying to help," Alison said.

"What help could it be to repeat what the salvage crew and Navy lot have done already? What Dr Anderson told us the diver found?"

"He might have found more." She turned to smile at Zemon, now dressed in his jeans and jumper and padded jacket. "So, any luck?" asked Alison, as if he'd called in to the travel agent to enquire about a holiday.

Irma was hugging him, as he sipped from a metallic flask, his teeth chattering so much that drops of coffee trickled down his chin. You could see him trying to get a grip on himself. He was so obviously distressed, so shaken, that my fury drained away a little.

"I think I was nearly there," he stammered. "I saw a bit of the wreck, I'm positive. It was so weird." He squinted at me. "I think I understand a little, how you feel about this, Joe. It was as if a hand reached out, and stopped me, just as I was about to make solid contact."

The cocky Zemon we'd met so far had been transformed for the time being into a subdued and confused fellow. It seemed he had more sensitivity than I'd given him credit for.

Irma took over at the stern, and Scanlon returned to the wheel, to guide us back across the firth and into dock in Newhaven harbour. I sat huddled at the opposite side from Alison and Zemon, trying to calm myself with the thought that this afternoon we would be at Eden Valley, one step nearer to my new goal.

CHAPTER ELEVEN

The house above Eden Valley was built for gales, with a stone-shingled roof crouched low over two stories of uncompromising stone. The window frames were painted a gaudy turquoise that, to my eyes, didn't suit the climate or surroundings. Worse, fresh paint had been slapped on over corroded old paintwork, and was peeling in many places. Weeds bristled from the edges of the gravel frontage where we had pulled up. A child's bright yellow plastic tricycle lay on its side beside the front door.

As soon as Kirsty opened to our knock, I could tell she hadn't been expecting any extras, only Zemon and Irma. Her smile was too tight. She was a tall, stringy woman in her mid-thirties, with frizzy hair in a plait, and red hands that she was wiping on a none-too-clean tea towel. Several kids' heads bobbed about, peeking out from behind her flour-streaked pinafore. In this out-of-the-way place, we must have been the greatest novelty since Christmas.

"Welcome," she managed. "Come right in now out of that sharp wind," as though we had trekked across the moors, instead of driving up nearly to the door. Her voice was a surprise: soft, mildly Scots, in a way I knew instinctively to be posh even though I'm no expert on Scots accents. A lot posher than she looked.

"Graham?" enquired Zemon.

"Back any minute."

Zemon folded her in an enthusiastic hug, from which she emerged with her ruddy complexion even pinker, but slightly more relaxed.

"This is Irma, and these are Alison and Joe, the treasure seekers."

That made us sound like something out of a children's book, but I didn't object. Kirsty, his friend, was welcoming us strangers. She kissed both the women on the cheek and shook hands formally with me.

"So what's this about treasure seekers?" she asked.

"Just the opposite," I replied. "We'd prefer they didn't raise the treasure of *The Blessing of Burntisland*."

"Are you crazy? You'll have half of Scotland up in arms."

So she knew about the wreck. Not surprising it was general knowledge around these parts, near enough to Burntisland, and to the Edinburgh museum that might be the home to the silver plate and other treasures, if they won out over the British Museum. If the salvage went ahead.

As though sensing my inward shiver, Alison said, "Well, to be honest, it's not so certain it can be raised. We spoke to the guy in charge, the day before yesterday, and he told us it might not be a viable project." She was frowning at Zemon. Would he understand?

"What Zemon meant was, Joe's a dowser, but for treasure not water," Irma said.

"Or old stones," added Zemon. "We've got a plan about that."

"Well, let's get you lot sorted and we can talk later," said Kirsty.

She asked me to wait in the living room, and ushered the others upstairs with their luggage, the children trailing after and from what I could see, trying to clamber up Zemon's long legs as he went.

The living room, off to the right at the front of the house, was a large disordered room hung with dusty woven panels, abstract patterns in lumpy wool, which I guessed had emerged long ago from an equally dusty loom that squatted in one corner. It seemed I had company when a Dalmatian dog strolled in through the open door from the hallway, and I made to greet it, stretching out my hand. However it stalked past with its tail held stiffly out behind, giving not a snuffle nor a bark, and disappeared through another door which must have led straight to the kitchen, judging by the smell of baked apples. I'd never been so snubbed by a dog before. It made it even harder to hang around trying to look casual. I glanced from the clutter of children's toys on the floor and battered sofa, to the uneven ranks of books on jerry-built shelves, then gazed idly up at the clusters of dried plants hanging from the ceiling beams.

Something very strange had been going on in the waters of the firth this morning. I'd never know, of course, what I'd have felt if Zemon hadn't interfered. That suffocating moment of entrapment, for example—was it my own or Zemon's panic? Or could it have been Newbolt's? Newbolt could swim, I knew that. Still, he may have doubted he'd escape. Or—there came a thrill at the thought—what if I'd picked up on Robbie's fear? A direct contact for once; and if once, then another was possible.

Then there had been my sense of the boat, *The Blessing of Burntisland* herself, a sense I'd never had before, a strange mix of the timbers and the cargo. It was hard to sort that out, because Zemon's dive had interfered with my own exploration. It wasn't his fault alone, of course; all of them had conspired, which showed that they didn't understand what I was trying to achieve—not even Alison. That was what hurt.

Simpler on my own—I'd always managed on my own before.

"Do you know about herbs?" Kirsty's voice made me jump, as if I'd been caught rifling through the drawers of the battered writing desk in the corner.

"Some. Can't recognize them dried." Actually I'd spotted rosemary, and sage, and tansy, but there was an eagerness in the way she'd spoken that warned me off. If she was into healing or worse, the white witch thing, then she might imagine we were kindred spirits. I decided to change the subject. "Your dog just gave me the cold shoulder."

"Oh, Dirk, don't mind him. He's barmy. His mum died when he was a wee pup, and he was hand reared, but kept company with a litter of kittens, and ever since he's thought he was a cat."

"No way," I said, unbelieving; a dog has a dog's nature, which will surely out, no matter how it's reared.

But Kirsty insisted. "Imprinting I think they call it."

I remembered the ducks that thought a man was their mother, Konrad Lorenz was it? One of those nights when I was recovering from Marjory, watching a programme in the OU "Introduction to Psychology" course, this had come up. The first thing the ducklings saw when they hatched was Lorenz—he must have removed the eggs from the mother duck—plus he gave them food, so they started following him around, and panicked when they lost sight of him.

"Does he try to miaow then, or what?" I ventured, and Kirsty laughed.

At that moment, the troupe of children—there were three, but they felt more like six—tumbled into the room. Julian, the oldest, demanded to know what the joke was. Kirsty explained, while the two little girls, Rose and Daisy, jumped around, getting in the way of clearing the sofa where I was to sleep.

Graham was a forester, Julian had told me while we were unrolling a sleeping bag on the sofa, and I'd expected a broad, taciturn bloke. I suppose I had a lumberjack stereotype in mind. Seeing him in the midst of his family and guests over the supper table, a plate loaded with a huge slice of meat pie held aloft in his right hand as he emphasized a point with his left, I realized how misleading stereotypes could be. He was very tall, but not a giant of a man, more a beanpole. Or a birch tree, maybe, with his floppy blondish hair, and his silvery brocade waistcoat. I wondered how long it would take before he passed the plate down the table.

"But I mean to say, Zemon," he went on, "have you thought about asking the locals? I do appreciate, no Daisy please don't pick your nose at the table, I do value your consulting us *of course* but even after—how many years is it, Kirsty?" He had an English accent, one I couldn't place, middle-class northerner of some species.

"Seven. Julian was two when we moved in, and I was pregnant with Rose," said Kirsty as she imperturbably continued cutting portions of pie. "And do hand that plate down the table, before it gets cold and our guests keel over from starvation."

What a wonderful woman, I said to myself, as the plate arrived in front of me. It was hard to hand it on to Alison but it had to be done. She muttered something about antediluvian chivalry, but before I could say "Pardon?" she was piling on the vegetables and tucking in. The kids, fortunately, had been served first. They wouldn't have had my fortitude.

"After seven years, we're still regarded as foreigners around here." Another plate circled around, and this time I turned it back when Irma offered it me. She gave a cheeky grin, which probably meant the same as what Alison had said, with trimmings. I resolved there and then to grab first turn next supper time, assuming we were still eating here tomorrow night. Our plans were fluid, and I for one was willing to decamp to an inn at Falkland if it turned out we were putting Kirsty and Graham to too much trouble.

Finally my helping arrived.

"Yes, foreigners," Graham insisted, "even though I joined their mountain rescue team the first month we were here, and Kirsty runs a very popular cooking class at the community centre, and they constantly come to me when they want to battle with the authorities."

"Maybe if you didn't still call our neighbour-folk 'them', Graham, they would be able to think of you more as one of the clan."

"The clan! What an outdated yet at the same time applicable expression."

He would surely have carried on like this, but the natives were growing restless. Julian, who had been holding out his plate for seconds even before all us grown-ups had been served, stood up, leaning towards his mother and the remains of the meat pie, at the same moment as the toddler Daisy up-ended her water glass over Rose's head. It was more or less empty but you wouldn't have guessed that from the roar that Rose set up, a babyish reaction for a seven-year-old. She reared back, knocking into Julian, so that he dropped his plate, and felled a wine glass. The red stain soaked into the blue cloth, making a purple pool that Alison and Irma vied to dab up with their paper-towel napkins. Rose's roar redoubled when she was sent down from the table, for giving her little sister a slap in revenge.

Kirsty slipped away for a minute, leading Rose out of the room. Returning with a furrow of worry on her brow, she settled down to eat the rest of her meal with little Daisy ensconced on her lap. She murmured something to Graham about Rose's temper or temperature—I couldn't tell which—but he was listening to Zemon.

"You're deliberately misunderstanding what we told you, Graham. We didn't come here to find a place. By the way, this is delicious," said Zemon, giving Kirsty a beaming smile. Again I saw her relax, basking in his charm as if it were a sunbed. It was astonishing how quickly he had recovered from his scare during that reckless dive; I was the one not fully recovered.

"Then why on earth come all this way? Surely not to witness the smooth operations of a commune consisting only of one nuclear family? You've seen all this before. And been good enough to point out to me that I've sold out by prostituting myself to the Forestry Commission, when I could be growing all my own vegetables in this god-forsaken climate, as no doubt you intend to do wherever you set up your utopia."

Graham's tone, in contrast to his language, was completely amiable. Irma perhaps missed some of the nuances, even though her English was near-perfect; she burst in as if to fend off an escalating row.

"Really, please, you must excuse Zemon if he sounds rude. We had this idea with our friends in Cardington, to make our next place a model for the alternative world we are struggling for, not messy squats like some of the comrades, though they have good ideals at heart really. So he told me I should like to meet you guys and see how you are living. Also to tap into your wisdom about harmonizing with your surroundings." She paused. "Do I mean surroundings? What is the word?"

Zemon looked at her with amusement, not helping her out.

"Environment," suggested Alison. I wondered whether, working in the Department, she had an awareness of the way campaigners like Zemon and Irma probably thought about global warming every time they used hot water or if, for her, "environment" was more a question of looking after the landscape.

"No, the environment is the whole world really. I mean more local." Irma furrowed her brow.

"Ecosystem?" offered Graham. Irma shook her head.

"Neighbourhood?" tried Kirsty, to the same response.

Suddenly I had it. "Homestead."

Irma looked at me as if I'd given her a small but valuable present. My satisfaction lasted only a few seconds. The others were staring at me with various dubious expressions.

"Home on the range, do you mean?" snorted Zemon.

"Tie a yellow ribbon on the old oak tree, maybe?" chipped in Alison.

"Or since we're in Scotland, how about croft-stead instead of homestead?" put in Graham. "Though our house is much too grand to have been a crofter's cottage, I'm afraid."

Kirsty's face was pink, either from suppressed laughter or sympathy. My own cheeks burned. Stupid of me to have imagined I might come up with the right word when everyone else was failing. For all that I scanned the world, listened in on conversations, read oddments of newspapers and magazines and watched bits of telly, I knew I lacked any orderly learning. My reading of books was too scattered, I picked things up in second-hand bookshops and devoured them piecemeal, often reading the end or middle at once, and the beginning years later. Stories I read forwards, but not many of those. My vocabulary was patchy, as I knew from the way it often let me down, like now.

"Getting back to Irma's point", said Kirsty slowly, "'about harmonizing, which was kind of her, in view of Graham's obvious distance from our neighbours, I think she was talking about our relationship …"

Little Daisy, who had been wriggling on her mother's lap, succeeded in slipping out from under her restraining arm at this point, and scuttled off through the door into the hallway. Kirsty turned to her husband. "Oh Graham, could you make sure she doesn't go near the stove? And bring in the apples. And the custard—mind, it's hot!" By this time he had disappeared.

Irma prompted Kirsty. "You were saying? About your relationship." Both she and Alison leaned forward, with that ill-disguised thirsty look of those who sense a bit of gossip coming.

Kirsty stood up and took our plates, stacking them while she spoke. "I was going to say, our relationship to the immediate landscape, the house, the vegetable garden, the hills around, and with Graham in a sense penetrating the forest in his work. Though he hadn't planned that." I guessed there'd be no gossip from Kirsty, but her next words set me wondering. She turned to Alison and me. "I suppose you know that we moved in here with two other couples, with the aim of self-sufficiency?"

In fact, the ever-casual Zemon had told us next to nothing about his friends; but I should have asked.

"I was wondering what Graham meant by 'commune'. It sounds sort of seventies, if you don't mind my saying so," said Alison.

"Oh, don't worry, everyone says that—except the few loonies like us who attempt to revive the idea. Only now we do things differently; there's a lot more ecological awareness, permaculture, that sort of thing. Anyhow, it went the way of most such dreams. In our case, the first bad winter was enough to drive the others away. So Graham took the forestry job and we manage the garden between us as best we can." I understood now the shabbiness, scattered toys, frayed sofa, and neglected loom—Kirsty could not keep up with the housework, let alone her weaving, on top of the gardening and other chores.

"But how did you all fit into this house in the first place?"

"Oh, we didn't. Dee and Robin stayed in a caravan out the back while they converted one of the outbuildings—they were to have an independent wee house. But the winter drove them in here, and then we were all too much on top of one another, and they fell out with Breslaw and Alice, and everyone fell out with us."

Alison had stiffened. "Not Jack Breslaw?" Kirsty nodded, and Alison turned to me. "That was Marazion's real name. I'd completely forgotten till now."

I remembered our first pub conversation, and her telling me about this lover from her past. It seemed an odd coincidence that he'd been here with Graham and Kirsty, but then again, these oddballs on the fringes probably circulated around the same sorts of activities and often ended up bumping into each other. Had Zemon known him, too? He was cocking an eyebrow in what might have been an enigmatic manner. But then again, I was probably tying my own eyebrows in knots.

"He's made it in the big world now," said Kirsty. "Wrote to us at Christmas to let us know. A PR consultant."

Graham returned with a tray bearing a large dish of baked apples, set cold in their juices; a steaming jug of custard; and a stack of assorted dishes. Kirsty gave him our dirty plates and said: "Spoons," at which he obediently ambled off kitchenwards again. It struck me as funny that Kirsty could boss her husband around so, when she was as mild-mannered as a ewe.

"Of course, it was a strain for Graham and me, too." Kirsty spoke hurriedly, as if to slip this in while he was in the kitchen. "That's why Daisy is so much younger."

I did a quick sum. Four years didn't seem much of a gap to me, but what did I know of family dynamics? Such things were never talked about back home in Thetford. As a kid, I'd somehow understood that Jean being ten years older than me was because our mother had miscarriages. Then again my parents might not have been getting on, what with Dad's temper; they might have slept on opposite sides of the bed with no touching, like me and Marjory in our last months together. Not together.

"But we're rock-solid now. What was that Icelandic book?" Kirsty asked as Graham came back, humming the theme tune from *The Sting* and rhythmically rattling a fistful of spoons.

Graham stilled the spoons, frowned, and then answered in that annoying telegraphese which couples often use. "*Independent People.* Oh, I see. That's us."

Kirsty turned to the rest of the company, as if we knew what they were talking about. "Well, Bjartur's place was called Winterhouses before he moved there, but he renamed it Summerhouses, just because he wanted things to be better. In a way that's like Joe saying 'homestead', isn't it?"

"Hardly a good model," said Graham. "Bjartur of Summerhouses was a pig-obstinate patriarch who considered his poor patch of land worth dying for, and his womenfolk and children his subjects."

Kirsty had finished serving up the apples. The combination of cold apples and hot custard was odd, but delicious. The set apple jelly, studded with raisins that had spilled out of the cored apples, melted in amber pools amongst the custard. There was a hint of cinnamon and nutmeg on the browned apple skins that peeled away from the pearly flesh at a touch. My spoon, I noticed, was silver—old, and striated with many a scrubbing, but silver.

"Summerhouses, homestead, whatever," Zemon drawled, looking from Graham to Kirsty, to Irma, to Alison, and myself. Julian was regarding him with wide-open eyes, meanwhile spooning pudding into his mouth very regularly. Little Daisy crept back onto her mother's lap. At the instant Zemon parted his lips to continue, I knew what he was going to say. "Doesn't it remind you of that Roman place, the one we visited on the way up here? Housesteads. Though presumably that wasn't what the Romans called it, doesn't sound very Latin does it?"

Hadn't they read the notices on the site? I could not resist the chance to put Zemon straight. "The Romans called it Vercovicium," I said, "and they—people thereabouts—only called it Housesteads long after, probably the fifteenth century."

"Sixteenth, actually," said Graham with quiet authority.

"The point is," Zemon shoved on with his own agenda, "Housesteads wasn't in tune with its surroundings. The Romans imposed their idea of an urban centre in the midst of the wilderness ..."

"Well, it was a camp beside the Wall," I protested. "You couldn't call that a wilderness."

"Exactly. The function of the Wall was a demonstration of their power against the wild Picts in a wild land. Then there was the camp, and that was orderly too, a whole town. It didn't fit in and yet it did. Look how they followed the line of the escarpment with their Wall."

"They had to." I was fuming. Zemon was taking over my territory, and I needed to contradict whatever he said. "Wouldn't have been much use building it in the burn below."

"That's my point. The Wall is alien, yet it grows into the landscape. And given enough time, the fort, and the settlement also, grow into the landscape."

"If you mean they collapse and get covered with turf ..." I began.

"What is old," Kirsty said softly, eyes gleaming, "whatever it may have looked like, however alien or raw to begin with, begins to harmonize …"

"Which was Irma's word," Zemon said, as if he'd turned up trumps. "So you can harmonize by being around long enough, like Housesteads or this old *homestead* here. Or you can harmonize by tuning into the place where you find yourself, in the here and now, like Graham and Kirsty have done. But how about combining both?"

Evidently he intended us to wonder what he meant. We all looked at him (I may have been scowling slightly), while he again scanned us all, a maestro of timing. What he said next was what I least expected.

"Which is where you come in, Joe."

It wasn't only the toy windmill, inexplicably missed in our making up of my temporary bed on the sofa, which kept me awake. I'm no princess, but it was no pea, and I don't know why it took at least half an hour before I realized this was no ordinary lump. After I'd dug it out from between the cushions and chucked it on the floor—which seemed the normal destination in this house—I settled down, and continued to mull over the issue that was bugging me. It chased itself round like Dirk chasing his own tail, a most unedifying performance I'd been treated to while I was helping with the drying up.

The young ones, as I privately continued to designate Zemon and Irma (though Zemon was probably as old as Graham and Kirsty, who however seemed older because they had the responsibility of house and kids), wanted me to do them a small favour. They'd come here to look over the closest example, in Zemon's view, to the way of life they were aiming at, not that it amounted to much judging by our tour of the gardens just before supper. Any one of my neighbours in Bishop's Stortford with an allotment was doing more in the way of sustainable lifestyle than these poor folk struggling with the inclement climate and lack of time. I reckoned Zemon must have been thinking of the ideal, the way his friends had aimed it to be, when they arrived above Eden Valley with the other couples, all starry-eyed with their hand tools and old-fashioned seed varieties.

The one bit that still worked, apparently, was the music circuit. Graham played the violin and Kirsty the flute. Whenever possible, they assembled with like-minded New Age types and a few tolerant locals in one or other of their houses in a radius of twenty miles or so.

The pubs round here were not generally encouraging, although in a couple of nights there was to be some live music at the Stag and Hounds in Falkland.

Where I came in, as Zemon put it, was when they got back home to Cardington. Of course it was purely fortuitous that they had met up with me thanks to Alison's good offices in the Rose and Crown in Newcastle. But being that way inclined, they thought it was Meant. They had set their hearts on establishing their hippy-type community on some site that had been sacred in ancient British times. They couldn't plonk themselves down on an English Heritage spot, not if they wanted to stay, so they needed to find their own. They were convinced—quite rightly, as I was able to confirm—that there were dozens, if not hundreds, more places with ancient stones beneath the surface, than those that had been excavated. So they'd got it in their simple skulls, or rather Zemon had, that dear old Joe here would trot along to their home at their behest, identify a few likely sites, and then tune into their chakra or feng shui or whatever tommy-rot they had on hand that day, and tell them which was most favourable for their new life. Like an ancient Roman chicken-gut diviner doing the auguries, or a Chinese astrologer predicting the auspicious day or place for a wedding.

Well, I wasn't going to do it. One, I'm not a quack, and though I could find ancient stones, I could not, repeat *not*, tell which would suit their intentions and fit their peculiar vibes. I don't deal in good luck nor in predictions. Two, as I told them plain, most land in England belongs to somebody—no, make that *all* land. So it would be a completely pointless exercise. There was no way they could start a settlement on whatever ancient sacred site they fancied. Three—what was three?

It was at this point that my mind repeatedly skipped the objections and snagged on the counter-irritants. Alison saying of course that isn't what Joe does. What business was it of hers if I went off for a few days' mystical dowsing jaunt with the young ones? After that daft diving business, she had used up her credit with me. She and I had no plans for when we got back down South. She might be returning to work, or if not, I presumed she'd need to look for another job. Probably she was jealous that they wanted my company—but it wasn't my fault if I had the special skills they needed.

Whoa, Joe. It wasn't just that I was contradicting my wiser self, which knew this was a non-starter. No, it was worse. A mad corner of my mind was running ahead, seeing myself as a kind of elder statesmen in the settlement: a cluster of round stone huts with threads of smoke curling out of their thatched roofs, surrounded by a wide circle of standing stones which we had unearthed and raised in situ. I'd have the biggest hut, naturally, and I'd be sitting in the sun outside, settling people's disputes, calming their worries, and laying healing hands on their sick. Small children play around my feet; their mother comes back from the bakehouse with a basket full of newly baked loaves. She has a long plait, dimpled rosy cheeks—and she looks remarkably like Irma. Or, whether worse or better I could not tell, like Alison.

Stop right there, I'd tell myself, and then the thoughts would start back at the beginning. Zemon lording it over us all at the supper table. Alison's tuppence-worth, the odd mention of Marazion. Kirsty all eager, as I had known she would be, about my dowsing. Zemon and Graham and Irma discussing how to set me up for the site-hunt back home.

I'd refused adamantly. Since adamant didn't seem to be in their rule book, I'd then cunningly deflected the conversation by asking about Falkland Palace. Although it was only twenty minutes' drive away, Kirsty hadn't been there since before Daisy was born, so the upshot of that decoy was that she wanted to come with us, with all her brood in tow, if Rose was well enough by the morning.

The waking dream swooped down on me like a night bird, soft and startling.

With the sun streaming in thus at an angle, catching the loose hairs in an aura of light, Susan indeed resembles an angel. She has on her face that half-abstracted gaze that I always associate with her inner music, since she told me of hearing it inside her, when I teased her for failing to attend to Brother Robert's declamation on the evils of Popery. I want to press my ear to her ribcage that I might hear the music for myself, almost as though she were the humming soundbox of a viola da gamba, but I know from experiments in this direction in our night-time sojourns together that the sounds are for her own, inward, ear only. Dearest Susan, my eternal mystery: so earthly yet with unerring channels into realms of the soul that most of us cannot even dream of.

I tap my quill to my page, making no mark for it is as empty of ink as my mental faculty of inspiration. I know so well, yet do not know, what it is that I have been burning to convey to a public that is all roiled with misapprehensions of our endeavour. Unlike our model and chief engine Winstanley, I have no longer any faith in moving the Parliament, the Lord

Protector, or even the Army from whose ranks I ejected myself. We must now appeal more broadly to the common people, and bend our words to fit their tunes, and for this I have time and again sought Susan's aid, since she is their representative in my house.

She has remained silent in face of my last query for a full two minutes now, and I break my admiration of her physiognomy to prompt her.

"Tell me, my dear, what is the instrument and what the melody?"

She turns with a little quiver to face me full on, and smiles. "No, I wasn't day-dreaming, I was puzzling where I am to find some yards of sea-green ribbon."

Her smile is wonderfully winsome, but she knows I do not care for this topic. If she will join the wondrous regiment of women planning to take their petition to Westminster—and I doubt not that it is a well-intentioned action, thought surely doomed to failure—then I should dearly like to witness the procession. But she knows as well as I that presenting myself in the capital would be to place my life in capital danger; though she has tried to argue me into recklessness, saying the mask was full protection and none could ever have guessed at my identity. I choose to think otherwise and even at times shudder at unfamiliar sounds at our door, imagining a spy sent from France to seek revenge and rip apart my idyll by ripping out my bowels.

"Look not so sombre, Master Newbolt," she says, advancing with her hands outstretched. "A bunch of ribbons is poor stuff, I know, but with our voices joined we surely shall be heard from Greenwich to Richmond, and then the ripples will run all up and down the country as when I shake my sheets to make them smooth after they have dried."

And with that she pats me on the cheeks like one of our children, and skips from the room, to attend to her laundry no doubt. Ah, but you are my Muse, my Susan, through what subtle process who shall tell, for despite your failure to address my question, and despite raising that matter of contention between us again, you have returned me to my fount of arguments. How to spread the word: by word of mouth, that is it, and it must be by practical example combined with stories of our new way of living, in language as colourful as the women's march will be. The stories shall start with my tract. I dip my quill into the ink-pot, ready to flow again.

I lay quaking, not sick or headachy but full of wonder and shaken to the core. Newbolt's fears seemed to me so frightful, I was all the more struck by how joyous he felt in this waking dream, very different from how I'd encountered him before. It was later, I knew somehow, later in his life than my previous glimpses. The mask.

I remembered the suffocating leather which coated my—his—face at the execution. So it was some time after that horrible event. Who was Winstanley? And Susan—a woman now, not the girl I recalled from the marshes—was she his wife? When she said "Master Newbolt", it was with such a light, teasing touch that I knew she could equally have called him "my dear".

Foolish tears welled in my eyes. What for? I could not possibly be envious of this man from the past. The one I felt close to, who reminded me of myself when I was young and full of promise, was Robbie. Where had he got to in all this?

One more phrase nagged my drifting attention: "our new way of living"—that was close to what Kirsty and Graham, Zemon and Irma had been talking about at supper. Objectively, I had to face the possibility that this had not been a genuine vision, but a mere figment of my imagination. There was only one way to find out for sure, and tomorrow I'd move towards it.

CHAPTER TWELVE

If Zemon and Irma hadn't wanted to see Falkland, Alison and I could have travelled in Kirsty's ancient Humber, along with the kids. Then, we wouldn't have chucked our bags in the back of Alison's car on the off chance we might stay over at the inn, the Stag and Hounds. We'd have come back to Eden Valley, and returned to Falkland the next night for the music, and I'd have taken myself off on my own for my hunt-the-trumpet venture. That way, perhaps I'd have kept it secret, Alison and I wouldn't have—well, it could all have turned out different.

You can't know, that's the truth. It's merely my hunch that that was the feather in the balance that tipped the scales. But I could not blame Zemon for coming to see Falkland Palace. He had more right than us to be in Kirsty's car, being as he was her friend, and Irma along with him.

Rose had passed muster at breakfast time, no sign of the malady Kirsty had worried about. Graham couldn't join the party because of work, but he stayed later than usual after breakfast, to see us off. After I'd thrown my stuff into a bag, I went out to find him having a smoke in the garden. I needed to ask if I could borrow a spade.

"I reckon the child's faddish," he told me. "Kirsty over-indulges her, for fear of leaving her out. Middle child syndrome."

He led me to one of the dilapidated stone sheds. In the dark interior, I made out a planked bin bulging with mossy firewood, with a range of implements leaning up against it. Among these were half a dozen spades of varying weights and types, immaculately cleaned. I selected one with a shield-shaped blade.

"I want to do a bit of amateur archaeology," I said, hefting it awkwardly. "Nothing that will leave a mark."

"As long as you don't dig up any ling," he said, grinding out his butt on the flagged floor. "Heather," he added, seeing my bafflement. "Virtually sacred round here."

There was so much of it about, I thought, why worry, but I promised not to harm a bud or twig of any heather bush, and left before he might ask about where or what I was planning to dig.

Coming round the corner to the front where Alison's car was parked, I saw her leaning into the boot, her dark red trousers stretched across her bum.

"Want to stow your bag, Joe?" she began, then took in what I was carrying. "Hang on, is there something I should know? You've finally throttled Zemon, and you want me to help bury him?"

"Funnily enough, you know that splash when he went in, it crossed my mind that Scanlon was disposing of a body."

"Why didn't you react then?" She gave her tartan grip a shove to make more room.

"I told myself I was being paranoid. Scanlon looked dodgy to me, but not that dodgy." I tucked the spade in.

"So what is it for?" Alison opened her grey eyes wide and scrunched up her nose, looking up at me.

"You may or may not find out, later."

"If it'll help, can I say how sorry I am for falling in with Zemon's infantile plot to discover the treasure? I realize it wasn't very clever."

"Yes, that might help. I'd better go and get my bag." It was disconcerting, standing that close.

My first and greatest shock at Falkland Palace came early on, when we passed through the gatehouse with its conical turret roofs, into the great courtyard. The outside looked much as I remembered from my waking dreams, and I'd expected the remainder to be the same—I knew it had been much restored. Once through the gatehouse, I looked towards the east wing where Thomas Newbolt had his quarters. It was present as a sort of ghost. Clearly the rebuilding efforts had run out of steam before they'd reached that side. The thick wall facing inwards to the courtyard was neatly broken off, as if someone had gone along with a huge circular saw, halfway along the upper storey. The windows had lost their glass; there was nothing beyond them. It gave me a very spooky feeling.

Zemon insisted on climbing to the top floor of the castle to start off with, and Irma went with him, while the rest of us followed the more usual route. The kids cavorted around, pretending to shoot one another with bows and arrows, and lasers. They obviously hadn't been listening to their mum's history lesson, and were in *Dungeons and Dragons* mode.

"These are on loan from Holyroodhouse," the blue-haired lady in the keeper's bedroom explained. King Charles I and Henrietta Maria flanked the windows. It increased my disorientation, seeing the king portrayed there in oil. The paintings were the only things I'd seen in the south range that were contemporary with Charles I and with Newbolt, but they looked too stiff and old to fit with my memories.

As I stared at the portraits I experienced a suffocating sensation of being neither in the present nor in the past. I had to take a few deep slow gulps of air to calm down. Alison looked over at me, and frowned. I gave a little shake of my head, to show I wasn't about to pass out. Kirsty was showing the kids the view down into the courtyard, and had not noticed anything amiss.

We wandered through a couple more elaborately restored rooms. "What do you think, Joe?" Alison asked. "Does it match your expectations—or should I say recollections?"

"Watch it," I whispered, nodding in the direction of Kirsty, who was preoccupied with stopping Daisy from climbing onto a brocade-covered sofa.

"There's no harm her knowing," said Alison, but she had lowered her voice, as people nearly always do when you whisper.

I'd explained to Kirsty before we set off that I might stay overnight, to explore the Falkland area in more detail the next day. She'd shrugged, saying Zemon could sometimes be heavy. Evidently, she had picked up on the tension between us. Maybe she also assumed I was trying to pull Alison away from him; which, maybe, was true.

"I'll tell you something for free," I murmured to Alison. "Those Bute lords who restored this place did a good job, but it doesn't feel right to me. Not for Thomas Newbolt's time anyway. He was quartered over in the east range by the way, the part that's just a façade."

I broke off. She and I, leaving Kirsty behind, had reached the entrance to the chapel, which for some reason was here on the first floor. Surely I had once run my fingers over those spindle-shaped rods on the carved screen of the entrance? As we moved into the body of the chapel, ranks of humdrum chairs underlined the intrusion of the present, but then I looked up. That ceiling! Geometric wooden mouldings, gold scrolls painted on the panels, all picked out in green and red.

"Ceiling executed for the visit of Charles I in 1633," Alison read out from the guidebook. "You recognize it, Joe—Newbolt was here?"

"I'm not sure." This all felt familiar, but I did not recall witnessing it in a waking dream.

Walking up the central aisle, we turned to look at the royal box halfway along the wall, opposite the windows. A gold-lettered frieze ran the length of the wall each side of the box; the words were in Latin.

"Look at that frieze—he must have stared at it often enough and he'd have known its meaning, but I can't decipher it," I told Alison.

"I thought they were only here a few days, for a hunting party. Perhaps Newbolt never visited the chapel."

"No, they were here for much longer. A fortnight, a month. And they had to come to prayers once a day."

She didn't question how I knew. How did I? It was as if I'd collected a faint tinge of other parts of Newbolt's mind, along with the scenes I'd actually seen.

"Go on then, try, you must be able to make out some of it."

"OVONIUM—no idea. REX—that'll be the king, I know that. SPERAT? Something to do with spears?"

"Hopes. It's something about singing psalms in praise of his virtues—the king's or God's. See, DOMINO there and then DOMINE later."

"As in dominate, rather than the dotty game?" I said.

She gave a cheeky grin; I found myself smiling back. As if suddenly overheated, she started to wriggle out of her parka.

"Keep that on," I said. "Let's look at the garden."

We had to pass through the tapestry gallery, a long walkway. At the far end, we nearly collided with Zemon and Irma bounding down the spiral stairs from the old library on the floor above.

"Don't bother with it," said Zemon in tones of disgust. "It's a shrine to the self-importance of the Crichton Stuarts."

"Oh no, it is worth looking," said Irma. "Very rich, with a lovely painted ceiling, curved like a barrel."

I asked if it was original, like in the chapel, and Zemon snorted. Alison and I looked at one another and shook our heads. Together, all four of us went down the stairs to the bakehouse on the ground floor. We had left Kirsty and the kids far behind.

I knew this place. Past and present overlaid, and fitted, like layers of a circuit board. Although the corridor was blocked off, this was the way Robbie had run when he was escaping from the palace—or at any rate, the way Newbolt had followed. The exit door was locked, but there was a peep-hole, and I could see out into the yard and garden. The past was tugging at me more urgently.

We stood together, Alison and I, on a circular dais of stone. Beside us was a low well-head, covered with a firmly bolted wooden lid. Zemon and Irma had scarpered into the royal, or real, tennis court, down at the far end of the garden. Fine rain dampened our clothes and hair. My right hand weighed the pendulum in my raincoat pocket, juggled it from finger to finger, as often when I'm thinking of dowsing, or just plain nervous. I looked sideways at Alison who had fallen silent. I nearly said: a penny for them. But it would have sounded trite.

"You're so lucky, Joe," was Alison's surprising gambit.

"What makes you say that?"

"Whenever I visit a place like this, I try to imagine what it would have been like to live there. Those reconstructions they do on telly, with computer graphics, they're good, and those re-enactments, people in costume with realistic period deformities or whatever, but it's not the same. I mean, when I stand here, I feel something." She trailed off and looked towards the intact south range, where we'd just been, her eyes as mist-filled as the air around us.

"The stones," I prompted.

"Sorry?" Alison's eyes swivelled to meet mine. Mist and distance dispersed.

I gestured towards the palace yard and surrounding walls. "You're sensing the imprint of times past, transmitted by the stones. All stones receive and transmit energies. Those that have been handled by human beings are affected by it permanently. That plus the intense traffic of people at certain times."

"Well, maybe. But that wasn't what I meant. You've actually seen, smelt, felt what it was like to be here, if your waking dreams are to be believed. That's what I envy."

"What do you mean, 'if'? Come on."

I grabbed her hand and tugged her after me, down the slope from the castle mound, across the lawn, and along to the little bridge, which I suddenly knew would be there, leading to the orchard. We were almost running, and she panted with laughter. It would have been easier if I'd let go, but she made no attempt to free herself.

At the end of the bridge, I released her hand, to open the five-bar gate and usher her through. From the way she looked at me, I wondered for a second if she expected a hug or a kiss. Before I could tell what I thought about that, she had slipped past.

I closed the gate slowly, then turned to her again. I thrust the pendulum into her right hand.

"You want to know how this works?" It was more of a command than a question. "Here, hold the string." I curled her fingers around it with my own, as I would with anyone. "Now, you have to tune in, like the kind of radio where you twiddle a knob to get the station." Her lips quivered, but I shot her a warning look. "It's not a game, Alison. Your target is to pick up on the energies of this stream. Hold the pendulum still, with your other fingers fanned out. Yes, like that. Now move slowly towards the stream. Very slowly. When you reach one of the energy bands, the pendulum will start to swing, either in a circle or side to side."

I kept my hand on her shoulder, to help the pendulum sense a familiar presence. As I walked behind her, unbidden there came to mind the sad lines of *Omie Wise*, about the cruel lover who pushes the fair maid in the river to drown, after he's had his way with her. It made me lighten my touch.

"Something's happening," said Alison, disbelief and excitement mingling in her voice.

"Well done. Here, let me check." I took the pendulum from her and felt with it each side of the invisible but definite force line. She'd located it spot on. "You're a natural."

I encouraged her to have another go, further on. She walked slowly, almost putting the heel of one foot on the toes of the other, towards the bank of the stream. She didn't notice a young alder near her trajectory; it reached out one of its lower branches and caught her sleeve. The pendulum started to swing madly. She looked at me but I shook my head and pointed to the branch. In the end she got a response at about the same distance from the water as before.

"Now we're going to start some serious hunting," I told her. "We're not just playing around here; we're looking for something. A seventeenth-century instrument." She stared at me, astonished. I told her then about the waking dream on Arthur's Seat, two days before.

"Why ever did the boy throw away such a precious possession?" she asked.

"I don't know. I don't see into his mind, only that busybody doctor's. But I think it was because the king had taken him up as a pet, and then turned his back on him." It was ironic, when he'd just been summoned to see the king again, I thought. But Robbie didn't know about that when he threw the trumpet.

An inkling niggled at the back of my mind: the boy was extremely anxious not to travel on *The Blessing of Burntisland*. Why? I remembered Newbolt writing a note to plead with the king for passage on his ship, but I wasn't clear whether this followed from Robbie's fear, or the doctor's anger at Soames's scheming to put him down. Or even whether the note-writing happened before or after this trumpet incident. I wished these damn things would come to me in proper sequence.

The stream would lead us, I hoped, towards the loch or pool I'd seen in the waking dream. As we pushed through the undergrowth, I explained about intentionality, which could make or break the hunt.

"We have to envision the thing we're looking for, in this case the trumpet," I began.

"Envisage," Alison interrupted, dodging around a root.

"Envision, as I said. Bring into your mind as clear a picture as you can." I described the trumpet's simple shaft of coppery brass, and the distinctive feature of the flared bell crushed from its open "O" into a flattened oval.

"But you can't know that."

I looked at her in puzzlement. Then I realized the problem. She thought I was describing damage that had occurred to the trumpet during the centuries it had lain buried.

"This happened before, perhaps a few days before he threw it away. He—Robbie, the boy—had a falling fit, and he clutched the trumpet so hard he squashed it."

It felt weird to be telling her. By passing it on I made the incident more real, yet at the same time, more distant. A bit like if you write about an intimate or horrible thing in a diary. I didn't mention Robbie's obscure prophecies. There was enough for her to take in already.

Alison stopped in front of me so abruptly I nearly bumped into her. A stone wall confronted us, the boundary of the orchard. More than a man's height, it ran right up to the stream, broken only by a solid wooden door in our path.

Alison rattled the catch on the door. "It's locked."

"Bugger," I said.

I had to try for myself. I reached over and grasped the latch, plus the handle, and tested them; the door didn't budge. Alison grabbed my wrist, tried to pull me away.

"Don't you believe me?"

I twisted my wrist in her grasp, and in an instant had hold of hers. "Bloody wall, what shall we do now?" I said, reaching for her other hand, which she whisked behind her back. She was laughing, and perhaps I was too.

A piping voice hailed us from some distance.

"Hey Joe, can you come back please?"

We sprang apart, and looking round saw Julian, Kirsty's oldest, running towards us.

"What's up?" asked Alison.

"Rose," said Julian, panting a little. "She sent me to look—Mum did—and I've searched everywhere for you, all the rooms and the garden and the old tennis courts, and they said you'd come this way."

So Irma and Zemon had seen us. We started to walk back. Had there been anything actually to see, I wondered? Yes, I'd grabbed Alison and dragged her to the orchard. What would that have looked like? Still, they had sent Julian after me so they can't have thought we were up to anything. Which of course we hadn't been.

"What about Rose?" I asked, "and what's the rush?" as Julian was starting to run ahead.

"I dunno, she's not well, and Mum says you can help!" His voice rose towards the end of the sentence, making it sound like a question. It's that Australian way of speech that youngsters pick up from soaps; I remember Emma going through a phase of it when she used to watch *Neighbours*. In my view, there should indeed have been a big question mark at the end of that statement.

CHAPTER THIRTEEN

I stepped up from the spiral staircase, Alison behind me, and emerged into the tapestry gallery. Kirsty was sitting with Rose and Daisy, one leaning against her from either side, on one of the chests. They made an incongruous threesome—Kirsty with her hair escaping in wild wisps from its bonds, and the kids' jackets bright primary patterns—set against hunting lords and ladies and fabulous beasts in faded blues and greens. Zemon and Irma were leaning against a transom in the window embrasure across from Kirsty, looking like a month of wet Sundays as Gran Vartin would have said.

"What seems to be the trouble?" I asked.

"It's this fever, she hasn't a sore throat or any other symptoms, and it's come and gone. You know she was fine this morning. And now it's come back again," Kirsty replied.

I asked why she didn't get some paracetamol from the chemist's, or take the child to a doctor if she was really worried. Impatiently, I listened to her explanation, which I could predict in view of the herbs, and the general New Age lifestyle at Eden Valley. She disliked chemicals for herself and her children, she thought they were too "strong" and prevented the body healing itself.

"Do you have an alternative therapist you go to normally?" I asked.

"We have a range, though not necessarily nearby, mostly for chronic conditions, Graham's asthma and so on," Kirsty answered. "But I have a hunch you can help, Joe. Please will you try?"

I was baffled. Beyond my plain straightforward dowsing, which I considered pretty practical and less intuitive than, say, playing the stock market, my special skills (for what they were worth) lay in the related area of locating lost people or things. Healing was something I'd never laid claim to. There were those who used dowsing for healing, asking questions with the pendulum hung over the patient's body, but I regarded it as a dodgy business. I'd have refused point-blank, but Rose stirred and turned her head, which was burrowed into her mother's side, and looked up at me with bleary eyes. Now I'm not, as a rule, very keen on kids, but as I looked uneasily away from the child's flushed face, Irma came up beside me and laid her cool hand on my wrist.

"Joe, why not try something? She's been moaning you know, and just seeing you made her go quiet."

I made one more appeal to reason, turning to Alison; surely she didn't think I could do anything? But she shrugged. With reluctance I knelt beside the little girl and placed my hand on her forehead. It was like a hot potato—boiled, not baked, being moist with sweat. I got out my pendulum, but couldn't think of anything to ask, and put it away again. I looked up at Kirsty.

"What on earth do you expect me to do?" I asked.

This is different. Even in the dim fumes of the boy's kennel, it is apparent that he is flushed, not pale as in his falling episodes. Nor is he gnashing his jaws together, but moans low and without coherence as though speaking in tongues. A coarse dew gleams on his brow. He has thrown back the paltry cape that serves as all his bedcovering. I am seized with sudden alarm; there have been rumours of a recurrent ague in these parts, this past week.

"Robbie, can you hear me?" I speak low, attempting to steady my voice. My simples will affect their work better, I know from experience, if served with reassurance. Almost always a sick man fears worse than that which is truly about to befall, unless there be a pestilence or he be severely injured of a fall from a horse or an accident in the chase, though these tend to suffer their woes most bravely, as indeed did this lad back in North Humber Land where we first encountered him.

"Of course," he murmurs, turning heavy-lidded eyes on me, then fretfully glancing away.

He is not delirious then; but his breathing is raucous, through mouth and nostrils at the same time, and the exhalations rank with some evil humour from his inner organs or it may be his throat. I have seen in children, and adults even, when I inspect the cavern of their mouths, the rear of that cave appear as a streaked or encrusted wall, not the smooth vault of the healthy part; moreover often with the pillars either side bulbous with white or yellowish excrescences. And my surmise is that this pustulation gives rise to the foul smell thence carried out on the breath, rather than any deeper corruption such as in the liver or spleen.

With some difficulty, and necessitating the application of my fingers to steady the boy's cheekbone and jawbone, I persuade Robbie to open his mouth to allow of my gaze penetrating inside; but the poor light baffles my eyes. I call for a brace of candles and whilst I wait in some impatience I use my own neck-cloth to wipe the boy's brow, which, however, rapidly exudes a further outcrop of greasy drops.

One of the charring maids stoops through the low portal and hands me a pair of candles—ready lighted, thanks be—with shy nervous glances at Robbie and myself. As she withdraws, I query for a moment what are Robbie's relations with the other underlings: the youths with whom he shares this bed space, and the kitchen girls, both the pretty and the plain, as this one. Doubtless he must seem to them an oddity, yet perchance an attractive one, both for his qualities of soothsaying and his position in the King's regard. That the latter has fallen off of late, they may not be aware.

The candle's rays reveal no visible disturbance in the boy's throat. This distemper is indeed some sort of an ague, for now he shivers and draws his wretched cover over his shoulders. I am as certain as I may be that his blood is affected, and requires refreshment. Ordering that he be provided with water to drink in case of the heat returning (for none had thought to minister even so plain a remedy), I hurry out, through the courtyard and by the postern gate into the orchard, to find again the hollow by Maspie Burn I explored two days ago. The open daylight, though weak enough as thick clouds obscure the sky, yet seems at first to dazzle my eyes that had grown accustomed to the dark interior of the boy's quarters. These under-servants' rooms are little better than prison cells, far worse even than my student rooms in Edinburgh, which we thought as dungeons compared to home, at least my sweet home in Lincoln before it burnt down.

Being late afternoon rather than early morning, this is not the best time for plucking botanicals. But needs must, I reflect, as I push between saplings of ash and elm and willow, whose leaves sprinkle me with fresh cold droplets garnered from the most recent outburst of rain. I try to dash the moisture off my sleeve but already half is soaking into the worsted—which is not close enough wove to repel water—turning its umber to a dark madder brown. Ah, here is the yellow flag I seek, in the shady corner as I recalled, curving its unremarkable spears of leaves over the brink of the brook. I kneel, despite the dampness to my breeks, and unsheathing my knife, use its strong short blade to burrow into the wet earth and ease out a part of the root. Pocketing this mud-streaked lump, I forage further afield and here beside the fence find a clump of yarrow, standing tall and frondy as is its wont. Not being the season for its flowers, I must make do with the aerial parts, which however serve quite well.

Now my boots are becoming sodden as far up as the shin, my right knee is wet from when I knelt, my sleeves very damp, my hair spattered, for I came in haste hatless. Would any doctor discommode himself more for any patient? Of course I could have sent a servant, but it would be difficult to describe the exact location of the flag, and besides I do not want word to circulate about my combining simples, such as any housewife might employ who can read an herbal, with my more esoteric remedies. Certainly Soames might twist such intelligence to his purposes, as further evidence of my heresies at which he is forever hinting; I must press on hugger-mugger and in haste.

Without further viewing Robbie, I speed up the stairs to my chamber. There taking a glowing charcoal from the fire to place in the copper cradle beneath my crucible, I apply my hand-bellows to produce a flame, and pour in a measure of water, to which I add fragments of the yarrow whose green fragrance stains my fingers and tingles my nostrils. As the water begins to bubble I am grinding pellets of antimony, then I rinse the flag root and chop a piece from it the size of half a walnut and mash this also in the mortar. Some would advocate separate treatment of the dry and moist elements, or chemicals and botanicals, but I never find it harms to combine them in the mortar, for why should it, since they will be blended shortly in the crucible. Now I stir all together in the boiling water, and though there is not more than a gill, my impatience is making it seem an eternity while the volume reduces by half. I raise the bowl of the spoon near my lips and blow gently, then taste a sip. Bitter, harsh, metallic (beyond the silver of the spoon's brim; that's the antimony) the liquid is imbued with a sleek texture which first sheathes teeth and tongue like a mossy coat, then peels away, leaving all refreshed. This will truly cleanse and tonic the boy's blood from its ague.

Within my damp worsted, I am sweating a little myself. Once I have strained the brew into a bottle, I shall call Hamish to carry it down and administer it to Robbie in small sips at intervals over the next hour or two. For I must lave all my utensils and store away the ingredients lest Soames's spies snoop in my room. Moreover I shall have to write up my notes on this episode, which I strenuously hope to conclude with Robbie fully restored before our departure and the ardours of the road. Perhaps I had best replace my wet garments lest ...

I registered that they were all staring at me, as if waiting for me to say something. Also, that I was kneeling uncomfortably. I staggered to my feet, my kneecaps crackling. To clear my head, I passed my fingers through my hair, cupped my palms over my ears and rubbed them, then knuckled my eyes.

Alison was regarding me with concern. If the others had not been there, I might have told her that for once a waking dream had come on cue, as if to help me out in my hour of need.

"In fact, there's a common plant or two that may help a little, though I can't promise. Do you have any dried yarrow, or flag rhizome at home?" I queried, but Kirsty shook her head to both. "Now, I suggest you all go and get snug as you can in the Stag and Hounds, while I see if I can find some hereabouts."

The three of the company who had become my companions, if not exactly my friends, all pressed to come with me, but I refused. This I needed to do alone, as much to think about the dream as to concentrate on plant hunting. But I whispered to Alison to enquire about rooms at the inn. If we were to continue our other, interrupted, hunt it would definitely be best to stay overnight.

"So, what is map dowsing? How does it work?" asked Alison, settling into the sofa beside me, a whisky-and-soda in her hand. My tumbler sat on a coaster graced with a stag, on a polished octagonal table nearby. I had the tourist map provided by the management open on my knee, folded down to show Falkland and its environs. There was no one else in the residents' lounge. Alison had chosen a good time to ask. I was in a mellow expansive mood, after indulging in a couple of pints along with the pub's game stew and a selection of exotic mustards.

We had checked into adjacent rooms, after seeing off Kirsty and her kids and our two hippy friends. The infusion of yarrow, which the landlord had kindly allowed me to prepare, seemed to have settled Rose, though any hot drink might have done the same. We'd both changed into fresh clothes before our evening meal, not because the Stag and Hounds was a posh pub—though it was upmarket in a genteel, Scots sort of way, as indeed I suspected this whole village was—but because we were damp and preferred dry clothes. In my case this meant old trousers and jumper and jacket, but Alison had a dress stashed away in her baggage, and had put it on, a soft brownish and greenish thing, and now as she crossed her legs I got a good look at them at last—for they hadn't shown at the supper table. Shapely pins.

As I slid the map partly over her lap, the back of my fingers touched against the cloth of her dress, and the knee beneath. Would she brush me off, snap at me, giggle, or throw her arms around me?

She took a swig of whisky, then grabbed the edge of the map and pulled it up a little.

"I can't see properly at that distance."

She didn't want to acknowledge the distinct tingle I'd registered. Well, maybe now wasn't the right time. I withdrew my hand.

"Well, you need to have the map laying flat," I said, biffing it in the middle where she'd buckled it up, "otherwise you'll lose track. You put your fingertip on the map, and hold the pendulum in your other hand, and ask the map if the thing you're looking for is there, moving your finger very slowly all the while, as if you were walking the land. You take it section by section." My finger described a circle over a quadrant, roughly above the point between our two thighs.

"Oh, I see, like a pond survey. But that can't ..."

"Wait, I hadn't finished yet. The great advantage, beside the ability to locate the area for your more exact search is—well, can you work it out?" It's always best to lead people to produce ideas for themselves, then they'll accept them more readily. But Alison wasn't following.

"No, because it's blatant nonsense. How on earth can moving your finger over a piece of paper have anything to do with—well, with all that out there?" and she swept her arm in a wide arc as if to indicate everything from Aberdeen to Midlothian.

My thigh seemed caught in an electro-magnetic field, radiating across the inch or two separating my leg from hers. I peeped sideways at her profile, and noted a frown. Was I imagining this aura of sexuality she was giving off?

"Look," I said, in my ultra-reasonable voice, "you don't think it strange when you read a map, on a journey, with a destination in mind, and at the end of the journey you find yourself where you want to be."

She stared at me. "So?"

"Everyone takes it for granted. But if you came from another culture, radically different, without paper and printing, the Australian Aborigines for example, it would seem very strange. You look at a piece of paper, you drive your car, and you're there."

"Leaving aside your outdated view of Abos, the point is the map corresponds to reality. The things on it have been seen and plotted, the map shows their relationships accurately. Your hidden treasure isn't on the map, for God's sake. I mean, anyway, how can your pendulum respond to a bit of paper?"

At least she'd ended with a question.

"Where does your map correspond to reality, though, Alison?" I tapped my temple. "There, only there in your mind. You have to locate yourself on that wiggly orange line, for example, and say 'I'm here now, this side of the junction with the Post Office on the corner'. But you're not on a wiggly orange line; you're on a real road. The only thing linking the two is your mind. It conjures a parallel reality out of the squiggles on the paper."

"Say that again—that last bit."

"It makes a reality out of squiggles on a piece of paper."

"Like reading a book." She rubbed her fingers over her forehead.

"Well, you talk of reading a map, don't you? With map dowsing, it's a bit like looking for signs on a map that help you locate yourself when you don't know where you are, only now you're trying to locate something or someone else. So you focus on each spot in turn, by moving your finger, just as you'd move your body if you were wandering the actual ground looking for something."

To illustrate the method, I walked my finger around the map, in a wide circle over my leg and hers.

She sipped her whisky. "It still sounds like baloney to me."

"Well, I've done it, and it's worked. I found *The Blessing of Burntisland.*"

"You think it's worked. You don't absolutely know yet. It depends on the outcome of the Naval Archaeology dives and tests."

"Anderson himself told us the diver touched wood."

Alison tilted her head. The underside of her chin was enticing, white and soft where it merged into her throat.

I jumped up and tugged her after me.

"Joe, look out. You've made me spill my whisky. That's probably a hanging offence up here."

"Only a drop. Here, I'll wipe it up."

It had fallen—a small splash, merging into the confused pattern of her frock—just above that magnetic knee. Falling to my own knees as in the gallery, I grabbed Alison's leg and dabbed at the damp place with a clean if crumpled hanky I fortunately had stowed in my pocket. She batted me about the head with the map, but she was laughing.

"Stop, Joe, it's ticklish. That's the worst place, you know."

"I don't know, do I, I haven't tried all the alternatives," I murmured, looking up. She gave me another cuff across the top of my head, ruffling my hair.

I stood up. "Now we're going to need a table. I'm not going to demonstrate map dowsing with the map on our laps. Too dangerous."

"But wait a minute, Joe—what's the other great advantage of map dowsing you asked me to guess?"

Tenacious mind, this woman. I'd almost forgotten. "Oh yes. Where was the wreck—where's any wreck?"

She stood thinking a moment, staring at the carpet, which was an unhelpful mixture of deep-cut leaves and thistles, then looked up. "Ah, I see, you can go over water as well as land."

"Exactly. But let's hope this baby's not too far out, or we're scuppered for tonight."

"Tonight?" She looked like a schoolgirl who's been offered a midnight feast.

When I told Alison I had experience of map dowsing having worked, I wasn't referring only to *The Blessing of Burntisland*. If she'd have let me explain, instead of distracting me with all those vibes, I could have recounted a whole catalogue of experiences.

Earliest was when we went on a school trip to London, and Nigel Poole, the only rich boy in our year, from the original more-money-than-sense clan, left his expensive camera behind. He started wailing on the coach home that he might have dropped it over the side of the riverboat. To save Miss Elvet a wild-goose chase, I got out the tourist map we'd all been given, and an old conker on a string—you can use anything in dire straits—and traced our whole trip including the stretch on the Thames. I still remember the thrill when the conker jerked itself around as my finger touched the Tower. Almost as good was the homing in, when I unfolded my detailed map of the Tower, and located the camera in the Gents on the second floor, south-west turret. Unfortunately Nigel Poole thought I was a dickhead and told Miss Elvet that he could not possibly have put his camera down anywhere in the Tower, as he had lost it before we got there; so when we got back she rang around all the other places we'd visited, and by the time she tried the Tower it was gone. I spent half the night going over the whole map of London, and got a flicker of response over Hackney Downs, but the map wasn't detailed enough to say exactly where.

Okay, so that was unsuccessful—but solely due to the obstinacy of that twerp Poole. From then on, I only did map dowsing for people who asked, or for myself. I found our Jean one time she'd stayed out the night, when she wasn't at her mate Helen's house like she'd told Mum she would be. For years after, she used to joke that it was my interference that had caused her to marry the first bloke she ever slept with. (Not that she got pregnant; but our Mum did not tolerate what she called "loose behaviour".) Strangely enough, considering I'd inherited my regular dowsing abilities from Dad, he was never much good at map dowsing himself. It might have had something to do with his general unfriendliness with the printed page, I suppose; he could read, but only with difficulty, and he found his way round the countryside by some innate knowledge, combined with practice, and never used maps. Mind, he never went further to "foreign" parts than Norwich.

Word really got around when I helped to locate that missing girl, the one with a boy's name, what was it? Sam Redbourne. Twenty years ago. She was being held to ransom by a nutter, over King's Lynn way, though they didn't know that of course, because he was deviously sending notes from all over the show. When he threatened to post one of her fingers with the next one, the family called me up, being desperate enough to try anything, including black magic if it would've helped. What I found was corroborated by bits of info the police had on file, but in a scattered way, so they were prepared to give it a go. These days they'll use so-called psychics, as well as regular psychologists, but it was adventurous of them to try me. Anyhow, it turned out I was right, and the kid—she was ten years old—was alive, thanks be, and not too mauled about, although obviously traumatized something rotten. Not as badly shaken by the whole thing as her mum, though.

So I'd built up quite a reputation, local at first, then on a national register with the Redbourne case. My fame, briefly, had helped in the romantic stakes, with Marjory. The missing persons business was only an occasional part of my work, for I found a bit of map dowsing a most useful preparatory step before treasure dowsing, when the people hiring me had only vague notions of where to look.

Contrary to popular opinion, as I explained to Alison, you don't need a hair of the missing person, or a sample of their clothing like you'd show to a bloodhound. Otherwise it wouldn't be much use for hidden treasure; you'd need a coin from the hoard you're seeking. It's the police who use their shreds of DNA or fibre to match with the assailant's coat—what I call the Cinderella's slipper approach: "Here, let's see if this fits. Right, you're nabbed." With map dowsing, it's more like radar: scan around and see where there is a disturbance on the waveband. Or that game in the infants' sand tray at our school fete where they'd made a sand island fringed with cardboard palm trees and surrounded by a blue paper sea. For a few pence you'd get a gold paper flag on a cocktail stick, and the box of chocs went to the one planted closest to the imaginary treasure chest hidden somewhere in the island. What had happened to that box of chocs? I'd given it to Mum, but she only got to eat one. Dad had come home in one of his states, and they got chucked about in the mêlée. She wouldn't let me eat any of the remnants, said the floor was dirty. You could see his point of view, he'd thought they were from a fancy man, he hadn't known about the fete. I didn't mention the treasure hunt to Alison, just the radar comparison.

For a lost person, it can work better if you have the relative holding your hand, but they can be a hindrance with all their emotion. Anyhow, for us dowsers with this particular gift, it's often enough to have a clear description of what we're looking for, so we can visualize it vividly while we're trawling the map. As with the dowsing we'd done by the stream, I told Alison, but even more so, the whole trick with map dowsing is an intense concentration on the image of the "target"; yet at the same time, an openness, not a demanding insistence on "I must find this". Too much demand and the pendulum goes dead as a plumb line. Too lax a focus, and the pendulum will swing about at random.

There's an art to it all right, and I was happy to demonstrate to Alison as we sat at the polished card-table. It's tiring, though, at the best of times, and after my botanical adventures that afternoon my attention slipped once or twice. Alison's musky perfume distracted me, her breath on my cheek, her hand on my free arm. I had to tell her to let go of me, and to try and relax her mind, simply holding the image of a trumpet, and if she liked, the general scene around the stream. After that I felt things smooth out for me. I was seeing the trumpet, and then there came the unmistakable twitch on the string as my pendulum started very gently to rotate.

"Got her!" I told Alison, and we both looked (she had to open her eyes first) at the spot beyond the castle grounds, quite close to the stream, a little short of a small lake or pool to the north-west. Not in the water, apparently. That was a blessing, though with this tourist map, it wasn't possible to be sure; scale and accuracy fell far short of the OS standard. Changes in water and earth levels over the centuries were common enough to make it feasible that the lake had shrunk.

Alison went off to ask the landlord about entry to the inn if we came back late, for we enjoyed midnight rambles. He must have thought we were crazy, but he gave us a Yale key for the side door. The burglary rate was clearly not high in this part of Fife. We decided to leave our ramble somewhat later than midnight, to avoid disturbing any courting lovers, supposing there were any inhabitants of Falkland young enough for that sort of thing.

Perhaps the landlord assumed that Alison and I were a courting couple. Let him think what he liked. Just so long as nobody nosed into what we were up to. Elsewhere and with another target I might have risked doing it openly by daylight but we would be (a) trespassing, almost certainly, and (b) if successful with the search, looting, for I had no intention of handing the trumpet over to the authorities, even for treasure trove.

As I lay down to rest on my solitary couch, I breathed a sort of prayer to the trumpet: please be there, please let me show her I'm not crazy, and let me get closer to Robbie. I only dozed briefly, and was awake well before my alarm could announce one o'clock. Lying in the dark, listening to the night noises of the old building, I guessed the louder creaks were Alison changing into her outdoor gear in the next room. I felt light-headed but remarkably alert.

CHAPTER FOURTEEN

We met beside Alison's Vauxhall, which she had parked near the squat village church, across from the Stag and Hounds. Sure enough, she was dressed in her parka and a dark pair of slacks, but ordinary shoes.

"Haven't you got proper boots?" I whispered.

"What for? We're not mountaineering," she said in a flat voice that discouraged further comment.

Opening the car boot, she took out a sturdy torch for use later. I shouldered the spade like one of Snow White's dwarfs. We could not enter the castle grounds at night, and anyway we'd encountered that locked door in the boundary wall by the stream, so I'd decided on a wide detour. We pressed on past the church and round the corner by the village green. There was another pub, securely shut down for the night, then a row of cottages whose grey stone looked oddly yellow in the lamplight, while miniature jonquils in one of their window boxes looked grey. Abruptly we had reached the village limits. Another hundred yards, and the street lamps gave out. The soft mizzle of the afternoon had cleared, but clouds still coated the sky. Alison switched on her torch. Where the road forked, we took the right turn, to keep closer to the grounds of the castle. We hadn't encountered a soul, but I was keen to get off the road as soon as possible. Our appearance would be bound to raise questions in the mind of any moderately sober passing motorist.

"Here," I announced, "this should do it. I'll climb over first, to check there isn't any barbed wire or a nasty ditch the other side. Hold this a sec." I handed her the spade. The drystone wall was lower at this point than alongside the castle grounds, about chest height, and provided plenty of toe-holds. I nipped over with no trouble, and landed in a bed of nettles. No problem for me, but I didn't want Alison getting stung around the ankles; I asked her to pass me the spade, and used the flat of it to beat down a patch of the nettles. As she clambered over, I offered her a hand, and would willingly have caught her as she jumped down. She waved me away, making torchlight flash wildly all over the show.

"Watch out, you'll alert the whole village," I hissed.

"Nonsense, no one will see us now we're inside this wall."

I checked the map briefly, but once I'm on site I don't keep referring to the map; map dowsing is your remote work, whereas actual dowsing when you're within range needs a different sort of concentration. I told Alison to hood her torch with her scarf and direct the beam downwards to help us pick our way across the rough pasture. I had a fairly good idea of where we were going, somewhere just this side of the stream, so it seemed best to find the stream first and work from there. We heard a dog bark, briefly, at a passing car somewhere back in the village, but no nearer sound that indicated danger of discovery.

Walking in the dark, you feel your feet connect with the ground much more definitely than in daylight, when your eyesight dominates and bombards you with messages the whole time. But you also feel less balanced because you lack that web of visual cues. Alison and I both kept stumbling on the tussocks of grass, and more than once she clutched at my arm for support, and once I returned the favour.

I felt a constraining sense of responsibility for her. I told her to cut and run if anyone did challenge us, for example a ranger out on his night rounds. (I imagined there were such officials on the royal estate. We were outside the castle precincts, but might still be on royal land.) I would hold my ground and delay him with some trumped-up story; tell him we were looking for our lost dog, a daft Dalmatian answering to the name of Dirk.

I sensed we were very near the stream, and said "Stop!" just in time, as water came into view in the torch's hooded beam. I laid the spade down just short of the bank and we started on the fine-tuning of the search, zigzagging back and forth along the designated area with the stream as the eastern limit.

There followed what felt like hours of my most frustrating, cold, and damp dowsing ever. My mistake was to let Alison have a go, after I'd been working the rods for about quarter of an hour. She was bursting to try, and I could sympathize. But when I took the rods back—she was having no better luck than me—my concentration was broken. We were, of course, both meant to be concentrating together, but I hadn't taken sufficient account of Alison's inexperience. That first try by the stream that afternoon, she had seemed to have the knack; I hadn't just been flattering her. But now she was all over the place. Finding the response to water is one thing, child's play really, whereas focusing on an unknown object and working towards it is quite another.

"Maybe you could describe it better," said Alison, after another half hour had passed in unproductive casts up and down the hinterland of the stream.

"It's a trumpet, it's squashed, and it's old."

"Come on Joe. Size? Weight? Any distinguishing features, birthmarks and so on?"

She'd managed to draw a chuckle out of me, but I realized with a wave of weariness that she really laboured under a huge disadvantage in never having actually seen the trumpet. I gazed at the torchlit puddle that had collected in my last footprint, which had been a particularly squelchy one. At any rate it was helpful to have her along to carry the torch, so I could use both the rods as I prefer, one in each hand. What we needed to do was keep moving.

After a bit more of this, I switched to the pendulum, because sometimes it can be the more sensitive tool. I kept feeling a tug towards the stream, which I thought was the wrong direction; increasingly, I suspected that this was an Alison chimera, an effect of her single success with water. Although she wasn't handling the rods or pendulum now, her mental state might well be influencing mine.

On the other hand, it felt companionable, with the occasional: "You getting anything there, Joe?" from her, or "Can you point the light more this way," from me. Every now and again we struck up a random bit of conversation. I found myself telling her about my Open University days, or rather nights—perhaps because this night dowsing, with its dreary tiredness accompanied by the lack of any wish to sleep, reminded me of those sessions. I had begun by being too excited, and was now too cold, to feel sleepy.

At one point Alison asked me about my mother.

"Mum? She had a hard time, but she coped. Of course when she was gone, it was my older sister who stood in her place for me, though I was nearly grown by then."

"Do you mean your mother had a hard time with your father?"

Spot on, but I wasn't about to admit that. "No, I mean we were hard up, and she took on cleaning jobs which tired her out. Then, after Dad died, she got cancer."

"How old were you when your father died?"

"Thirteen. He got caught in a swamp and drowned. Bit of an occupational hazard. He had this idea there was a bit of treasure in the swamps near home and—well, he fell in, or got sucked in, wandering off the path at dusk. Even the locals don't always know all the safe pathways and the dangerous bits."

"How terrible."

Why had I told her—why that burst of confiding? I fell silent, trying as usual to distract myself from that horrible memory. By association, I thought of my waking dream by the river in Edinburgh; Thomas Newbolt treading a boggy path and stumbling off, and a girl helping him. That was Susan, a very young version of the woman in that lovely waking dream above Eden Valley. And earlier, when Newbolt wondered where to flee after the execution, the person he thought of was Susan, living with an "earthly sect" somewhere secret and safe. That safe haven must be where he was living with her, and I wondered where it was.

The bulk of the clouds had lifted, the last rags were blowing away in a freshening wind, and glimmers of starshine and gleams from the crescent moon spread thin silver across the ground. I checked my watch, the illuminated face showing nearly three in the morning. The battery was running low in Alison's torch, so I told her to switch it off. Then I faced her, putting my frozen hands on her shoulders. I was wearing my fingerless gloves, to allow me to detect the instruments' response, if there had been any. I could feel her shivering, and was sure it was more from the cold than my account of my father's death.

"Alison, this isn't working. You'd best go back. If I walk you to the wall where we climbed over, do you think you can find your way back to the inn all right? I'll give you the key and you can leave the side door on the latch for me." It was a lot to ask; she'd have to make her way back alone and unprotected in the dark with only that dim torch, but it wouldn't be far and this place felt pretty safe. If she objected, I would walk her all the way back, but I was reluctant to lose yet more time.

"Joe, if you think I'm going to give up now, after all this, you don't begin to know me. I will go back if you will, but if you're going to carry on, then so am I."

"Even if it means more of the same till dawn's on its way and I have to give up?"

"Even so." She shivered violently, then gave herself a shake, and pulled my hands off her shoulders, and gripped them tight in her own mittened ones. "Joe, are you quite, quite sure that we are in the place you identified on the map?"

I was indignant, but a sudden doubt seized me. I pulled out the map, and switching the torch back on, studied it again by the feeble beam. I could hardly believe my eyes.

"My God, Alison, you're right—it's completely mad, but we're on the wrong side of the stream altogether!"

I snapped the torch off and explained that the stream's twists and turns, combined with the angle of the lane as we approached, must have thrown me off course. When I was map dowsing back at the inn, I'd been thinking of the way we'd approached before, via the orchard. All the same, it was idiotic of me not to have checked and double-checked, once on site and actually ground dowsing.

"Stop apologizing," said Alison. "You know what I think it is, Joe. When you checked our orientation just after we entered the field, I bet you were holding the map upside down."

"No way! Only you women do that." But there was a chink of possibility that she was right. Tonight, I seemed to have forgotten all the rules.

In mock annoyance, I growled and lunged at Alison, clutching her waist and giving her a squeeze to tickle her sides. The effect must have been somewhat muffled through her quilted jacket, but she uttered a satisfactory yelp, and then biffed me on the chest. Considering how dark it was, she did well to make contact. I lifted my arms in surrender and we both stood there laughing.

Then I realized that in the fracas, I'd dropped my pendulum.

"Buggerdamnshit," I mumbled.

Alison wanted to help me look, but I told her that it would be more helpful if she stood to one side. She walked off, as I started to make passes with my two rods over the area where we'd been standing. Pendulum, I kept telling myself, pendulum. The dots and nicks on that brown ceramic surface, a meaningless but rhythmic pattern.

I heard a faint splash, and wondered if Alison was chucking pebbles in the stream. It was a disturbing reminder of the splash I'd heard on the boat. Damn, I'd lost my focus. With an effort I conjured up my pendulum, then had a distracting moment of seeing the trumpet in my mind's eye, at which point the rods swivelled towards the stream just as I heard another splash. I swore black and blue, did my dragon huffs, thought determinedly of the pendulum, and then my rods swung in and crossed one another. A quick scan the other way confirmed the spot. Reaching down to the turf, I felt the pendulum. Joe, I told myself, you are brilliant. Needle in a haystack and you just home in on it, no trouble, always the way.

With that cheering thought, I softly called out to Alison, whose dark shape I could barely make out against the lighter water, as I approached the stream yet again. "I found it, no problem."

She gave a grunt, and heaved a large stone into the water.

"What the hell?" I asked, slightly alarmed.

"It may have escaped your notice," she panted, "but the only bridge we know about is the wrong side of a high wall, back in the Palace grounds, and this stream isn't exactly a trickle. I'm trying to put in some stepping-stones. Trouble is, there aren't many big stones round here. You could help by fetching some from the wall back there."

"Not on your nelly. A drystone wall is a sacred object. Tell you what, Ms James, I'll tote you across, the old St Christopher stuff."

"Joe, don't be ridiculous. I weigh a ton."

"I doubt that. Besides, it can be my penance for misreading the map."

Alison treated it like a joke, but I meant it. I had good boots on and anyway I didn't mind if my feet got wet, whereas she only had those shoes. Also I quite fancied giving her a lift. Perhaps she sensed that; anyhow, she refused.

What could I do with this woman? I picked up the spade, and blundered across the stream in three giant strides, aiming for the stones, which were barely visible in the moonlight, not taking much water on board my boots. I turned round to find Alison already dodging from one foothold to another on the rocks midstream. With a pathetic wail, she wobbled, attempted an oversized step forward, and landed up to her shins in water, just below the bank. She would have fallen full length, but as she toppled I jumped down, caught her by the armpits, and hauled her out. Now we were both soaked up to our knees.

"Thanks for that," I said, with irony heavy as a policeman's boots.

"No, I have to thank you, Joe." She was near tears, I could tell from her voice. She pulled herself together, shivering though she was, and gave the torch a shake. "Lucky I didn't drop this. We might need it when you find the spot and we have to start digging." She tried switching it on. The faint light was almost completely dead.

"It's okay," I said. "We'll manage." I would have offered her a hanky but there wasn't one in my pocket.

After that it was like a dream, or a switch from a bad dream where everything's blocked to one where you know what to do. Cold, wet, and terribly tired though we were, we now worked in harmony. Alison took the spade to ease my movements. I cast about with my pendulum and found the energy line emanating from my target, with that old thrill that I don't know how to describe—it's like hearing someone pluck a string that vibrates at exactly the frequency you were imagining in your head, or how your finger feels when a wine glass rim starts to sing beneath it. Why I hadn't felt it before I don't know, except maybe I had, in those odd tugs, which I'd discounted as being an interference of water-energies. Apart from one diversion caused by an acute bend in the stream, and a scramble over an officiously high fence, we were able to move fairly straight across spongy pasture to a shallow dip in the ground. After that, the pendulum's direction of rotation went into reverse.

"Here," I announced.

Breaking up the darkness a short distance ahead, there lay a pool, sheeny with gleams of starshine. This must have been the pool, which Thomas Newbolt thought of as a loch—perhaps because it was more extensive in his time—where the boy had thrown the trumpet. It had silted up over the years, and the water level had sunk as it had become cut off from the stream, which bypassed it now. And so the spot where the trumpet had fallen had become dry land—dryish anyway—a small distance from the pool.

Adjusting the length of string on the pendulum, by winding it around my fingers, I again and again made passes over the spot, with different lengths corresponding to different depths. The most positive response came at the equivalent of about eighteen inches. Half a metre.

Working by moon and starlight, we took turns at digging. Alison wanted to do her bit, to warm herself up, and I could see the sense in that, though naturally I grabbed the lion's share. Once I'd chopped through the resistant turf to the slightly spongy ground beneath, the job wasn't desperately hard. We cut a trench about two and a half feet square and laid the cut turfs to one side so we could make good afterwards. As we worked down, we let the sides slope in gradually. It felt odd at first, to be digging in the near-dark almost like a mole, but after a while we fell into a rhythm, and if sometimes the blade missed its mark and brought up next to no earth, the next cut would make up for that. Within twenty minutes or so we'd reached a depth where I felt we needed to go cautiously. I laid my hand on Alison's arm—she was about to step into the hole we'd made, for a better angle of attack. I asked her to direct what little light the torch could still muster down into the hollow.

Kneeling on the edge, my head almost below my knees, I started gently scooping away at the peaty soil with the point of the spade, which I now held by the blade. My arms were soon aching like mad. I crouched, braced myself with a foot each side, and carried on that way for a few minutes.

A slight clunk, a different quality of resistance for a moment, and I knew we were there. I threw the spade aside, and looked wildly around for a better implement.

"Oh Joe, have you found it?" Alison was jigging up and down.

"Still, woman, keep that light pointing down"—though it was so faint now as to be almost less than the moonlight.

"Haven't you got a penknife?"

Yes, of course, I should have thought of that myself. Doubled over again, I scraped away to free the object I'd struck. It felt like stone, a big flint maybe, or ossified wood, which might be more likely in the peat. I felt a lurch of fear in my solar plexus. I pulled the thing out of the sodden hollow, holding it out for Alison to inspect.

"I don't think ..."

"Knock the mud off," she said.

It's odd, I'd been present at so many digs and I should have been far more confident than Alison, but perhaps I was flummoxed by having last seen this object in daylight, flashing through the air and falling into water. Now it was so dark I couldn't really make it out, but for sure there was no lustre, until—

"There, that's where I struck it with the spade," I said, pointing to a brighter line which just caught the moon's gleam.

We simultaneously looked towards the pool, and without having to say a word started to jog towards it, at an awkward stumbling run, so stiff were our legs.

Alison soaked her feet again, stepping with me into the soggy edge, where grass gave way to reeds and waterweeds. A nearby clash of wings: some roosting bird rose on our right. Alison clutched me around my midriff, whether to steady me or herself, as I bent over to bathe the trumpet, to free it of three and a half centuries of silt. Freezing water on cold fingers. The muffled clang as I prodded with my penknife's blunt prong (the one for removing stones from horses' hooves) to loosen dirt from the mouthpiece and crushed bell. It was only a preliminary, a very rough and ready job, but it made all the difference in the world to me. When I'd finished, and held the trumpet up high in both my hands towards the heavens as if I was offering thanks to the moon, which indeed had helped us towards this find, I knew for certain that this was what we had been looking for. I also knew I was not mad, the pictures from the past which had been plaguing me were not delusions, and by whatever strange mechanism they came to me, they were to some purpose.

Now we staggered like drunks, clambering back out of the shallows. Only a few steps onto the turf we turned and embraced. I still had the trumpet in my right hand as our lips met, clumsy with cold. I was shocked at the heat of Alison's mouth and my left hand was drawn under her jacket, to find where her shirt and trousers met, there to burrow into the warm gap to meet the flesh of her belly. She barely gasped at the cold of my fingers, a murmur of protest lost in our urgent kiss. Without words, we fell onto the ground and each helping the other we loosed what was necessary of our clothing so we could join our bodies. I was astonished by the heat inside her, then there was no more thought, just the two-backed beast, the ancient ceremony. Only after the inevitable explosion, which this time seemed to take my spine and blow it through the top of my skull, did I return to my senses enough to realize that my bum was freezing. And where was the trumpet?

"Oh, shit," we both said together.

At what should have been a moment of transcendent harmony, or some such, we were at cross purposes. While I was finger-tipping the grass nearby, Alison scrambled to her feet, piling oaths upon the inconsiderate cow which had left its dung in precisely the spot where her legs had resided during our coupling. I felt so wobbly I wondered if I were about to have a waking dream.

"I'll have to wash these trousers, pronto," Alison muttered.

"Got it!" I said at the same moment, scooping the trumpet into my arms.

By the time we finished repairing the hole we'd excavated, the sky was shifting from indigo to mauve, the stars had weakened, and a dawn wind was tossing the bare branches. As we made our way back to the inn, I tucked Alison's arm under mine to support her.

Back at the inn, without needing to consult, we both went into her room. Too weary to wash, we dropped our filthy clothes into a couple of carrier bags, laid the trumpet reverently on a bedside table with my scarf underneath it to catch the mud, and fell into a deep dawn sleep. As I drifted off with my arms around Alison, I looked ahead to making love in bed when we awoke. A fuck in a field had been fantastic, but not to be repeated at this time of the year.

CHAPTER FIFTEEN

For the first time since I had located *The Blessing of Burntisland*, I woke without The Dread springing onto me. I couldn't immediately remember what had happened, but I felt protected. Then it came to me: the trumpet, and Alison. There was a contradiction there, which I had resolved in the night in a very dodgy way. Perhaps it had been a dream. Meanwhile, I felt randy, and even before I opened my eyes, I swept my arm across the bed to find that warm body. But she wasn't there. Back in panic mode.

But then I realized where she was; the bathroom door was shut. I also realized I needed a pee. I wrapped the bedspread around myself and tiptoed out of her room and into mine, which likewise had its own small bathroom—shower room really.

I brushed my teeth while I was about it. Nothing worse than a furry bad-breath kiss to kill passion.

I rushed back to Alison's room and jumped into bed. When she emerged from the bathroom looking lovely and fresh in her silky maroon wrapper, I patted the pillow next to me.

"Come back to bed, you gorgeous thing. But do me a little favour first."

"What would that be, Joe?" she said, almost shyly.

"Drop that gown."

She frowned, not at me, but at the bedside table.

"Joe, where is the trumpet?"

Ah, there was a delicate question. Well, it had to come up sooner or later. Pity it had to be sooner.

I had a formula of words that didn't lie, but didn't reveal the truth either.

"I took it back."

"You what?"

"We did two crazy irresponsible things last night, Alison. One was absolutely great and I want to repeat it as soon as possible. But the other, well, I woke up and thought about it and I realized we must have been off our rockers. It was more than madness, it was badness. You could easily lose your job over something like this. And I'd seriously damage my reputation."

"By sleeping with me?"

She used a mock-incredulous tone. She was winding me up, but the mere thought that the digging could be the good bit, and the sex (I didn't know whether to think of it as love-making) the bad bit, cast a chill over me.

"Alison, I discovered something more important than an old bit of metal last night. I discovered you. I don't want to jeopardize that." It might have sounded convincing.

She was staring at the crumbs of dirt on the bedside table again. "Joe, you can't have re-buried the trumpet. You didn't have the spade. You didn't have the car key so you couldn't have got it. The car key is in my purse under my pillow and I would damn well have known if you'd tried to sneak it out."

So that was how far she trusted me. She was right, of course, but I chose to respond with another non-lie, non-truth.

"Maybe I didn't re-bury the trumpet, darling. Maybe I copied Robbie, and threw it in the water."

"Oh Joe!"

She looked at me, her eyes wobbly with tears, and I almost regretted what I'd done. I longed to take her in my arms and comfort her, but that had become impossible.

"Sometimes one person has to make a decision for both," was all I could offer.

"Yeah? So who made the decision not to use a condom last night?"

Feeling suddenly too naked, I pulled the sheet over myself, and stared at Alison.

"I didn't think. Got carried away. Listen, you must tell me if …"

"Just get out, Joe. GET OUT. Before I call the management."

This was not what I'd intended. At that moment, though, I told myself it was Alison's choice to part company with me, and really not my fault.

In my room, I dressed rapidly in the less damp of my two sets of clothes, packed my muddy boots wrapped in plastic into my bag, and was ready to leave. I went down and returned the pub key to the landlord, and asked him about transport to Edinburgh. There was a noon bus, to a place called Ladybank, where I would have to wait for the stopping train along the branch line to Edinburgh. The journey would take a couple of hours, and then there was the onward leg, another five or six hours, but I wasn't in too much of a hurry. I had nothing else to do that day, and it would be better to arrive at my destination after shop closing time.

First, I rang Kirsty from the phone on the reception counter, to check on Rose's progress. To my relief, not only had the child's feverishness dropped, but Kirsty had arranged to take her to the doctor. When I told her I regrettably could not enjoy more of her hospitality, as I'd had an urgent call back south, Kirsty apologized for the way she'd pestered me over Rose's fever. Yesterday seemed an age ago. She asked after Alison.

"Yes, she would like to come back to your place." To wash her mucky stuff, and then what? None of my business now. "I'd best go. Thanks again."

"Hold on a mo," said Kirsty, "here's someone wants to have a word with you."

Oh no, my un-favourite gypsy king.

"Hi Joe, what's this about you not coming back? We've got some unfinished business in Edinburgh, mate. Not to mention that little project of Irma's and mine. We scratch your back, you scratch ours, that's the deal isn't it?"

"Sorry Zemon, I'm behind schedule on another job. I have to go home and sort stuff out. Look, it's been great meeting you and Irma—give her my love, won't you? But the boat affair is a wild-goose chase, that's what I've come to realize."

"It's because I did that dive, isn't it?"

We hadn't discussed it since his shivering return from the depths of the Forth, except for immediately afterwards, when I couldn't help mentioning a few times that he was completely crazy. I'd kept off the subject since, but if it helped him to believe I was still bearing a grudge, that was fine by me.

He asked to speak to Alison, and seemed puzzled when I said she was not around, but would be at Kirsty's place within the hour. From his reaction, I realized Zemon must have thought Alison and I were "an item". I replaced the hotel phone in its cradle, with a sudden urgent need for coffee to wash away a bitter taste in my mouth.

I did see Alison again, very briefly; I offered to carry her gear downstairs and she accepted. I also offered to pay for both our rooms but she wouldn't allow that. We made our farewells out beside her car, in the quiet street with the inn on one side and the palace gatehouse on the other. As she struggled to fit her key into the lock of the car boot, I noticed the shadowy aura around her eyes. She seemed unable to look at me directly, as if she were the guilty party, not me.

I heaved her bag into the boot and turned for a final handshake. At least she granted me that. Her hand was cold. I caught a whiff of lemon soap but none of her usual musky scent. The way she said goodbye sounded horribly final.

As I sat in the shelter at Ladybank station, gazing at the oil-coated weeds struggling to survive at the edges of the single track of railway line, I reflected what a fragile thing trust is.

Had the fact that we'd had sex sealed a pact between us; did it mean that I should have shared everything about the trumpet with her? But I just could not do it. I could not accept that the trumpet belonged to her as well. It was Robbie's, for all that he'd thrown it away, and I had to find some way to return it to him, or use it to call him to me. Alison could not understand that, because she had no idea of how I was groping towards contact with Robbie as a lifeline maybe to my own salvation, maybe his. No comprehension, either, of what my waking dreams felt like, the turmoil and anxiety they brought me. Odd that. Since she'd come on board with me, she had rarely asked about them. I suspected she had always remained sceptical. Perhaps she gave some credence to my dowsing, but not the waking dreams, despite the bits of evidence.

Bits! What about the trumpet? Now we'd found that, she surely must believe. In fact she had seemed very impressed with the find last night.

Perhaps I should have told her I was sorry, this morning. Perhaps I should have taken her into my confidence.

I looked around to see if there was a phone booth on the station. Nothing on this platform. Perhaps in the ticket office? I picked up my bag, hesitating whether to rush back and have a look, when a two-carriage diesel pulled up. This was my train, and if I missed it, I'd blow my chances of making the onward connection. Anyway I could ring Alison later, I told myself, as I clambered into the overheated interior. A couple of teenagers sat sharing a bag of crisps, little black plugs in their ear-holes emitting a tinny pulsation that would have driven me mad. Luckily it was drowned out when the engine throbbed back to full throttle.

No, we could not have carried on; nothing I could have said would have mended the broken trust. Alison was bound to come to her Departmental senses soon enough, and then she'd have shopped me, and the Government or the Scottish Office would have bagsied the trumpet. Or failing that, if she had chucked in her job—which was a very big if, for most people set a lot of store by a steady career—why then, she'd have been on my hands and wanting to decide what to do next, as she had shown a tendency to do all along. Miss Bossyboots.

At the point where the line approached the Forth Bridge, I crossed over the carriage to look out of the left-hand window. A squall of hard drizzle blew against the panes and ran back in diagonal rivulets. In the mid-distance, the jumble of buildings, the sea front defences and railway line, and beyond that the spread of the green, seemed to shiver in my view. Burntisland. I regretted ever having heard the name.

Unless. Perhaps it had been meant, after all, and perhaps I was carrying the key right now, in an inside pocket of my gabardine.

At Edinburgh Waverley, I had to wait ten minutes to get my ticket, hopping mad because I still hadn't had my coffee. The man behind me in the queue, a scruffy individual with stringy hair, who looked oddly familiar, didn't share my annoyance when I muttered about the ridiculous lack of staff.

"Where you going?" he asked.

I turned my back. What business was it of his?

At last I was at the ticket hatch. "Single to London," I said.

So I was more than a little annoyed when this same chap came and plonked himself in the seat opposite me on the train. True, there weren't all that many vacant places, but I had managed to put off all other comers with my prize Norfolk scowl which matches my poacher's mac a treat.

"Mind if I join you?" That was a cheek, considering he'd already sat down.

I tried to carry on as if he wasn't there. I had my back to the engine, on Uncle Vernon's theory that if the train had to stop suddenly in an emergency, I wouldn't get whiplash. Edinburgh was disappearing behind us, the core and the fringes of that great dark city, its packed stones reeking of age and confidence and solid wealth.

"So, did you find what you were looking for in Edinburgh?" said the greasy man opposite me. It was an odd thing to say to a stranger. I glanced at him then, sharpish.

"Excuse me, I don't think we've met." That would have shut up anyone with a shred of common decency.

He continued to lean forward with a vacuous smile on his pasty round face, staring at me through plastic-rimmed specs. "Or perhaps it was a trip across the water that you were after?" he continued.

Now I was staring back at him. I bit my lip—unlike me, but I sensed I had to go careful on this wicket. A corner of my mind envisaged the train braking sharply, giving his neck a little wrench, so he'd have to wear one of those big padded collars for a while, and couldn't go around rubbernecking into other people's business.

"Sorry, I don't think you said your name?" I asked. It wouldn't surprise me if he knew mine.

He held out a bony paw, white with bright red knuckles and yellow tips to the index and second fingers. "Dooley. Call me Kevin. Pleased to meet you, Joe."

It took me a second; then as I shook his hand I recalled who he was, though of course we had never met. We had spoken on the phone, way back in the time before I'd made this second trip to Scotland, before Alison had fully entered my life. Dooley of the *Ouse News*.

"You're not telling me you followed me all the way up here? Surely you have better things to do with your time, and your employer's money."

"No, nothing better at all. I have relations up here I wanted to visit, anyway."

That was the line I'd taken when I was impersonating Dave Berry. I wondered how much he knew about me. And why he was so damn interested.

"Is that so? Now, if you'll excuse me, I need to get myself some coffee."

"No, let me." He was half out of his seat but I stood up and blocked the gangway, pressing down on his shoulder.

"I'll get yours too, Kevin, it'll be my treat." That bony shoulder, the specks of dander on his blue anorak, the smell of stale fags. "How about a snifter to brighten up the journey?" I added.

His eyes lit up behind their windscreens. "Wouldn't say no to a brandy. Settles the stomach. I take milk, one sugar. Ta."

First off, I washed my hands, struggling to keep steady on my feet in the cramped, swaying toilet. Already at the start of the journey there was a slick of some unidentifiable liquid across the floor. I'd realized too late, in shaking hands with Dooley, that I had defiled that final contact with Alison. I'm not usually obsessive, but I washed and dried my hands twice, afterwards rubbing till the coarse blue paper towels disintegrated. I patted my lining pocket to check the contents were still safely there, just managing to resist the temptation to have another look.

The smell of disinfectant soap clung to me as I tacked my way down to the buffet. Leaning on the high counter, I ordered two double brandies, poured one into Dooley's coffee, and kept the other to give him on the side.

Of course the coffee was scalding, so he'd started on the brandy, and then by the time he came to the coffee he could not tell the difference. Not that it went to his head, or not fast enough for my liking.

"So you were there in the pub witnessing Zemon's performance on the tin whistle. What a coincidence," I said. Not such a coincidence, given that he was in touch with Alison, of course. At least it accounted for why I'd thought I'd seen him before—it turned out I had.

"Yeah, funny bloke your friend Zemon. Potty about his little theory, isn't he? Just as convinced as Ms James is about hers."

I was trying to keep my face neutral. So he'd spoken to both of them, and in some depth. When?, I wondered. One thing was for sure; but for Alison blabbing, he would not have known about our quest in the first place, or about our movements in Edinburgh. She had betrayed me—hadn't I made it absolutely plain from the start how much I disliked involving the press? This was helpful in one way, making me feel less guilty about deserting her.

"What theories would those be, then?" I asked.

"Come off it, Joe. You're the one that started all this."

"No, honestly. We've bandied ideas about, but I'm at a loss really. In fact I've given up on the whole thing, that's why I'm going home."

"Via London?"

"What other way is there?" I had not asked for a through ticket, because I might not be travelling home today. How come I had barely been able to hear the ticket seller at Waverley through the racket of announcements, but our Kevin behind me in the queue had heard every word?

"Then there's that nice young foreign girl, she likes the bones angle."

Nosey-parkering Dooley had probed further, and discovered more about people's motivations, than I'd managed recently. Tender-hearted Irma thought *The Blessing of Burntisland* should stay on the sea bed because it was the watery grave of thirty Stuart servants. Dooley elaborated the general argument about disturbing bones, versus leaving them in situ out of respect. Archaeologists, no longer so blasé about long-dead people, were having debates about this all over the place.

"Lot of mileage these days, way they went with the *Swan*," he continued.

Either the guy was more generally knowledgeable than he looked, or he'd been doing a thorough bit of homework. I wouldn't have heard of the *Swan* myself, but for the salvage crew. She was another of Charles I's ships, built in 1641, shortly before civil war broke out. She'd fallen into Parliamentarian hands, and Cromwell sent her north to subdue some Royalist Scots, but she was wrecked off the western isle of Mull, a sad end just a few years after being commissioned. Divers found the wreck a decade or two back, and since then the archaeologists had been on the case. I knew they had decided not to raise the *Swan*. Why hadn't I thought of that as a simple precedent for *The Blessing of Burntisland* to be left in peace?

"Yeah, but they are still raising the contents," I told him. That was why. There had been news of one or two promising bits of ordnance, though no treasure as such.

"No harm in that is there? At least they won't be radioactive, like your other friend hinted the *Blessing* might be. Is that what you think Joe?"

What I thought was, this fellow was too sharp by half. When would the brandy kick in?

"Would I have allowed Zemon to dive if I'd believed that?" Oh blast, I chastized myself, did he know about the dive? I was handing him stuff on a plate.

"You didn't have much choice, from what I gather. Of course, he was taking a risk, considering the plague or some other deadly disease may be lurking down there. Presumably it won't revive unless it comes in contact with the air."

I took a gulp of what could have been sweetened bathwater, and raised an eyebrow at Dooley. It seemed everybody had more theories than I did—annoying, considering I'd done my first method acting in Dr Anderson's inner sanctum the other day, and imagined I was ahead of the crowd. Not that it had been exactly crystal clear to either Alison or me what the Navy, or the archaeologists, thought was going on, down under the firth.

A sudden light bulb switched on in my brain. That name Dr A. had been struggling to remember, and kept getting wrong ...

"Seems we both visited Dr Anderson the same day," said Dooley. This man was making a habit of reading my thoughts and I didn't like it one bit. "But you and your friend Ms James maybe were more on his wavelength."

"I'd have thought you'd have had the advantage in door-stopping him. Tricks of your trade."

"All I got was some bunkum about what this was going to contribute to our knowledge of the life and times of the jolly old court of Charley One—as if I didn't know that already. Zilch about why everyone was suddenly as nervous as a virgin in a lap-dancing club."

"Tell me what it is you want to know, Kevin."

"Okay, it's this. I can't figure out why all these people are under your spell. Apart from your obvious charisma and animal magnetism, of course. What is your angle on all this, Joe? You must know the real reason why this wreck is a threat."

He looked almost genuinely bewildered.

"Just remind me why I owe you any help?"

"You don't want them to raise this wreck, right? Zemon thinks we need a campaign." This was news to me; it had been Alison's idea. But then I remembered the two of them were in cahoots. "I'm willing to start it up, I've got the contacts, and if it rolls I'll get the credit, so no mystery as to my motives. I don't care if you're right or wrong, as long as it's good copy. Ms James clearly embarked on this thinking she would be a whistleblower, that her Department was colluding in a shady deal. She was onto the nuclear sub angle though she also mentioned to me the chance there was a fishing vessel tangled up in a Royal Navy propeller down there. But now I think her real bugbear was the Scottish thing." A flush had crept into his cheeks.

I wondered if the *Perseus* could have been a small boat, instead of a sub. No, the diagram of a submarine I'd seen in Dr Anderson's file had been a clincher. Yet it hadn't altered my sense that there was something else, some threat that was far more nebulous yet more deadly.

"The Scottish thing? You've lost me."

"Oh you know, this business of who does it really belong to now?"

"*The Blessing of Burntisland*? It belongs to the Crown, that's obvious. It was King Charles's treasure and as far as I know we are still a monarchy. So it's literally crown property. When treasure is found that is crown property, it belongs to the nation."

"The British nation, is what you mean. But the Scots don't see it quite that way, do they? And that's what Ms James was worried about."

"I think you'll find that was only a cover. If it had really been that, she'd have had the blessing of her Department to negotiate over it or whatever. She's onto a much bigger issue."

Good. He was leaning forward, interested, not knowing what was coming next.

"She has some proof about the nuclear sub. She's been cagey because she knows that New Agers like Zemon will make a big fuss about this, but she seems dead serious that it might be irresponsible to carry on with the excavation. If it's a Russian sub, it may be highly unstable—you know what they were like."

"Then why the hell does she come here undercover? What's wrong with her Department?"

"It may not be a case of nuclear armaments, but nuclear power. It will raise ructions about current British nuclear-powered subs. She has to gather the info quickly, before the people here realize that she's not acting on orders. And I happen to know that she made a breakthrough. She saw something in Dr Anderson's lab that I didn't see, something that convinced her there's a sub down there, practically alongside *The Blessing of Burntisland*."

"What do you mean, you didn't see?"

"Seems Anderson was ever so slightly suspicious of me, so he waited till I was in the Gents to show her some sonar scans—hasn't she told you all this?" I had no way of knowing how far Alison had gone in blabbing to the lizard.

He had pulled out a notepad and was scribbling in what I guessed, from my upside-down view of it, was shorthand. How old-fashioned, right up my street, not an electronic pad like I'd have expected. Not that it endeared him to me. He shook his head and waved his biro, a gesture I took to mean "Carry on".

"He also showed her a plan of a sub which had disappeared in those waters in 1984," I said, not knowing where I had snatched that date from. "It wasn't covered in the press at the time, part of the Cold War fog; they were hoping to track it down and exhume its secrets without the Soviets knowing."

"How does this link in with your wreck, then?"

"It doesn't. That's why I've lost interest."

The feeling of relief when Dooley alighted at Newcastle, to catch a train back to Edinburgh and follow up his story with the redoubtable Ms James of the DoE, was so marvellous that I didn't really need to celebrate with a can of Newcastle Brown from the buffet, but I did anyway. I was still resisting the temptation to look at my find because I knew once I started I wouldn't want to stop, and I might give the game away. But the feel of it clunking away against my leg as I wandered down the train was wonderfully reassuring. The only cloud came when I tipped the beer down my throat, and a brief flash of recent memory flooded with it: Alison and I in the Rose and Crown in Newcastle, me being sick and she holding my head and helping me clean up. She'd been really great then. She'd been really great last night, if I was honest. Why did she have to spoil it by making a fuss over the trumpet? Her reaction when she saw it was gone showed how possessive she was already feeling towards it. OK, I'd lied a bit, but she hadn't trusted me, so why shouldn't I?

And now I knew she'd been conniving with this Dooley behind my back, I was glad—yes, glad—that I'd done a runner. My god, what if he'd known what I had in my poacher's pocket, right here under his nose?

Yes, it was lucky I'd broken with Alison just in time. Now he was running back to her, demanding to know about the nuclear submarine.

What if she told him about the trumpet? It was a risk, but I didn't think she would. As far as she knew, there was no evidence now that it had ever existed, and it would be awfully difficult for her to explain our illicit night dowsing and digging expedition.

Mentally, I communed with my precious burden: You're safe now, my lovely, and I'm taking you where you can be made as good as new, as you were in Robbie's time.

Between York and Doncaster I fell asleep, and slept most of the rest of the way, waking befuddled shortly before London. I took the Underground from King's Cross to Mile End, changing at Liverpool Street, hating the sense of suffocation as always, and emerged onto Mile End Road to breathe in the traffic fumes with relative pleasure.

CHAPTER SIXTEEN

Brokesley Street is, as Stepan would say, a funny one, with the Royal London Hospital halfway down, and Tower Hamlets cemetery at the end. His shop was just inside the street, but being off the main road no one came there by chance; only his "cognoscenti". He had a half-shop, with half of the display window, his instruments all crammed in on top of each other on one side of the partition. Barqa's florists had the other side. They did rely on passing trade, of course—both hospital and cemetery visitors—unlike Stepan. He also had half the premises above, the top two floors (or one and a half really, for the very top was cramped attic space), with Mr and Mrs Barqa and their seven tiny children in the floors immediately above the divided shop.

There was a drab house-door, set back a little from the street, next to the left-hand shop entrance. I rang the top bell, marked "Divac" and counted slowly to ten, then rang again. Footsteps limped down the stairs, the door was flung open, and a long face with dark deep-set eyes looked out, at first astonished then delighted.

"Joe! Joe, my friend. Why you didn't ring to tell me you coming? Come in, come inside anyway."

Stepan led me up the three flights of stairs coated in sticky lino, past the tasty curry smells and wakeful child squeals of the Barqa apartments, to the stuffy little living room which also served as his kitchen.

I remembered him sitting there in his one armchair, sobbing, head in hands. Stepan owed me; he would not refuse what I'd come to ask. That time, I had found his son who was lost, not even in this country, but in one I'd never heard of and could not have located on a map if I'd been asked. He'd had the map, luckily, and a picture of the son, out of date but enough for me to do the job. Or maybe, just maybe, it was the tin whistle, the one that Georg had played the one time he'd been allowed into this country to visit his father. He'd been twelve then, and when he went missing he was eighteen, running away from the call-up Stepan guessed. Their people were not likely to survive long in the army. It seemed mad to me that Stepan couldn't just demand to have his son with him, if he was in such danger—after all, the British authorities had recognised that Stepan himself was entitled to safe haven here. But it doesn't work like that apparently. And from what Stepan said, it sounded as though the mother wouldn't let go of her son before he turned eighteen and went missing. Eventually, after I tracked him down, they got him out of the country and over here.

Now this lad Georg was living in Stevenage, at college in the daytime, working in a bar at night, and making money from selling mobile phones at weekends. He'd be a successful businessman in a couple of years. Stepan didn't see much more of him now than when he was back home, but he was happy, knowing he was safe.

A delicious savoury smell wafted around the living room. There was the square table where I had spread the map, with Georg's photo to one side, the tin whistle laid in front of it, like a little shrine. Stepan had suggested I play the instrument, but I'd refused, I don't know why. Stepan himself played it often enough, a good deal better than my new friend Zemon.

"You want eat?" asked Stepan, ladling some chicken goulash out of a big iron saucepan as though I had been invited for supper. The grey streaks in his hair were much more pronounced now than last time I'd seen him. He was about five years older than me, but looked much more worn.

I did want eat, very definitely. Stepan himself had finished already. While I was gobbling, he gave the trumpet a look over. He tactfully didn't ask where or how I'd come by it, but he remarked on it being very old, much older than the gear he dealt in, the lovingly restored saxes, trombones, slide trumpets and all the rest. I explained I wanted it cleaned and back in shape so it would sound like it used to, as close as possible.

"How long?" I asked.

Stepan gave a low whistle. "She's not very happy, this little one. Full of mud, then the bell all flat, this old metal maybe a bit how you say, birtle, could crack if I try to make it round again."

I worked out what he meant and corrected him. "Can't you do it then?"

Stepan pushed my plate aside, and laid out first a piece of oilcloth, then an old towel folded many times, and cradled the trumpet on that. He put on a pair of horn-rimmed spectacles and studied the trumpet minutely, gently probing to loosen more of the dirt clogging up the bell.

It was my turn to sit in the leaky armchair with horsehair itching my backside through my trousers, my head in my hands. If a broken trumpet isn't as serious as a lost son, you probably wouldn't have known it from looking at me.

"Course, the metal might be more softer, being probably more pure, I didn't do one so old before. But you brought her to the right man, you know that, Joe. Hey, you wanna stay over?"

"How long, Stepan?"

"So's you can rest up to catch your train in the morning, longer if you want. Oh, I see. This beauty. A week, maybe nine days. I got my regular work and the shop to run. That okay?"

I tried to hide my disappointment. It was a long time to wait for my key to the past, and perhaps to the future too. But meanwhile I could try tuning myself in to Robbie through visualization, so when I got the trumpet back it would work more smoothly.

"Sure. And when it's mended, can you give me a quick tutorial on how to make the thing sound notes?"

Stepan ducked his head and gave me one of his rare smiles of almost childlike glee. He had a gift for working on musical instruments, and hated selling them because it was like parting with his children, but he was a musician manqué he'd told me. I'd heard him a couple of times, when I'd come round to check on progress with getting Georg over here, and I believed him. He could play anything. "Not so anyone will pay to hear me," he'd said, but I wondered. If he'd had friends to help him, maybe he would have made it. The jazz scene's loss was my gain, now.

There was a most peculiar episode in the night, given that I am not a sleep-walker.

In the first place, I had trouble getting to sleep. The half-room where Stepan insisted on putting me was overheated and claustrophobic, though not cluttered. He kept a divan permanently made-up there, with a blue quilt and embroidered white pillowcase, for such time as Georg might remember to pay a visit. Apart from a couple of hangers on a hook on the back of the door, there was nothing else—there was no space. It was neatly plastered, painted white, but a damp patch stained one corner a mushroom shade; and to stand up properly I'd have had to open the skylight. In fact I'd tried but it was stuck.

After a while I drifted off and then, not sure if I was asleep or awake, I heard a sound, like a voice. In an unaccustomed room in a strange neighbourhood, you cannot expect to identify noises like you could at home. But I was convinced this was in the house, not outside, and probably just downstairs, not in the prolific Barqas' apartment below. I got up to investigate.

Soft. I pause outside the door of my chamber, for there is some movement within, subtly more regular and therefore more human or mechanical than a rat's scurrying. And if mechanical, therefore human. And now a wheeze of breathing. All my frame freezes, but for my right arm and hand which draws out of its sheath my dagger (for I am not dressed with my sword) so silently none could detect the motion from within. There being no means to open the chamber door with equal stealth, I make to fling it wide of a sudden, for surely Soames or his spies will have broken the lock to enter. But no, it is secured still, and I must fumble with my key, transferring the dagger to my left hand, meeting resistance from another, doubtless counterfeit, key in the other side. What is my astonishment when the other key grates, the door opens before me, and Robbie appears, his face rosy in spots as it were with shame. I peer behind him, expecting Soames's men with poniards to his shoulder-blades, but he is alone in my chamber and there is a fire in the coals beneath my alembic; and bellows but now laid aside, for I guess that was the regular noise I'd descried—the wheezes of the little bellows breathing life into the fire.

"What the devil?" I shout as I push past Robbie ...

"What on earth, Joe?" Stepan switched on his bedside lamp as I blundered into his bedroom, which was next door to mine.

"I didn't mean to disturb you. Thought I heard somebody downstairs."

Stepan was great, came down to the living room with me to reassure me the "dear little trumpet" was tucked up safe and sound, and gave me a slivovitz to settle my nerves.

Thinking how much more worried I'd have felt if the trumpet had been in his back-of-shop workshop, I made him promise to bring the instrument upstairs to his flat every night.

"But Joe," he said, "I have my whole livelihoods down there, I have burglar alarm, everything. Why you so paranoic?"

Stepan now knew, if he hadn't guessed before, that the trumpet was extremely valuable. So I told him an essential bit of the truth: that I needed the trumpet to help me find a lost boy. No more questions after that.

Travelling north to Edinburgh and Falkland had taken me half a season backwards, so I really noticed the progress in my garden when I got home. All around the borders and under my two apple trees, clumps of daffs had opened. Celandines shone among the grass. Leaf buds were gently opening on the hawthorn and birch hedges. The hedges had aroused scathing comments when I'd planted them, but were now an accepted part of the neighbourhood scenery.

That lawn needed a mow. I couldn't bring myself to wreck the starry flowers so I left it. Onion sets ought to go in; I could not be bothered. There was a fair bit of post accumulated on my hall floor; I opened one shrieking envelope that informed me I'd won a prize cruise to the Bahamas, threw it in the bin and stacked the rest in the toast rack on the kitchen table.

I'd dumped my bag in the kitchen. All my clothes from the journey could do with a wash. I checked the box of powder and found not more than a teaspoon left. I really could not face the supermarket. I would have to go soon, for food, but for the moment I showered, changed into my softest old shirt and trousers, and retreated into the shed. Treadling the lathe, I set to work turning another white pawn, to replace the one I'd ruined the day before I'd set out on my travels. As I worked, I pictured Stepan's workshop at the back of his store, and wondered when he'd get around to starting on the trumpet. This evening, maybe. Or perhaps even in his lunch break, if he had a lunch break.

It had been stupid, blundering into his bedroom last night. I had known I was in the wrong place but could not figure out why. The waking dream had come over me in the tiny bedroom, just as I was making my mind up to investigate that random noise I'd heard. Possibly, I now realized, Stepan's snoring. My foot slowed on the treadle, as it came to me that I'd followed the movement Dr Newbolt had made during the waking dream, right to pushing through a doorway. It was lucky that I'd found Stepan's door, rather than stumbling on the tiny landing and falling down the stairs. I could easily have broken my neck. What was to become of me if it went on like this?

Now here I was at home, and although everything looked skewed, too old or too new, or the wrong size, as it does when you've been away a week or two, as if the table's been out dancing and the carpet's had its friends round, at least I knew I was safe here. If I did any more sleepwalking (or waking-dream-walking), my feet would surely find their way around without hazard. I started to relax, working the lathe a little faster, and even hummed to myself in an experimental way as I worked.

I'd spent on the trip up north as if there was no tomorrow. Not that most places we'd stayed at had been expensive but it mounts up, and then there was paying for meals out. Normally when I travelled for dowsing work I got all expenses paid but then, normally, the client gained a big reward. That last B&B, in Falkland, had been expensive. I should have paid for Alison, but I understood why she wouldn't let me. At least the night at Kirsty's had been free. Ah, but Kirsty deserved something in return—I personally didn't set much store by my amateurish attempts at herbal doctoring for Rose. I'd send her a present. Now, what would she like?

I thought momentarily of sending Kirsty one of my real treasures, a ring or brooch I'd been given as my share from my two most valuable finds so far, Anglo-Saxon grave goods, but that would be seriously overdoing it. How about something I'd made? I took my foot off the treadle, let the lathe whir to a halt, and looked around the shed. I contemplated a neatly joinered beechwood box, whose lid closed perfectly over an inner lining layer of rosewood. The trouble with a box, though, is you want it to contain a nice surprise; but two presents would be too much. Also, it would be heavy to post. So I went into the house, and ferreted around in my desk, in the spare bedroom which doubles as a kind of study, not that I study anything much.

Among the jumble of old photos from the family, and the paperweight I'd been given by Uncle Vernon when I was twenty-one, the fountain pens that didn't work but might be fixable, the broken balsa model aeroplane from when I was eight, the bits of green blotting paper covered in doodles, and the treasures I'd picked up from junk shops when I was a kid just starting out to be interested in old stuff, I found it. An ivory carved ball with seven smaller balls disappearing inside, each punctured with circular windows so if you were very patient you could line them up the way its maker must have done when he started with his carving. On the outside of the outermost sphere, stylized dragons and lotuses intertwined. (I imagined they were lotuses; I had no idea of what lotuses looked like.) You cannot get these balls new, now that the ivory trade has been banned. It gave me a twinge, realizing Kirsty probably disapproved of anything made of ivory, so I put in a note saying she could think of it like old piano keys, made before we knew any better. It wasn't personal, just a pleasing object I'd picked up from an antique fair years ago, not even a real antique; probably forty years old, or a bit more, like me. Kirsty's kids might like to play with it. Presumably Alison had left Eden Valley by now, but Zemon and Irma might still be there, and they might tell Alison—no, I was being ridiculous. I parcelled the thing up with bubble wrap and brown paper, then realized I had no proper postal address for Kirsty.

I had her number in the back of my notebook, from when she left us in Falkland. She answered straight away. My stupid knees felt jelly-like. But it soon emerged that Alison had only stayed one more night, and had left with the others that morning.

"Joe, you missed a treat with the lads playing at the Stag and Hounds—they were brilliant." Alison had also missed the music, pleading a headache. All three visitors, to Kirsty's best knowledge, were now in Edinburgh. She had no idea how long Zemon and Irma planned to stay there. Alison aimed to return home by the end of the week at the latest.

I'd made myself a cup of tea to steady my nerves. It sat cooling beside the phone on the hall table as I punched in Alison's mobile number. I wasn't prepared for the mechanized female voice offering to take my message, and rang off straight away. But I should let her know I'd tried. I took a sip of tea, rang again, and said: "Alison, it's Joe. Just wondering if you're okay. I'd like to talk."

The right words would not come, the words that would convince her that all our mateyness, our joint efforts over *The Blessing of Burntisland*, our night dowsing and impromptu sex, surely outweighed a little squabble about a disappeared trumpet.

She would have another grievance against me, I remembered, now not feeling so proud of the way I'd turned the sleuth-hack Dooley back onto her.

I dialled her mobile number a third time. "Hi, it's Joe again. I forgot to say, Dooley got on my train, asked a lot of nosey questions, and then got off—said he was going to see you. I told him the story's a dead duck, there is no story, but he seems to want to make something of it. I let slip a mention of the sub. He's very tricksy, so beware, don't answer him if you can help it. About that or anything else."

She had contacted him in the first place. But would she still want to pursue the idea of a media splash now that I had dropped out of the *Blessing of Burntisland* affair?

Had I dropped out? I mused on it as I sorted my dirty clothes for washing, and stowed my bag in the understairs cupboard. It might depend on the trumpet, on contacting Robbie, on what the boy would tell me if we actually managed to speak to one another. He would know the significance of *The Blessing of Burntisland*—he had so much more second sight than me. But I had some, and he would recognize that.

Perhaps my fears had been misplaced; perhaps The Dread was really around Newbolt's and Robbie's near-drowning, rather than any disaster that might arise from raising the wreck, or the treasure.

I sat at the kitchen table, sipping at my cold tea, and thought back to the other day, out on the Firth of Forth with Alison, Zemon, and Irma. I had been avoiding this, it was too difficult or too odd. And I had been too angry. My visualization, linked perhaps to Zemon's dive. What had I seen or felt, exactly? It had been truncated at that moment when I had realized the gross deception Zemon was perpetrating on me. Just before that, there had been a powerful sense of a precious object, or substance, concealed in a box, yes, a sealed box, in a saddle-bag wasn't it, on one of the dead horses, the skeleton horses.

A box, like the ones I made, but bigger than most, and more closely sealed than I could ever hope to achieve.

The contents, though, were a mystery.

To be fair to Zemon, it was unlikely I could have identified what was down there through my visualization. I'd have had to start on my refined dowsing, testing for the materials in the cache, and that would have been next to impossible with so much wreck and treasure and bones heaped together in close proximity, and with us rocking in a little boat hundreds of feet above. No, I would not even have attempted it. I would have to wait till they raised the wreck to find out ...

Raised the wreck! Now I was positively welcoming the idea, for the first time. How extraordinary.

I remembered once when Todd and I were skiving off school, fishing on the Little Ouse where it flows close under the old railway embankment. As I struggled to reel in a drowned shoe, I'd told him with amazing sincerity that I didn't fancy Evie, the girl he was going out with. Miraculously, the ache of longing had starting to recede from that moment on.

Now, by telling Dooley that I'd given up on stopping the raising of the wreck, I'd seemingly convinced myself. Four months of The Dread, and it had evaporated overnight. Almost, I felt cheated. That snippet of waking dream at Stepan's might be the last. If I'd known, I would have tried to hang on in there longer. There was definitely more to see. What had Robbie been up to?

Robbie. Would I still be able to contact him? Did I still want to, now the urgency about the boat was receding? Yes, I discovered, very much.

Taking a risk, I drove to the supermarket to stock up. Not a quiver or a shadow of a waking dream troubled me, but I realized when I pulled up in front of my house that I'd been sitting bolt upright the whole way there and back, and had developed a nasty twinge between my shoulders.

With the washing machine chugging away in the background, I settled down on the sofa and let myself be lulled into a semi-doze, where I could work on envisioning Robbie. That was the first of half a dozen sessions over the next couple of days, initially without much result. I would lie down on the sofa with the curtains shut, day or night, and close my eyes, slow my breathing, and allow my mind's eye to travel over my "sightings" of the boy, but above all the one where he had looked in the mirror and—I was sure—had seen me. I would leave out, so far as I could, that self-important doctor. When he popped into my head, which he inevitably did since it was through his eyes that I had seen Robbie, I told him fair and square: "Bog off, Newbolt," and refused to listen to his inward chatter if I started to recall it.

One way he could have been useful to me, if I could have chosen which bits of his experience to sample, was in writing those notes about Robbie. What wouldn't I have given to be with him while he did that, I told myself the first time, but then pulled myself up sharp. What need for Newbolt's interpretation of Robbie, when I could have my own?

I became a proper little housemaid, between bouts of Robbie-gazing. Normally, I keep the house reasonably shipshape, but I'm not over-fussy. Now, I was taken with an urge to clean and set to rights, and even ironed my shirts as soon as I brought them in off the line. I dug the garden, and made another two pawns for the chess set. And I avoided the pub. It was like being in training for a race. Or perhaps an initiation, I thought with a slight shiver.

I had told people that I was likely to be away for a week or ten days, so the phone didn't ring much. The first time it did, I was polishing the one and only mirror in my house. It was a long one that I had fixed on the wall at the end of the upstairs corridor, soon after we'd moved in, to brighten up a dark corner. Marjory wasn't satisfied with it; said she couldn't get a proper look at herself, what with the lamp at the head of the stairs back-lighting her. She went on nagging at me to install a new light fitting where it would illuminate her prancing up and down, trying on four different outfits before we would go out, last as usual to meet up with Marvin and Janie and the others down the pub. I couldn't imagine Alison parading in front of a mirror like that. She'd choose her clothes carefully and make sure the buttons were done up straight and then stop worrying about how she looked. Anyway Marjory left me before I got around to putting in a new light.

When the phone rang, I saw my face with a comically open mouth gawping in the mirror. I dropped my chamois in the bucket, and leaped down the stairs three at a time. The normal laws of motion must have been suspended or I'd surely have gone head over heels.

But of course it wasn't Alison.

"Hello, Joe, Stepan here. Thought I should let you know how things is progressing this end because you seemed so anxious about your little beauty." I had previously indicated it was better not to mention the trumpet on the phone. You never knew who was listening. "Say, you all right Joe, been running? Well, I got a fairly good idea I can do it in a week. I got a half day early closing I forgot about when you asked, and I made a start already in the last couple days so we talking next Tuesday, say Wednesday on the safe side, okay? Give me a ring Monday evening to check it up. See you soon."

After my heart stopped thudding I realized I should be very pleased indeed. Stepan had sounded optimistic that the trumpet would be playable. Whether I would be able to play it was another matter.

I chided myself for getting worked up. Much better that Alison and I had gone our separate ways.

On the second morning, I started by reading all my notes about the waking dreams. There was too much Newbolt in them. I took the notebook out to the shed. There was one box that would serve my purpose perfectly. It had been an experiment; sycamore wood, lined and covered with lead sheeting left over from a repair I'd done on the valley where the bathroom roof joined the main one. The box was heavy, and ugly. I'd made it years ago, after I'd seen a *Blue Peter* programme about time capsules at the millennium. My idea had been to choose my own items, to reflect a different side of the twentieth century from the video game, Nike trainer, toothpaste, and whatever they had chosen. But what would I put in it? Dowsing rods, a second-hand copy of *The Maltese Falcon*, a photo of Emma as a fat baby? I had left it empty.

I placed the dream diary in the leaden box, returned to the house and settled on my sofa. It occurred to me the box I'd sensed on *The Blessing of Burntisland* had been heavy, too. It felt heavy, in my memory. I wanted to go and add that to my notes, but no, I told myself, relax. Deal with that later.

I went deeper into myself, focusing simply on my desire to touch base with Robbie. The images came slowly, one replacing another, like lantern slides projected onto the inside of my eyelids as I lay there in the darkened sitting room.

Shimmering like a mirage through a heat-haze, a handsome woman with tawny hair bends over a pot in a low space glowing with firelight.

The same woman but shrunken, horizontal on a bed or bier, her skin waxy-pale in the dimness of a shuttered room with one candle burning.

A long pause, nothing but darkness, and the sound of my heart thumping.

A hulk of a man, bearded, a cast in one eye, swinging at a tree in a thick forest with spangles of sun on the shuddering trunk.

The same man with a hatchet-blade embedded in his temple, blood streaming down his face, toppling over like one of his felled timbers.

Darkness, silence. The smell of my morning kippers drifting through from the kitchen. Should have washed up the grill-pan straight away.

For half an hour after that session, as I brewed myself a restorative cup of tea and drank it and set my kitchen to rights, I flattered myself I had tapped into Robbie's most vivid memories of his parents. But then I remembered "hearing" in one of my waking dreams that he was an orphan. The florid images I'd seen could have been conjured up by my imagination.

Perhaps I had been trying too hard. The inward tremor that had followed one of my earliest waking dreams returned. That horribly vivid image of the woodsman's axe had disturbed me—echoing the ghastly experience of "seeing" the king's execution.

Towards dusk that same day, when I was in the gloom of the corridor downstairs, Newbolt revisited me with a vengeance.

In single file we march into the narrow courtyard surrounded by high walls so it seems as though we were at the bottom of a well where no sun ever reaches. As we halt there a moment I observe a small fern growing at the level of my eyes, from between two blocks of stone, and I wonder at its intense green, and notice how on the underside of each finger or frond sits a raised brown spot like a tiny cushion. The order comes to continue and as we defile through a dark doorway shaped like a spearhead into the even deeper gloom of the interior lit by flares that gutter as we pass by, I surmize that the fern may have been the last living thing I shall have ever seen; apart from men. For such has been the secrecy and solemnity of our summons to this benighted corner of some benighted engine of State—is it indeed the dread Tower itself?—my mind is fixed on the idea that they intend to make us vanish from the face of the world. Whether all or only a selection of our company, who can tell? Our execution will be immediate and huggermugger, else why no trial?

Now we are halted and told to fan out into a line all facing the door ahead. I expect men with firearms to enter—but surely at least we will be afforded blindfolds? I look to our commander, Hewson, standing off to one side, and see his face is grim but he stares straight ahead so I may not question him with my eyes. The others either side of me, two dozen men in all, look troubled but not as men about to die. None but myself has grasped the seriousness of our predicament. Half are from my company, the most rebellious, bold, and anti-authoritarian souls, some with a record of misdemeanour and punishment. Is it too late to call on them to join me in overpowering Hewson and the three guards, and breaking out of this place? But we are unarmed, there's the rub.

The door opens and a man clad in iron walks in, a man I recognize even before Hewson steps forward to present arms and announce: "Men, salute General Ireton!" We obey, myself at least with puzzlement as well as awe. Since he most certainly has not come to execute us, what dealings has he with our raggle-taggle band of miscreant and rebel soldiers?

Yet, it has to do with execution.

"Men, as you know the Parliament has tried and sentenced Charles Stuart for treason." The word hangs heavy in the air as Ireton scans our faces. Most are turned to him in some reverence. Here stands one among the half dozen most powerful men in England, almost on a par with Cromwell and Fairfax. Yet he speaks directly and with a Nottinghamshire intonation as if to his comrades, like any hedge parson. "You all know how long and bloody a war he has brought upon this country through his obduracy, setting neighbour against neighbour, brother against brother. All is nearly over now but for one more brave deed your countrymen ask of you. One man here will have the valour to step forward for this task."

I shiver in this vault of a room. Is this a premonition?

"The law requires that we appoint an assistant to the chief executioner, that all may be seen to be fairly done. It is not a task any man will relish, but it is an honourable one nonetheless. Because the traitor Stuart still has friends, your identity will be protected. The executioner himself goes masked and so shall you. And you will be rewarded. Now who will volunteer?"

I dare say every man's visage is cast down as mine is now. Hewson barks, "Come, do not be shy. None here will ever tell, you have my word for it." That was foolish of him, for it opens the idea in our minds that one—not myself, I dare say each man thinks—might betray this assistant executioner to those friends of the King for a pouch of silver or gold. No one moves a muscle.

Ireton beckons Hewson over to his side, and now comes the most extraordinary station in this charade, as one by one we are called forward to confront the general. Each is held to attention with a guard beside him, for perhaps half a minute, as Hewson mutters our name and a word or two about us. When my turn comes and I hear the word "Woolaton" I know I am lost.

I hadn't moved, this time, just slumped against the wall. There, I told myself, at last I had the answer to why Newbolt was on the scaffold that January day in 1649. Thanks, Newbolt, I muttered aloud, you have well and truly buggered up my progress with Robbie. Hiding the dream diary had not helped a bit. I would have to be really careful, and cunning, if I were ever to bypass Newbolt and succeed in reaching out to Robbie.

This was driving me crazy—almost, I felt, literally. When the phone rang that evening, with Zemon at the other end, I think he was surprised by the friendly response I gave to his request. It was that business which they had touched on in Scotland, about needing to move house and wanting me to dowse for a new location. Yes, I would be happy to come over and help his people with their quest. A long weekend away from home suddenly seemed not only attractive, but essential if I wanted to hang on to what was left of my sanity.

CHAPTER SEVENTEEN

Farthing Lodge, the detached house of Victorian red brick, which Zemon and Irma shared with a motley crew, was on the edge of the small village of Cardington. It was dark by the time I arrived by taxi from the station at Church Stretton. Despite the differences, it reminded me of arriving at Kirsty and Graham's place above Eden Valley. There was a similar air of genial domesticity inside, and general tattiness as to furniture and fittings. Ethnic music strummed from someone's CD player in the common room—you could hardly call it a sitting room. There was only one easy chair, but a plethora of cushions, a beat-up day bed or couch, and a painful-looking kneeling stool. Zemon told me to dump my bag there, and led me through.

In the adjoining kitchen, three or four people were engrossed in eating their supper. Irma looked up and nodded a greeting, telling me to help myself. The huge wooden table was laden with half-empty bowls of wholefood, and an array of both clean and dirty plates, no two matching. Perching on a paint-splashed dining chair with a broken leather seat, I scoffed a mixture of bean curry, alfalfa sprouts, roast pumpkin seeds, and brown rice with currants scattered among it. Surprisingly tasty. I could not hold my own in the conversation, which wended around and over me. It had been a long journey.

Irma said, "I think Joe's falling asleep. Let's show him his room."

Zemon went ahead with my bag. As I traipsed after him, a memory struggled to surface. Of course, our room swap, in Newcastle. On the landing, I half expected Alison to appear.

I turned and whispered to Irma: "Any news of Alison?"

"She went back to London, to her job. We thought you and she had fallen out, but it isn't our business, Zemon says."

"What do I say?" asked Zemon, from the doorway of my room.

"About Alison and me. I'd be grateful if we keep off the subject."

"Fine by me, mate. Far as we're concerned, you are our welcome guest, no questions asked. Here you are, a room with a view, but you'll have to wait till morning for that."

What tact. Had he changed, or had I misjudged him?

I slept all night, undisturbed by dreams, and awoke to find my head near a curtained window. Pulling back the russet-coloured hessian, I gazed up from my pillow at the sunlit crest of Caer Caradoc, standing like a painted scenery flat against the blue spring sky. A blackbird sang, "Bear with me, bear with me."

"There's a Roman villa five miles over there, as the crow flies," Helena said, her outstretched arm indicating the south-west. "Zemon tells me you're partial to the Romans."

Helena, the matriarch of the clan, was filling me in on local features, before launching me on the solitary walk I had prescribed for myself. She seemed to understand that I needed plenty of time alone, before I could help the Farthing Lodge crew. We were standing halfway up the garden behind the house, on a slope leading to fenced-off woods, and I was twisting a frond of juniper, still damp with dew, around my fingers. The air tasted of larch shoots and lichen and juniper. My eyes kept wandering from Helena, and the ceanothus which was blooming as blue as her eyes, to the shoulders of Caer Caradoc glowing in the morning sun.

"That's news to me," I muttered.

Helena's eyes were piercingly sharp. She sounded like an upper-crust dame, not what I'd expected in this latter-day hippies' den. She eked out a living by doing "body-energy" therapies, and organizing the collective smallholding, whose produce they sold in a local farmers' market. She must have been getting on for sixty, dark henna hiding the true colour of her short hair, still a handsome woman whose clear-cut features and accent spoke of refinement and decisiveness. Despite her homespun woolly cardigan.

"Well then, you might favour the rebels. Caer Caradoc is a name derived from the ancient British for the hill of Caratacus, the last British king to stand against the Romans. There's a ring fort on top of the hill, as on many others round about; on Wenlock Edge in Mogg Forest and beyond that on Clee Hill."

"Whoa, one's plenty for now."

She set me along a footpath that dipped through woods, rather grandiosely called the Wilderness, and across a gurgling stream, before the land began to rise again. The stream was bridged with a single slab of granite that looked as if giants had installed it before Caratacus's time. I stood there relishing the sound of the running water, and the broken sunlight on angular, rough arms of hazel and scrub oaks. Some of the trees were so draped with ragged lichens that their new leaf-buds hardly showed. The occasional hum of vehicles on the minor road half a mile away scarcely interrupted the peace. Listening very carefully, I fancied I could detect which birds were still establishing their territory (robins, blackbirds), and which were building their nests already (blue tits and bullfinches). Probably I was just kidding myself. Neither my hearing nor my bird-lore was especially acute.

The steepening path took me up a bare flank of the hill, coated in cropped grass. Halfway up, I stopped a moment, bracing myself with hands on knees, to catch my breath. Looking back I saw farmland and heath that lapped around the hill's rise and stretched back across the vale to Wenlock Edge in the east. There was no distant view of water, but I was reminded of my climb up Arthur's Seat, and then I saw again, in a momentary flash, Robbie casting away his trumpet. I envied myself the clarity and pleasure—and hope—I had felt after that waking dream, in contrast with the muddle and fear I felt now.

No other walkers were about on the hilltop. Deep ditches defined the banked-up ridge of the ancient circular defences. I walked that grassy rampart widdershins. When I came to the northernmost point I checked I was alone, then lay flat and let my body roll down the inward slope, as a child might. As I scrambled up, I dug my fingers in the sweet-smelling turf spotted with vetch leaves and plantain.

Each of the following mornings, I rose early to take the same walk. It certainly helped calm me. Although no morning could be as magical as the first, I loved the hill, open yet hiding its secrets, changeable with the clouds or rain or sun, but beautiful.

I offered my opinion during the evening meal. "You needn't leave here. You've an ideal location—okay, so you're not actually sat in the middle of a stone circle, but with these hill forts all around, you surely already have the vibes you're after." I forked another heap of soya mince and potato in tomato gravy into my mouth. I had built up an appetite through digging their vegetable patch all afternoon.

"Of course we don't want to leave Farthing Lodge. I thought Zemon explained," said Helena patiently.

Zemon had gone off mid-afternoon to fetch more supplies with Steve, a tall young man with a sharp Adam's apple and uneven eyes. They were late back, so we had started supper without them—we being Irma, myself, Helena, and a dour silent girl with the unfortunate name of Myrtle. I wondered if she had peculiar parents, or had chosen the name to represent some plant-like quality she admired, having been christened something perfectly reasonable like Jane.

Irma smiled. "Probably we made it sound like we wanted to move on, actually," she said. How come Irma always understood me?

"Ah. I see. You don't know our situation then, Joe?" asked Helena. I shook and then nodded my head, to indicate half-knowing, and raised my eyebrows to indicate curiosity. It was quite a performance, all to avoid opening my mouth while chewing the veggie delights.

"This house was loaned to me for an indefinite term, about thirty years ago. I was a very fortunate young woman. Naturally, I wanted to share my good fortune, which I did, with a succession of friends and my own partner and children over the years. Now the owner has died, and his nephew, who inherits, wants to sell. At a price we could never dream of affording."

I swallowed, and risked butting in where it might not be my business. "Irma told me it was an uncle of yours let you live here. Surely that gives you as much right as the nephew …"

"He wasn't my uncle. It was, how shall I put it, a liaison, the wrong side of the blanket."

Myrtle muttered something, plucking at the edge of the table covering. It was less a tablecloth, more like a sari, deep green and vibrant pink with gold threads in the border.

"I beg your pardon?" asked Helena.

"I still say you should fight it." We waited, but nothing more emerged from beneath the hanks of dark hair.

"Myrtle wanted us to invoke natural law," said Helena. I pictured the Natural Law Party ads, with guru types levitating, and had to hide my smile. Helena carried on: "I'm afraid I cannot bear the thought of a court hearing. It would be bound to drag on for years, like *Bleak House*. We would have lost anyway. I did consult a lawyer. Beanie just hadn't thought about it, about me, for the last thirty years or so, since Mummy died. So far as he was concerned, he'd paid for my education and provided me with a super house, and I'd filled it with my hippy friends, which I was entirely free to do, that was my affair, but I was no longer his responsibility. He hadn't seen me since Mummy's funeral."

She spoke evenly, no trace of bitterness or longing for the man I presumed was her father. I wondered what her real feelings were; if there was another layer beneath the controlled persona she showed us.

My early morning walks on Caer Caradoc were mine alone, but I was happy to accompany the others on one of their regular hikes along Wenlock Edge on a crisp Sunday morning. Helena drove us up to Roman Bank in the van. The valley below lay spread out like a map come to life, perspectives shifting as we walked, every tree and field and house gable sharply defined. My favourite hill kept pace with us for a while and I strolled a little apart from the others, musing on the mysteries of parallax.

Presently, the path squeezed us into pairs and I found myself for a long stretch beside Irma. She asked me about my waking dreams, which had intrigued her from the little she had heard. As if the place, the moment, unloosed my tongue, I found myself pouring out my memories of them. I told them in the order they had come to me, in as much detail as I could muster.

"Sorry," I finished, holding aside a straggling branch of gorse, beaded with a few early blossoms. "It's a jumble, I know. I can't make sense of it myself."

I had reckoned without her inherent sense of how things worked. "Give me a bit of time Joe, and I will retell them in order. Do you mind if the others also listen?"

Until then I had kept the dreams to myself, confiding only a little in Alison. I had worried that people would think I was crazy, or that they would read their own stuff into it. But something had shifted, and I felt reckless.

I shook my head, giving her permission.

Halted at a natural hollow, which acted as a sun-trap, we all tucked into our picnic of vegan sausages with mustard in baps, date loaf, and flasks of maté tea. When the group lay sprawled about in digestive mode, Irma said she would give the after-dinner speech.

"This is the story of Joe's dreams."

Everyone settled to listen. Steve and Zemon, each lying sideways and propping their heads up on one hand, made mirror images of each other.

"First, Thomas Newbolt, a young doctor and alchemist, is befriended by a patron, a woman who becomes Lady Woolaton, who helps him wiggle his way into the court of your King Charles the First, which is pretty good for a young guy of poor family in those days. He's with this court on the journey to Scotland, and some place along the way, maybe in North Humber Land, out hunting the stag, the king shoots instead a boy called Robbie. Now, Robbie has magic powers, to tell the future and meaning of dreams, a bit like *Joseph and his Technicolour Dreamcoat* I think (but Joe didn't say that), or they believe so anyway. The doctor of yours gets in charge of him after a while. Because this boy Robbie has fits."

"Do you mean, like, epilepsy?" asked Steve.

"They called it the falling sickness," I said.

"That probably was epilepsy," said Helena. "But like with lots of those terms they used then, we can't make an exact correlation with our present day categories. It might have been something else entirely."

Irma continued. "So the king's main doctor, Soames, is angry in case Robbie can give Thomas Newbolt some power with the king. He is very popular, this boy, and the king likes his singing as well as his dream sayings and fortune-telling. And people know it. For example the king's chief of music gives Robbie a beautiful little trumpet. By this time they are in Scotland processing around, taking the royal treasures to everybody's castles to show off the king's mightiness. For a break, for some more hunting, they go to his Falkland Palace, where we have been, and to get back to Edinburgh they have to cross over the Forth of Firth ..."

"Firth of Forth," murmured Zemon.

"So this guy Soames tells the king to put the bothersome alchemist, Newbolt, and the boy on the luggage boat, it doesn't matter, they're servants really. Robbie is scared and angry so he throws his trumpet in the lake."

"Loch." It was my turn to correct her. But it's only a pool now, I said to myself. Shrunken water. Silting of time.

"Anyway Thomas writes a letter to persuade the king, but he's too busy to pay attention or maybe the other guys, the Soames lot, have it prevented, so they go on this boat, *The Blessing of Burntisland*, which we also know about because we went to where the wreck is sitting. So the boat went down with all the king's treasures …"

"Probably because it was overloaded and a storm brewed up," I intervened again.

"… and everybody drowns except for Thomas and Robbie, because Thomas can swim and he rescues Robbie. And the king is very sad. Then a couple years later maybe, Thomas is in the queen's court, and he must run away because he's making romantic meetings with a lady of the court which he's not allowed to do, and besides this Lady Woolaton is suspicious, she is in with Soames and the priest Cawley. They are right actually, Thomas has turned against the king. They could get him killed as a traitor. But the serving maid, I forgot her name," and she looked to me.

"Martha," I said. Dark eyes lit by the lantern as she leaned over him, the feeling of trust. He was better with people than me.

"Martha warns Thomas in the night, and he escapes across the marshes and these men in a hut rescue him, they must be rebels."

"Hang on, where is this?" Zemon asked.

"East Anglia. Not sure exactly," I replied. Was it close to my home? Loads of land was marshy back then, before the great eighteenth- and nineteenth-century drainages. Perhaps my fear, around what happened to Dad, had prompted the marshy waking dream. Which way did the association work? When I had that snatch of waking dream I was in Edinburgh, walking the riverside path with Zemon. I'd wished to know if Newbolt survived fleeing the court. No thought of Dad, or marshes.

Irma was talking about Susan. "This young girl, he takes no notice of her although she guides him when he's lost in the boggy place. And now a big gap, perhaps ten years, and then Thomas is fighting in the Civil War, against the king's side. The Roundheads are suspicious of Thomas, Joe thinks maybe he saved the life of that Lady at Woolaton Hall. Even though she had tried to persecute him before. Anyway to prove he's loyal to the Roundheads, he is forced to be assistant to the executioner who cuts off the king's head."

This provoked an all-round gasp. It was like the conjurer pulling— well, not a rabbit, more like a bloodied head, out of the hat. There were murmurs of: "You saw that, Joe?" and, "Never, man!" and,

"God, this is an amazing story." I grimaced, a mix of pride and revulsion. Irma carried on with a little frown.

"Thomas does that with a mask on, but afterwards he has to flee again and he joins these more revolutionary ones, maybe because he's met Susan again. Joe saw them together in a little community where everybody helps to grow the food."

"Where?" A single, deep note of interest from Helena.

"Again, location uncertain," I said sorrowfully.

"Now he's getting old," Irma continued.

"Hang on! In his forties."

"Thanks Joe, yes, quite young still. Susan is even younger and they have kids, so I guess Thomas wasn't fighting in the war all the time? Anyway the war is over, the king is dead, the Parliament is ruling. Susan is going on a demonstration of women in London, and Thomas wants to see her on this march, there has never been anything like it, but he is busy writing a pamphlet ..."

"Plus he's afraid he'll be recognized as the second executioner, and lynched."

"... so he forbids her to go to London, and we don't know what happens, but she is a determined woman so I think she'll go."

Irma, sitting cross-legged, put her hands on her hips. Finished with her narration, she looked at me with shining eyes. The others were gawking at us. There was a general shifting of cramped limbs, Steve rolled over onto his belly, Zemon cracked his knuckles.

"Thanks, Irma," I said. "I never put it all together like that. It's like editing a film after they've shot it in any old order. You've done a great job."

Zemon had a question. "Did your doctor not have anything to do with the magic boy after the wreck, and if not, why not?"

"Good question. I can't choose what I see. I simply haven't seen him in any of the later time-frames." Though it was him I wanted to see.

Irma butted in. "Thomas was under attack from the other doctor. Perhaps that one got the boy back under his control, so when Thomas fled, he lost touch completely."

Steve's turn. "Joe, I gather you didn't want them to raise the wreck, or the treasure. Why not?"

"A strong intuitive sense that it would lead to disaster, a bad feeling about it." I relied on these people having a healthy respect for intuition.

"Anything specific?" Steve pressed.

"I don't have a specific theory, but if I tell you that each of the waking dreams, however interesting they may seem to you, felt to me like a nightmare, that might give you some idea."

Zemon nodded. "Of course, they haven't raised the *Blessing* yet, so you can't make that connection."

Helena cleared her throat. "For what it's worth, I'd guess that your Newbolt chap was in a Digger community. They were a more radical offshoot of the Levellers, you know. Would fit with tilling the soil. And with writing tracts, though lots did that. Plus Susan's radicalism. Oh, and they might have been more likely to accept a dubious character like Newbolt than most groups."

I stored that bit of info away, nodding thanks to Helena, not sure whether I liked her definition of Newbolt as "dubious". Yes, damn it, she was spot on.

Myrtle jumped up. "Freezing," she said, and started to march off. The rest of us stuffed the last bits of paper wrapping away in our day bags.

"What's up with her?" I asked Irma out of the side of my mouth, as we trudged in Myrtle's wake.

"Oh, she thinks you are making it all up," said Irma blithely, as if she considered Myrtle a little crazy.

The first time it came around, the Sunday evening, I shook my head. Bang, draw, what I called weed. But an old smoker is always tempted, and so I took a little puff, and then another, seeing as how it eased the flutter of anxiety below my ribs. The others were more used to it than me, but I was fully aware of what I was doing, just a bit more inclined to laugh. One minute we were reclining on cushions and sofas in the lounge, the next we were sat around the great table in the kitchen. Instead of the fancy table sari, we had a map spread out before us. Five pairs of eyes gleamed at me in the light of candles arranged at one end.

"There's only one way I can think of to do this," I said. I put my finger on Caer Caradoc. "I start here, and work outwards in a spiral. But I shall have to make it a tight spiral and I'll have to go slow, as this map covers such a huge area. The whole fucking country in fact." Steve and I both had a giggle at that. "Then when we get a hit—if we do—you'll have to get a larger scale map, and we repeat the process."

Before starting, I arranged them how I wanted, Irma one side of me and Helena the other, lightly touching my shoulders with their fingers; Zemon next to Irma, then Myrtle; Steve next to Helena. All holding hands in a ring. They were to say to themselves, like a mantra but silently: "We are looking for a place to live the way we want, among ancient stones where people long ago worshipped." If I hadn't been slightly stoned myself I could never have believed in this New Age stuff. But somehow, temporarily, I did.

"Don't blame me if you end up in a converted chapel in the Home Counties," I joked, and they variously shuddered and giggled. That launched a discussion that could have gone on all night, about whether to insert "in pre-Roman times" into the mantra. To cut it short, I told them to carry an image of ancient stones in their mind's eye, and I'd do the same, and we'd be covered.

I stuck a map pin, which Irma had reclaimed from the communal notice-board, into the map, just above Hope Bowdler to the west of Wenlock Edge, the nearest I could make to Farthing Lodge in Cardington. It was a large pin with a spindle-shaped green head. Driven in hard so it bit well into the wooden table-top, it made a firm centre. Around the shank, I tied a thread of white sewing cotton, long enough to reach to Land's End on the one hand and Edinburgh on the other. If they wanted to go any further north, they could join Kirsty and Graham up Eden Valley way.

I was sitting at the Wales side of the map, to reach the pin easily at the outset. The thread looped around my right index finger once, the rest curled ready for release in my palm, I started to trace tiny circles, aiming to create a smooth spiral. But the thread wound itself round my finger so I had to keep stopping each time I came back to my side, to release it. There was no way to avoid this. If I'd left an ink trace, it would have looked like a series of stepped circles, rather than a perfect spiral. The others didn't know that I'd never done this before, that it was my own spur-of-the-moment invention. (For a wide sweep to find a missing person, I'd normally quarter the target area and would never attempt to cover more than one OS map at a sitting.) Not that it mattered. I glanced up at their faces, lit up by the candles. They were focused on outcome, not process.

When my finger reached about two inches from the centre pin, it was sweeping over Newtown in Wales, then Oswestry, Market Drayton, Wolverhampton, Stourbridge, and Kidderminster where I had changed trains on my way here. Then more open country, especially on the Welsh side, for a couple of sweeps. How rapidly the spiral moved. Helena's brow furrowed as my finger swept across heavily built-up zones: Aberystwyth, Liverpool, Manchester, a break across the Peak District, then Nottingham, Leicester, Rugby, Newport. Soon, we were into sea areas: Cardigan Bay, Irish Sea, Bristol Channel. More land to the east, now, than to the west.

The sheer effort of concentrating on country-wide dowsing was making me shaky. My finger skirted Greater London, and I saw Helena frown again. I sensed that she was willing me to stop over Exmoor, but there was no twinge there. Straight after that, though, I felt a quiver go up my finger as it brushed Pembrokeshire.

I picked up the pendulum and went back across the area, and it responded with a swing. Right, we were in business. "Here," I said, touching the map.

Just to be sure I continued on with the spiralling for a bit, not wanting them to miss out on the Lakes, Pennines, Yorkshire moors, or Cornwall. But the only other response was Leeds. Well, that was a surprise.

My fingers were fuzzy like pipe-cleaners, and it took a great effort for me to pull the pin out of the table. It left a hole in the map that looked huge. I turned the map over, aware of the others breaking their linked hands and turning to one another to comment on the "find". I tried to smooth out the punctured bit. The cloth backing was like loose-woven muslin, stiffened with sizing; my fingers kept brushing over it, enjoying the comforting feel of the old fabric, a grid of tiny ridges and hollows. The hole in the table was almost indistinguishable from the numerous woodworm holes nearby.

The tremor in my hands had grown into a full-body juddering that Helena and Irma evidently noticed, for they asked if I was cold. Zemon was declaring Pembrokeshire the winner and asking Helena if she had a close-up map. There was a buzz of excitement around the room that I could not share. I slumped in my seat, utterly exhausted. How long had it taken? It didn't matter; it was the distance I'd covered that was so draining.

"Joe needs to go to bed." That was Irma.

"Not without a hot drink inside him." Helena. "And then some restorative therapy."

Cocoa they gave me, which I downed at once, and then some very good twelve-year-old malt whisky in a thin tumbler of unevenly-blown greenish glass, with a spiral of spun glass just below the rim that caught the candlelight. Neat coincidence with the virtual spiral I'd been tracing over the map. The glass and the classy whisky must be Helenaisms. Even after the drinks, I was shaking, though not so badly.

Helena led me into the little blue-painted room that she used for her therapies and which they all used for meditation. The ceiling was dark blue at one end, sprinkled with white stars, merging into a thrush-eggshell blue at the other end, all barely visible by the glow of three candles which Helena lit as I settled back into the reclining chair. She tucked a heavy tartan rug firmly around me, then sat at my feet and clasped them in her hands. An oddly reassuring sensation with a surprising amount of heat. I began to relax, to become aware of flute, harp, and drums making a faint skein of sound from a CD player in the corner, and some woody scent, mixed with frankincense which I recognized from the high church Mum took us to for a brief period after Dad went. There was an essential oil burner on a small table like an altar at one side of the room.

There must have been a bowl of water there too. I heard Helena washing her hands. They felt cooler when she put them around my temples and forehead. Pure touch, without pressure. Tingles, not erotic at all, but pleasant, rippled down my scalp and the back of my neck. She kept her hands there for maybe five minutes, building up a comforting glow. Just as I was wishing she would shift her hands to my shoulders, she did so, as if the need in my shoulders had sucked her hands to the right spot.

The trembling had retreated from my extremities now to deep inside me. My arms, though, ached from holding them out over the map for all that time. I was an empty vessel, grateful for the refill Helena channelled into me. At that moment, I believed in "body-energy", and drank deep.

The boy walks towards me, holding out the trumpet, which has the appearance almost of glass. Robbie, too, is translucent. He opens his mouth. I strain to hear.

There is a buzzing in my head. Only one sound will clear it, I know. And then I shall hear his voice clearly.

"Play it, Robbie. Blow a note for me."

He shakes his head, and holds it out again, pleadingly, with both hands. Does he want me to play the instrument? But I cannot.

Then he raises the glassy trumpet to his pale lips and blows, and an eerie note throbs through the air and beats between my temples.

He lowers the instrument and holds it out again.

"Please, I cannot, I have to go," he says or thinks.

Now I realize it is perfect, if hard to see fully. It is no longer deformed from the time he crushed it in a fit. Am I dreaming? I pinch my thigh and register the feeling, but dully. Where in fact am I? All seems dim around me.

Robbie appears to be walking backwards, his eyes fixed on mine, with an expression of the most pitiful bafflement in them. His arms drop to his sides. Is he still holding the trumpet, or am I?

CHAPTER EIGHTEEN

I walked around the corner into Stepan's street. There was something wrong with the way the shop-front glinted in the dull light. Only after I crossed the road and was almost there did I see with a shock the glass of Stepan's half window shattered in a pattern like a spider's web, spokes and wheels of cracks, a hole as hub in the middle. A stone, or a bullet? Who, and why? I honestly believe my heart missed a beat. Someone had come for it, was all I could think. A thief who knew about my incomparable treasure.

"Is just kids, wanting make trouble, or maybe a petty thief get his hands on one a my accordion, or mandolin more like," said Stepan, as he led the way upstairs to his flat. It had happened three days ago, but it might be weeks before he could afford to get it fixed. His meagre insurance would not cover that sort of malicious damage, and it wasn't the first time. Shatterproof glass was too expensive. His reassuring, sad patter of explanation failed to sweep away the ill-omened greeting of that window; for me, it hung over the flat as a bad dream hangs over the entire following day.

If a burglar, hoping to raise a couple of hundred quid from the classier instruments in the window display, had known what lay upstairs in a green velvet pouch, he might have been more persistent in trying to break into Stepan's premises. Stepan drew the trumpet out of the bag like a magician producing doves from a silk scarf. He held the flanged end with a soft cloth, a duster. "To stop fingerprints. See how I burnished it up?" Lamplight gleamed in long ripples along the bell and shaft. "A little beauty."

He held it out, on the cloth, in his two hands, and I thought of Robbie in my most recent vision. It had been my own vision; that was how it felt, not a waking dream, for there had been no Thomas Newbolt making me see things through his eyes. A haunting.

That had propelled me back to Stepan's, though the Cardington household had clamoured for me to accompany them to the Welsh hills, to prospect for a hidey-hole in the landscape. They'd had to make do with another map-dowsing session, on OS 145. The Preseli Hills. A patch of woodland, near a stream, just below a peak across the valley from Carn Iglis. Very laden with remains, those hills, they should have no trouble stubbing their toes on ancient stones. But, I told them, slim chance of erecting so much as a tent without a park ranger turning up at the tent flap, ordering them to take it down. Besides, what would they do for running water, heating, toilets? They would use the stream, wood stoves, composting pit latrines, they'd replied. I'd packed my holdall and asked them to drop me off at Church Stretton station.

Stepan was grinning hugely, in contrast to my poor ghostly Robbie, whose uncertain look and retreating steps lingered on my inward sight. The trumpet itself looked so much more flesh and blood, if you could apply such a term to a thing of metal. I remembered it had been glassy in the vision.

I rubbed my hands on my trousers to clean them, then reached out and took the trumpet from Stepan. He quailed, but there was no way I could avoid touching the instrument if I was to play it.

"The brass has come up lovely," I agreed, turning it this way and that to examine the play of light along the curves. It was by no means immaculate, there were scratches and grainy marks that Stepan hadn't been able to smooth out, but it had cleaned up well. There was no sign of where it had been flattened. The bell had regained its flare, like a convolvulus flower. For the first time I noticed a silver decorative band just below the mouthpiece; otherwise, it was all plain.

"I dreamed it was made of glass," I blurted out.

"That's funny, they did used to of made them from glass, two, three hundred years ago. Course, in them days it wasn't so special, a glass one, you didn't need a licence to play them kind. But they all broke, so I guess if you'd of found one of them in one piece, you'd make a fortune."

Neither of us referred to the possible value of what I held in my hands. Stepan knew that for me, its market value was immaterial.

By tacit agreement I could not offer payment to Stepan for repairing the trumpet, which was a return favour for the one I'd done him, but I did insist on paying for the replacement of his shop window. "As an old friend, to set my mind at rest about your other instruments," I said, writing him a cheque for £500. My elation at reclaiming the trumpet made me reckless.

Besides, I might not need money much longer. In one corner of my disjointed mind, there lurked the vision of myself with a brood of followers including my own kiddies, in a New Age settlement that miraculously would work, with a woman who was a cross between Irma and Alison at my side. In another, even more misty corner, I saw myself with young Robbie, roaming the byways of seventeenth-century England, offering people amazing prophecies in exchange for our supper.

There now remained the music lesson. Stepan pushed the table back, stood with his legs straddled, took the trumpet from me and drew a full breath. As he exhaled on the mouthpiece, an unearthly, clear bray filled the room, wavered, sank, and rose again. It was a hunting cry, a challenge, a shout of pride. Stepan lowered the instrument. He'd emptied his lungs too much, tempted by the rich resonance of the old brass. He held it out again to me, with a wobbly smile.

"Your turn," he puffed.

I wiped the mouthpiece with my sleeve, took the same stance as Stepan had done, heaved a lungful of air, and blew firm and full. Nothing. Again: not a squeak. Third try: a feeble fart. Stepan doubled up laughing. My brain swirled.

"Okay, I show you." This time, Stepan stood sideways to me, so I could see how he pursed his lips and just touched them to the mouthpiece, not trying to grasp it like a bottle-top. I remembered that scene in *The Commitments* where Lips Gillespie tells the lads to imagine they are kissing Sophia Loren's nipples. But Stepan was on a different track. "Don't try to swallow her. You ever do that noise with grass between your thumbs?" I nodded. Everybody has done that. I could make a fair racket. "Like that. It wants to vibrate, you just got to blow right frequence, then it can't help, it has to make noise."

Like the wineglass that sings under your finger. Or the silent vibration of the dowsing rod finding its target.

This time blowing neither too hard nor too soft, in a split second I woke the spirit of the trumpet, and a full-toned call rang out. Without giving it conscious thought, I raised and lowered the note, the way you do with your voice, the way Stepan had done. He clapped his hands, grinning at me.

"Sure you don't want to take up saxophone?" he teased.

He explained the simple straight-shafted trumpet might have started life as a hunting horn, then the shape was refined so it could serve in an ensemble where it would provide a strong highlight. But it lacked the range of the looped trumpet; and the slide trumpet of course was far more versatile, "Almost like the one we have nowadays." This baby was pre-Baroque in style, he reckoned. That short history was as close as he came to identifying the age of the trumpet. I could tell he longed to know more.

To make up for my reticence, I told him the nickname I'd devised for the trumpet: "Sophia". As with my other little mysteries, Stepan forbore to ask why.

It was late, so I accepted Stepan's offer of a bed for the night. We ate another of Stepan's delicious beef and paprika concoctions, and chatted about music, Georg's progress, the pros and cons of living in London, and life in general, over a bottle of deep red wine.

It was well past midnight when I lay down, placing Sophia under the bed for total security. Sleep would not come. I lay musing on my Cardington vision of Robbie, and then, although I tried to avoid it, the waking dream from last time I stayed at Stepan's. At some point, trying to escape into sleep, I thought how Helena's touch had made me relax. Rapidly I was overcome by a woozy sensation that made me grateful I was already lying down. I knew it was not the effect of the Tokai I'd drunk.

I was half in Stepan's spare room, and half in Falkland Castle in 1633, revisiting the moment when Newbolt disturbed Robbie in his room. This time it was as though I was able to see for myself, rather than through Newbolt's eyes. With photographic clarity I noticed something I didn't remember seeing before. Over Robbie's shoulder, it was possible to make out the corner of a large volume, lying open beside the alchemical apparatus. There were signs at the top of the page, next to the heading. Although the heading was not legible at that distance, the signs were large and clear.

The vision faded, and I was more wide awake than ever. I switched the light back on and made as good a copy of those signs as I could. In the intuitive way I "knew" odd things about Newbolt, I was convinced these were not Newbolt's ordinary "chimestrie" nor even his alchemical symbols. There was a jangling feeling to my vision, as though I'd caught Robbie out. Newbolt had been angry, hadn't he, when he saw what Robbie was up to, whatever it was? These symbols might provide a clue.

Next morning, with the parting gift from Stepan of a bottle of superior metal polish tucked into the green velvet bag alongside Sophia, I set out on the underground for Charing Cross station. From there, using my mental map, I made my way through alleyways and twisting streets to Kofer's café. For one instant, my footsteps nearly turned the wrong way, towards the huge building that housed Alison's department, but I resisted that urge.

I had a hunch that Abed, the waiter I'd chatted to before, when I wandered into Kofer's after first seeing Alison, might be able to help me now. He'd mentioned that his father, who was a professor, often deciphered old inscriptions. Abed might have picked up some knowledge, or he could give me an intro to his father. I wanted, at least, to identify what manner of symbols or writing they were.

Fortunately the café was almost empty, as before, and Abed not only remembered me, but greeted me like an old friend. He insisted on making me a dense black coffee on the house, then entered into the spirit of the quest, leaning over the counter, studying the squiggles I'd drawn.

"It's very ancient, this, I think," he said. "I was born in Lebanon, as you know, but my father, he's from Egypt, where these come from."

"Hieroglyphics?" But they didn't look like pictograms.

"No, no, not that old. From the desert all the same. My father had interest in this subject. It's some medieval monks, they took the old Egyptian knowledge, and used it for their purposes. Very secret. They called it after one of the old gods." He stared at me as if perplexed.

My knowledge of Egyptian deities was limited. "Anubis? Thoth? Ibis—no, Isis?" I pictured men and women with heads of jackals or vultures.

Abed shook his head, his dark curls bouncing. For a moment I was reminded of Zemon.

"It was a Greek version of Thoth. What was the name? I know, it was Hermes. These signs are from the cult of Hermes. Where did you see them?"

"An old manuscript." That much was obvious. What could I safely tell him? "In a museum in Scotland. It came back to me in a dream, so I may not have got them right. But I am intrigued."

"Intrigued?" He clearly did not know the word.

"Interested, want to know more."

"Ah. Well, we have internet here."

This was new to me, electronic technology I'd always resisted, but with Abed as my guide I was willing to set my prejudices aside and enter the esoteric world of Google. There was a laptop behind the counter. I sat beside him while he tapped away and then, when he had to serve a customer, I jotted down some notes on the back of a paper menu.

- *Ancient Greeks knew of Egyptian guru they called Hermes Trismegistus, but his writings were lost when the great library at Alexandria burned down. (When?)*
- *Later—in 14th or 15th century—this esoteric lore "rediscovered" in Arabia, filtered through Europe, became origins of alchemy, influenced mystics etc from Sufis (Asia Minor) to John Dee.*
- *Texts found 1945 in sealed jar at Nag Hammadi in upper Egypt, 1,600 years old, included hermetic writings.*

"Hermetic" seals on the jar containing the writing, and alchemical lore. I had the connection. That was what Robbie was up to, in Newbolt's room: making a hermetic seal on the box, to keep the notes safe. He had known they would be at risk, even if he didn't know exactly how. Or perhaps he did. He was blessed, or cursed, with second sight, better than mine. Was that not why I was so desperate to contact him?

And there was something else. Since my vision in Helena's room, I felt that Robbie was calling to me as much as I wanted to call him. I had the means now, in the green velvet bag in my baggage. There was no way I could fail to use it.

"Did you find this helpful?" Abed asked, leaning over my shoulder.

"Some leads to follow up. Thank you ever so much."

"My pleasure," he said, and he shook my hand like an old friend again, before I left.

Back in Bishop's Stortford, I appointed myself exile from the world in my home, taking solitary walks into the country to practise far away from prying ears of neighbours. By the hedgerows of Boundary Lane, frothy waves of hawthorn blossom tickled my nostrils with their insidious scent; clouds of midges were my audience. Wandering into the middle of a field of flax in full flower, I played sweet notes to their billow of azure, and lofty notes to the cobalt of the cloud-spotted vault above. Day after day my mood grew more elevated, till I could scarcely eat, or tell what day of the week it was.

What brought me down was reading my dream diary, retrieved from the shed, for it showed me how few sightings of Robbie I'd had. The evenings still held a chill and I was averse to putting on the central heating, so I'd light a fire, wishing to live as close to Robbie's ways and days as was possible in my thirties semi. Of course that meant reading by candlelight, so on the second or third day I ventured out to buy in a big supply of candles and night-lights. That was about the only time I did talk to anyone, for Mr Patel asked if I knew of a planned power cut, and should he stock up.

On an afternoon when grey clouds covered the sky, out in the long grass of a distant meadow, I succeeded in making a pattern of seven notes; a very simple, repeatable tune. As if I'd called them up, black clouds rolled in from the west. I hurried homewards before their lowering threat, but they overtook me and loosed a burst of huge drops, drenching me to the skin. I ran the last stretch of the way home, changed into dry clothes, and downed a brandy or two. It was only four o'clock but felt like dusk on a winter's evening. I lit a candle and took it around the house with me for good cheer, although the light strengthened again as the cloudburst passed on.

It had come to me in a flash as I was running: the only waking dream where I had been certain that Robbie could see me had been that time when he'd looked into the mirror while Newbolt was shaving, as I looked into the mirror in my bathroom. They were in another place—Falkland—as well as another time, but that had not blocked the contact. Ergo, the notion came to me, to play Sophia in front of a mirror, and hope the glassy surface would act as an interface between our worlds. I would have my intention honed to a firm point, and I'd be calling on Robbie's trumpet. Surely I stood a chance of reaching him, wherever he was most receptive to me in his own life.

I chose the mirror on the landing for two reasons. Being in the innermost part of the house, my noise was less likely to attract the attention of nosey neighbours. Second, the mirror being three-quarter length, it was more like a door than a window. That excitable corner of my mind saw one or the other of us—Robbie or myself—stepping over the lower edge as a threshold, and entering the other's world. The sane bit of me knew that was fanciful. At the least I dared to hope for direct contact, a chance to talk.

There was no precedent for what I was about to do, no books to look up, no wise men to consult. But I mentally checked it out with Gran, and I worked out a plan for myself. First off, I ran a full tub of hot water and chucked in an armful of rosemary branches from the big bush at the corner of my vegetable plot, and soaked and scrubbed myself into a state of alertness and purity. Or such was the idea. Then I polished Sophia with Stepan's special brew for brass, while listening to Van Morrison's *No Guru, No Method, No Teacher*, ignoring the breach of my no-modernity mode that the CD player represented. Sitting in my study with Sophia back in her bag on my desk, I re-read my dream diary one more time, all the way through. Then I set about a series of rough drawings—well, any drawings I did were going to be rough—using a 2B pencil that I had to keep sharpening as it blunted so fast. Robbie holding the trumpet when all was well and happy with it (with her, I tended to think); Robbie falling on the heath and crushing the trumpet's bell; Robbie casting her into the waters; Robbie holding the barber's bowl for the doctor (but I didn't draw *him*) and looking startled but not too much so.

I hesitated whether to draw Robbie clinging to Thomas Newbolt as they both rose through the bubbles to the surface of the firth. Better not, I didn't want any image of that pestiferous Newbolt to distract my mind. Robbie in Newbolt's chamber, brewing up a concoction with Newbolt's apparatus. That was tricky, and I grew engrossed with the details of the stand, the charcoal-holder, the retort or whatever they called it. Was there something else? My mind, well soothed by now, roamed the scene. Of course, the bellows! I drew them in, between Robbie's hands and the little fire. I had to rub out his hands twice, to position the bellows right. Then I worried as to whether I had seen this. It was an inference, wasn't it, for I hadn't actually witnessed Robbie at work; Newbolt hadn't burst through the door and seen him thus, he'd heard the bellows and then the key turning, and Robbie had stood there looking guilty. Oh well, I wasn't going to scrap my drawing after all that effort. Poetic licence shall prevail, I told myself. Newbolt had spotted the evidence of Robbie's alchemical mischief over his shoulder, for sure. Come to think of it, he'd spied a box out of the corner of my eye, his eye, whoops, I'd drawn it in before I could stop to think. Like one of my boxes on the inside (for I drew it gaping open) but covered in lead on the outside. Where had that come from? My own lead-covered box, was I copying that? I wondered about putting in the book with the hermetic symbols, but that was too fiddly, I decided.

Now dusk was falling in earnest, and I got up to draw the curtains. As I did so, Mr Sissons from next door gave me a cheery wave. He was coming through his front gate, coming home to his tea, supper, or whatever, after a hard day handing out parking tickets. What must that feel like, a day job, a wife at home making your tea? Secure, I should imagine. Not like my life. Especially now. My old dowsing life had felt in a way almost as secure as Mr Sissons's imagined life, but not any more, not since *The Blessing of Burntisland* showered her dubious blessings on poor old Joe Fairlie. Why me? I guessed the answer. Without me the searchers would have wandered the deeps of the Firth of Forth for years to come, and most likely would have given up. More than the diver who confirmed there were timbers down there, I was the first to touch her. Plus, my abilities, my gift or whatever, made me the unwitting, often unwilling channel for the wreck's strange cargo of dreams.

Well, now I was in control, I was doing the willing.

Seven o'clock. Time was running on, running out. At any rate I didn't need to make myself anything to eat; I'd decided the task was better undertaken on a fasting stomach. I'd set myself a mental witching-hour of eight o'clock to do the deed. Midnight would be better, but no way would the neighbours ignore Sophia's braying then. There would be knocks at my door, windows flung open, shouts of: "What bloody time do you think this is?" Whereas, at eight, they would not even be worrying about the kids waking, they'd all have their tellies on full blast and the teenagers would have their music going. Perfect.

I'd fixed Robbie firmly in my mind's eye with my drawings, for all that they looked more like sketches for a woodwork project, all angles so that he resembled a wooden boy, a Pinocchio. I now set about firming up the questions I would ask if I managed to make contact. I lit additional candles in two jam-jar lids on my desk, replaced the plain pad I'd used for drawing with a lined one, and picked up a biro. Should have been parchment and a quill. Oh well, I thought, chewing the end of the biro, a quill would soon look mangled if you chewed that. I tried to think of a heading for my list, couldn't, and just started in with:

1. *Ask him if he knows who I am. Tell him not to be afraid.*
   He'll know what a dowser is, won't he?

2. *Was the wreck of* The Blessing of Burntisland *an omen? For his time and/or mine?*
   This could be tricky, I realized. What if he doesn't know about the wreck yet, at the point in time when I contact him? A thrilling thought: what if he finds out *from me*?
   I got up, cracked my knuckles, wandered to the bathroom for a pee, washed my hands, returned to the desk.

3. *Can you tell me what is going to happen to the royal Charles in my own time; will he become King Charles III okay?* (No, OK is American isn't it, and after his time? I crossed out "okay".) *Is there anything important we need to do in our time to make sure this happens? E.g. stop the wreck being raised?*
   God, will that slim lad from the seventeenth century know, or care, anything about my time? There had not been any indication that his prophetic powers stretched any distance forward. I was expecting too much. Still, I had been drawn in, and that made a link between the centuries. I wrote down the biggest question of all:

4. *Will we be heading towards civil war in my time, as in yours? Between England and Scotland, or who? If so, what can we do to prevent it?*
   Perhaps I was barking up the wrong tree. Perhaps *The Blessing of Burntisland* sinking wasn't an omen for those disasters of Charles I's time—where had I got the idea it was? I slid my chair back, went across the landing into my bedroom, drew the curtains then opened them again. People would think I had a lover if I closed my bedroom curtains at 7.30 pm. Crossing back I caught my reflection out of the corner of my eye. Hair wild from my soaking, and from running my fingers through it.
   Newbolt was the one who saw the wreck as an omen. He was sure that King Charles thought so too. He'd even recalled it on the scaffold. I shuddered as I sat down. Attempted to shut all thought of the execution, of the king, of Newbolt himself out of my mind. But I knew I could not achieve that by myself.

I crossed out all my questions, and wrote just one:

How can I get Thomas Newbolt out of my mind?

Sweet-smelling applewood, a small fire in the living-room grate. Night-lights either side of each tread of the stairs, leading the fire smoke up to the landing. Beeswax candles, ones I'd saved from a part-payment in kind by a beekeeper I'd helped years ago, in my pair of three-branched candlesticks, on the floor, one each side of the mirror. Those six candles, doubled by their reflections, gave a dozen candlepower: a decent light. We'd be illuminated for Robbie, me and Sophia; all beyond in gloom, so no modern appurtenances to startle him. He'd be startled to see the trumpet, of course. No avoiding it. My route to him.

Eight o'clock. Into my study, put matches down. Don't even look at my writing, I know what I want to ask. Wipe hands on trousers, slide Sophia out of velvet bag, touch her smooth cool surface here and there with tenderness.

On the landing, standing a yard away from the mirror, Joe looked back at me, under-lit by the six bright candles with their six bright reflections. Scary? Too late to stop now. Raise her to my lips. Dry. Should have drunk some water at last minute? No, better so, fasted and a little parched. Empty belly, empty mind. Heart racing. Breath in. Blow.

A muffled call from without. Who would be out there at this hour, on so blustery a night? No, it must be the wind.

"Cataclysm." Is that too great a word for my readership? Otherwise the passage reads well, yes I believe it does, unless perchance at the last my phrasing becomes a touch too Biblical.

Again the call. A note—no, that cannot be, it must be my imagination at play, fired by my composition. Were Susan here, she would have tempted me from my desk hours before, claiming that over-long writing at night will bring on the ague. Such a sound I have not heard since I left the court, unless it be its cousin in battle; this though is not the battle-horn but the angel's voice as that boy used to call it.

I should have pulled the shutters close at dusk, before I lit my candles. I'll do it now. Carry this sconce over, to see the bolts sit tight.

That face at the window. Who? Cavernous eyes, beard, unkempt hair. A spy come to slit my throat, all this way from London? Slow, my heart, cease lurching so. A spy would not show himself thus openly, for sure. He mouths at me angrily. He knows me, I hear my name. "Not you, Newbolt." As if in great agitation, he waves some object in his right hand. Not a dagger. Worse.

Pain in my shoulder, pain down the arm.

No, it cannot be Robbie's trumpet. It cannot be. Yet I see the signature band clear as clear. The boy gone near twenty years, his trumpet jettisoned before, and none but I know—it cannot be. And yet I see it, whole, as it was.

The man's face contorts. I shall scare you away, foul stranger. Susan shall not return to find one of them has broken in, to defile our home. With the last of my strength I hurl the sconce at the window, and it flies through. The coward quails, he's going, fading away, and I too, with the glass shattering and my candles passing into the darkness without, I feel the pain overwhelm me and I slide into my own darkness.

Susan, Susan, do you know how much I love you my dear? There is no more I can do.

My forehead hit the mirror as I lost my footing and pitched forward, slumped down. There was blackness and there was light. Pain seared my left arm, so intense I could not tell if it was cold or hot. Flames on my sleeve. Hot. Still clutching the trumpet in my right hand I shuffled in a stumbling crouch into the bathroom. Lucky so near. Put it down a minute, tap on, splash water onto. Not enough. Turn on shower, low, yes jump in, all soaked good. Out now, pick up trumpet, oh flames all around mirror end of landing, lucky I'm wet. Barge through, quick no time to fetch anything, run down stairs—no, can't run, bump down and open front door, out onto front lawn, collapse.

The pain followed me, came with me, even though I'd left the flames behind. I knew there was something I must do, not lie there forever. But I wanted to carry on lying on the lawn so I tried yelling "Fire! Fire!" Nobody came. TVs on loud, of course. My shouting quiet, choking. Fire not showing yet, nobody looking anyway. But it would soon spread, and then they'd feel it right enough. Hauled myself up; still the pain was growing, gnawing. Why hadn't it been so bad at first? Was water bad for burns? Gran put on butter when I was scalded from spilling soup that time; how little Joe screamed. Want to scream now. Up next door's path, how to ring bell? Left arm too sore to lift, right hand too full of trumpet. Very slowly, taking care with my balance, I lowered my face to the door knocker and gripped it between my teeth, lifted and dropped it, one time, two times, three—the door flew open and I was eyeballing Mr Sissons's flies.

"What the hell? Oh Jesus, look at the state of the man."

They rang 999. The fire engine arrived first and I had the joy of watching my blazing upstairs go under the hose. By this time I couldn't speak, my jaws clamped tight over my pain as if they'd been wired shut. Then the ambulance came, men in pale blue overalls, marvellous men with a syringe of kindness.

Inside the ambulance, as they pushed me horizontal, I unclamped my teeth and my fist.

"Sophia. Bring Sophia. The trumpet. Wherever I go."

One of the lovely men nodded, sliding her from my loosening grasp. Their morphine dampened the shock of noticing that at some point—as I fell against the mirror I dare say—I'd crushed the poor darling, so its mouth was once more Robbie's flattened "O".

CHAPTER NINETEEN

I shifted against the pillows in an attempt to ease the pain in my left arm and shoulder. It was exacerbated by the lump under the pillows, but no way would I let anyone remove my prize possession. Despite my pleas, they'd cut out the morphine almost straight after they'd admitted me and treated the burns.

Jeannie had been enumerating all the steps "we" needed to take, from dealing with the loss adjusters and finding a reliable builder, to choice of wallpapers and paints. It was soothing enough but I decided to intervene as she branched into her ninth degree of digression on the builders angle. The usually reliable Martin Baxter had developed a crush on his sister-in-law and gone right off colour, even joining the batty church she went to, did I know about them, the Plymouth Brethren, nothing to do with Plymouth in Devon of course, being as these were in Norwich, but she'd been to Plymouth once with Dad before I was born, had I known that? It was Navy Day and they went on an aircraft carrier first and then a submarine ...

I cut across her flow. "Jean, I'm not sure I want to go home."

I felt the warmth of her trusting brown eyes on my face as she tried to read me like a riddle. Those eyes had been a constant, in all the years she had cared for me, and even now while the rest of her face was sliding into middle age they hadn't changed a bit.

As I'd lain two nights and days in that slippery high bed, wrapped in my pain, unwelcome gobbets of memory and reasoning had swirled around in my brain. I knew I had killed a man as surely as if I had run a sword into his heart. Unintentional, but I had set out to contact the boy, and with all the choices of questions and exchanges at my disposal I had focused on just the one: how to rid myself of the pestiferous doctor? Well, I had got my wish, not through seeing Robbie, but through seeing Newbolt directly, and more to the point through *him* seeing *me*. I knew he'd died, because something in me had given way at that instant. He'd fallen, dying of a heart attack, as I fell, swooning, gashing my head on the mirror—not at the same time in a conventional sense, since we were in different centuries, but at the same instant of our contact across time.

I knew now that The Dread had been about this: about the horror I had caused. I knew, too, with all the certainty of my best intuition, that there would be no going back, no more dipping into episodes of Newbolt's life, now I'd been in on his death. That thread which had drawn me into his mind so unpredictably and inconveniently, however it had been established, had now snapped off. I had broken it myself. That was fine. But I had broken the man, too, and that was ghastly.

Ghastly; that was how he had seen me. A ghost-like figure, if you can be a ghost, coming from the future. Poor Thomas Newbolt. And poor Susan, and the kids, when they returned to find him dead. Though the other comrades in the settlement would have found and buried him by then.

The plan was that I would stay a fortnight at Jeannie's in Thetford, but in the event I was only there three days. It was odd how it happened.

I was sitting in an armchair in her living room one afternoon, beside the nicely convincing gas-fired coal-effect fire, when Emma swanned in. I had not seen my dear niece since Christmas. We'd spoken on the phone a couple of times, most notably when she had given me the contact for Alison James back in February. She saw me struggling to rise, one-armed.

"No, don't get up Uncle Joe," she said. She blew me an airy kiss, obviously mindful of my injury. "How's the convalescent?"

We had a little chat, mostly with me asking about her work, trying to avoid talking about how I'd set my house on fire.

There was an awkward moment when Emma said, "You know, Alison tells me you abandoned her in Scotland."

"Does she? We fell out, I'm afraid. A pity, because we had become good friends. It was my fault, I don't mind admitting. Though she had been a bit sneaky, putting this awful newshound onto me." I thought, Joe stop there, you will dig yourself in deeper if you carry on.

Luckily, Emma showed no inclination to pursue the topic, and a moment later Jeannie called her, to prepare the vegetables.

While Emma helped Jean, I laid the table one-handed. It was tricky, lining up the cutlery straight. As I went to and fro between kitchen and dining room, I heard snatches of Jeannie telling Emma about her plans for refurbishing my house. Emma and I caught each other's eye at one point, and had a quiet chuckle.

Norman entered on cue, as Jeannie decanted the plaice from its baking dish into a clean pottery server. The key clicking in the lock, the briefcase slung under the hall-stand, the peck on his wife's cheek, big hug for the daughter, and a manly shake of the hand for me. Norm, whom I'd always privately despised for his safeness, his mainstream banking job, his boring love of model boats, seemed admirable now; more admirable than me anyway. I pumped his hand, as though this was a fond farewell, and we were destined never to meet again. The handshake was a bad idea. It joggled my sore arm, and a sweat of pain broke out on my forehead.

When we sat down to eat, Jeannie offered to cut up my food for me. "Although," she said, "I did select plaice with you in mind Joe, for easy eating, you can't really ask for a softer fish, but the carrots may cause you trouble, Emma took them off a bit sooner than I would."

"Thanks all the same, I can manage. Lovely meal, Thetford's finest."

"No, Uncle Joe, that's Tom Paine," said Emma, with a twitch at the corners of her mouth, knowing I knew; there was a statue of Tom Paine in the middle of town, after all.

I decided to test her on Tom Paine, suspecting the younger generation might not have had his words drummed into them like we did. "Go on then, quote me some."

Emma laughed, shook her head, and looked at her mother.

Jeannie obliged. "My teacher used to make us recite: 'The world is my country; to do good is my religion.' But she didn't totally approve of him."

Norman, an incomer who had not grown up with the town's pride in its famous son, frowned. "Not bloody surprising. He was a revolutionary."

Long enough ago for it not to matter now I thought; the American Revolution. But "revolutionary" jolted a connection in my mind. Winstanley, the man Newbolt had thought about as a model, was he one? Gave off the same sort of feeling, wanting to change everything.

Usually, I would have agreed with Norman, but I found myself saying: "What's so bad about that? There was plenty that needed changing. Not only back then, either."

Norman started choking on a fishbone. Jeannie went into a flurry of backslapping, water-pouring, and trying to force dry bread down Norman's throat. I slipped out of the room and fetched a bottle of Soave that I'd put in the fridge. Jeannie had told me that it wasn't necessary, they didn't drink that often, but I thought it would provide a useful distraction at this point. For myself I brought through a bottle of Badger's bitter, also my purchase.

In a way I was right about the drink being a distraction. Jean took a thimbleful only, Emma a single glass, and Norman drank the rest. In his cups, he turned vituperative in a way I could not have believed if I hadn't witnessed it. He vituperated about the gypsies camping at the seaside, near Great Yarmouth, and when Jeannie spoke up on behalf of their ancestral rights to meander the land, he vituperated at her. It made me wonder about the times I'd rung up when Jeannie had not been her usual chatterbox self. When I stuck my oar in, muttering about people needing to keep their hair on, he turned on me.

"And you can keep your nose out of this, you bloody arsonist sponger."

I knew he was angry with me because of what I'd said about Tom Paine, but there was also an element of truth, which hit home.

There was one of those frozen moments like someone's put the video on hold. Jeannie's reproachful eyes fixed on Norman. Emma curled over, her head ducked down, as if looking for a bolt-hole under the table. Norman's hand thrust out towards me, the oratorical gesture; he'd forgotten he was still clutching his wineglass but miraculously not a drop spilled.

Every move felt fast in that dead moment. I pushed back my chair, placed my napkin on my plate, stood, drained the dregs of bitter from my jug, turned, and walked out of the room.

Ten minutes later, I walked down the drive, Jeannie on one side holding my good arm, Emma on the other, carrying my bag as far as the taxi. It seemed best to go, but I was worried, now I'd seen the other side of Norman. Of course they were used to him, and Jeannie said it was only when he was drunk, and only verbal.

"Still, verbal can be hurtful," I said. "I mean, for you—I'm not that bothered."

We had a gentle three-way hug at the gate. They had their issues to face, and I had mine.

Back home, I could not bear the filthy smell of burnt and water-soaked wood and carpet, so I camped in my shed, lying on a thin bed-roll with my sleeping-bag zipped up around me to keep the evil spirits at bay. Here, the wood smells were blessedly fresh. Each day, hampered by my left arm still being stiff, I worked on the house. The insurance people, called in by Jeannie, were dragging their feet, on the grounds that it had been careless of me to leave so many candles around. I rang them to say don't bother, it was an accident but I didn't want a protracted enquiry. I drew on my savings, and called in my old pal Martin Baxter to help with the bigger stuff, on condition we kept off personal matters in our inevitable chats.

Clearing away the burnt mess was the worst part. Every bit gave off a stench that clung to the insides of my nostrils. I slept poorly, with bad dreams, and the arm still sore. One night, I dreamed of demons driving me into hell. They used their long fingernails instead of pitchforks. Funnily enough, hell turned out to be not an inferno, but a dark garden, with tombs all around, great ugly catafalques. The paths of cold, sodden clinker were lined with dead plants: blackened stalks bearing a few damp brown leaves. The sky—for there was a sky in this hell—was charcoal-grey and sat low above my head. I wandered looking for somebody, hoping to find them around each corner, but fearing they were in fact in one of the tombs. I awoke to wonder if it were Newbolt I had been searching for.

After Martin and I had stripped out all of the burnt and singed and water-rotten rubbish, he replaced the essential timbers of the door-frame, the flooring on the landing, and one joist which was distinctly dodgy, being above the central inferno site. I asked Jack in, to replaster extensively, and when he'd done, I began to trust the house would become habitable again. I'd started on the downstairs redecoration while Martin did the major structural work upstairs. The downstairs rooms, like my bedroom, weren't burnt, but the smoke had penetrated everywhere, discoloured the paintwork and tainted the furnishings. I got carried away. Once I'd started chucking, I could not stop. I filled three skips in quick succession, first with debris, then fire-damaged goods, then furnishings, from curtains to sofa, and finally just about every damned article in the house. The sofa left the skips almost as soon as I put it in, and good luck to whoever took it. After the last skip had gone, I loaded the leftovers into my van and took them to the tip, as a break from decorating. Martin finished his share of the work and I paid him off.

The rhythm built: broken nights in my shed, days of laborious cleaning and painting. I began to feel this was my penance, yet I almost enjoyed the work, seeing the house grow new around me. I had almost completed the white emulsion in all the rooms when the notion came to me. It filtered through my consciousness with the clarity and definition of the early summer sunlight. There was a further penance I must make, for the wrongs I had done to Newbolt and to Alison.

After I'd wrapped my brush in a damp rag, I found a sheet of plain paper to write a covering letter, and packed up my most precious possession, which I realized was not mine after all.

Dear Alison,

I'll be lucky if you read this, I know. You probably feel like chucking anything from me straight into the bin.

This is to say sorry and explain about the trumpet. I'm more sorry than I can say, about walking out on you. I can see how that must have hurt you, considering we had been so close.

Fortunately it seems I am free of the waking dreams now. I have had none since the fire and a hunch tells me I'll have no more. It was because of those dreams I took the trumpet. I was obsessed about the lad Robbie, and thought it was a way to be in touch with him. Of course I should have told you what I was up to, but I was afraid you would try to stop me.

I gather from Emma you are back in your job. I suppose you have contact with the Scottish end who are dealing with the wreck. Even if this trumpet was not on The Blessing of

Burntisland it is part of that treasure in the sense it originally belonged to Nicholas Lanier, one of the king's chief musicians on that 1633 tour. There may be records, I don't know, your experts can sort all that out.

It's up to you how you present the trumpet but you know where and how it was found. If you don't mind telling them it was a dowser who found it, I'd prefer that, for it's the truth. But I realize it might be hard for you to explain you were there at the time and therefore can verify the location etc. Anyhow I should tell you a good friend of mine restored it for me, so I could play it (my idea being to contact Robbie that way; crazy wasn't I?) but then I squashed it again when I fell.

Yours truly,

Joe Fairlie

P. S. For what it's worth, I think Robbie put Newbolt's notes into a box and sealed them. I don't know why exactly, but he foresaw disaster. How he persuaded N. to co-operate I don't know. Nor why he was so keen the notes should survive. The box is on one of the horse skeletons in a compartment on deck.

The difficulty of striking the right note to Alison was as nothing compared with the difficulty of parting with Sophia. The only way was just to do it. When I returned from the post office I had to shut myself in my shed. The lack of that briefly familiar lump under my pillow made me fear I'd never sleep again, but that night I slept soundly and dreamlessly.

Painting the woodwork takes a whole lot longer than the walls, what with stripping, priming, and painting. Days and weeks went by. I had done top coats of gloss on the outside woodwork, and first coats on most of the inside, when a package arrived for me one Saturday morning. My name and address were typed on a label, not hand-written. Inside the large bubble-pack envelope was another package, this time wrapped in brown paper, with an envelope taped to it, addressed simply: "Joe". I recognized Alison's writing from the few times I had seen it, starting with upside-down when she took notes in our first interview. I tore open the envelope, to find a handwritten letter.

Dear Joe,

You will be surprised to hear from me so soon. Enclosed is a photocopy of the most unexpected find from The Blessing of Burntisland. (Well, the only find so far, though progress is expected soon.) Yes, papers! Unbelievably, to most of us, there was a package of papers, preserved inside a hermetically sealed casket. Guess where?

I had to fight tooth and nail to be allowed to make a copy. You must treat it as confidential till we go public on this one—you'll understand. I know I can trust you.

Don't get *too* excited; this is not a copy of the *original* (I certainly wouldn't have been allowed to handle that, it's very delicate) but of the rough transcription done by Dr Marcus Bond of St Andrews for the Scottish environment office who are handling things that end. Actually it's probably helpful to have this version, as the original is obviously in that funny old writing which is very hard to read. Though you might be better able to figure it out than most. They're still trying to work out who wrote it, but I think *we* know.

Also I should warn you it's not complete—he's only about halfway through so far but I thought you'd like to see what's been done.

Best wishes,

Alison

I had to read it twice before any of it sank in. One sentence seemed to fly off the page into my breastbone and almost crack me in two: "I know I can trust you." This letter was like balm.

"Hermetically sealed", Alison had written. It was a standard expression for double-glazed windows, and I guessed she was using it in that standard sense: tightly sealed, so nothing could get in or out. For wrecks, there was the precedent of the *Mary Rose*, now in Portsmouth, where they had opened jars of ointment untouched by seawater after some 500 years below the waves. Nobody had anticipated that there could be documents preserved down there in *The Blessing of Burntisland*. But I, of course, had practically seen the hermetic seal in the making.

I brewed myself a coffee, and took the package and the drink through to the front room where I perched on my tool-box. What were the originals like, of the Newbolt notes? I could imagine pages of vellum, cured calf-skin, supple and stippled with follicles where the hair had been stripped off the hide—but no, vellum was for fine manuscripts, books and the like. Newbolt never wrote on vellum, to my recollection. Nor true parchment, made from sheep or goat skin, next best to vellum. Paper then, "vegetable parchment", thick and creamy, yes I could recall that, how the ink used to stand on the surface a moment, gleaming till it dried and I—he—blotted it with rag or scattered sand. He'd a fine knack of shaving and splitting his quills so the ink ran thinly enough to last a line or so. Now, though, the paper would be dusty with age, the blacking pigments of the ink rusted to brown. My, that is, his crabbed writing would be hard to decipher; because paper was costly, he wrote very closely. I should be pleased I'd been presented with a typed transcription. Yet I'd love to see the original.

I tugged the notes out of the brown paper parcel. How many sheets? They were numbered; I glanced at the end: 32. Widely spaced, big type. I glanced at the first sheet.

> Wednesday the 23rd of March 1633. Stirling castle. As the* King has commanded me I am to keepe note of the courses of illnesse and alle thinges concerning the boy Robbie that now is intrusted to my care I shall commence by taking stock.

I stopped there, wondering what the star was for. Oh, a footnote, at the bottom of the page: "*Here and in most cases throughout, 'ye' in the original." Why had Dr Marcus Bond of St Andrews made this bow towards modern spelling? Perhaps they had asked him to do that because they were planning to release some of this to the media, and didn't want too much of a "Ye Olde Worlde" approach.

The last entry in this bunch was dated 3rd May. The wreck was July 1633. Robbie had been with the court a few months in all. Months of intense interaction, observation of the boy by Newbolt, himself under pressure from the rivalry of Dr Soames. I wondered again why he never seemed to think about Robbie later on. Had he any idea what had become of him, or did he not care, because his own life had become so fraught? Well, best begin at the beginning.

> The boye is circa 16 or 17 yrs aetat altho lookes younger being of slight stature. Has loste both mother and father nr where we found him on King's demesne in North Humber Land when he was shot for an hynde.

I stopped reading for a moment, rubbing my brow. It had been a stag they were hunting, I was sure. I recalled the tined antlers. Although I was not sure what a hind was, I thought it was a female deer. But as I'd read that phrase, "shot for an hynde", a plunking sound of plucked strings and a thin high voice had momentarily echoed in my head, and I knew that Newbolt had in mind a song about hunting "the hynde" while he wrote that bit. Slipshod of him, if I could recall his own experience more accurately than he did! It put me on guard. The fact this was a written record from the time didn't guarantee that it was totally correct.

But perhaps that is always the case. Writing, speaking, we all put a version of the truth out, our own version, even if we're not deliberately lying.

> I can understand his speeche well enough, having been much practised in difft. partes of the countrie through my travails, esp. yrs in Edinboro where the common folke have as broad an accent tho of difft. nature than Robbie's tongue, but moste of the courtiers deem him a savage that doth not comprehend English which is *their* ignorance not his. Halfe the troubles he had experienced w. Dr. Soames was due to gd Dr. refusing to listen or to comprehend the boye's utterances; besides wishing to dose him w. clysters, emetics & c.
>
> As I tolde the King, I have studded the Fallinge Sickenesse thro' that vol. of von H. and beleeve gentilnesse is all, holding the pt while fitting, administering little doses of mine own concoctions bye the bye. [These I durst not write even here. Eyes are everywhere.]
>
> Thurs. 31st Mar: The first time Robbie fell since I took over his care. A small time lying trembling on the ground, they called me to the kitchen but it was allmost over when I reached him. I told the girl next time to put his head on her lappe lest he hurt himself. All were stood back in a circle watching in fright, many crossing their selves. I said: nothing to fear, sweet churls, this is a gift he has, for with the fittes he oft fortells future happenings and more, he can reade dreams. He spoke nothing this time, but I was foolish, for now we are persewed everie hour by another servant asking for Robbie w. their silly dreames.

I read on, feeling a mixture of pride and estrangement. I could see that this was a rare and (in parts, for much was routine) fascinating insight into a seventeenth-century "case history", with glimpses of court life for good measure. And Dr Newbolt's approach, by his own estimation, was pretty much cutting-edge for his day. But this was my Dr Newbolt, whose head I had actually inhabited. Those waking dreams had given me so much more vivid an experience of his interactions with Robbie, through his own eyes, that the written record seemed distant and dusty by comparison. Also, much of it was new to me, and felt alien.

It was with a surge of joy that I came across a passage describing an incident I'd witnessed: the boy's interpretation of King Charles's dream about the young woman hiding the jar behind her back. Here it stood alone, whereas in my waking dream, Newbolt had recollected it, linking it with a judicial matter—aha, two pages on, there was the second incident:

> 10th Apr. Tho' not strictly a medical matter I muste record the ill effects on Robbie of being called, well paste tyme for his sleepe, to sing for the court as a noveltie while they feeste. And to-daye what is wurst, calling him to soothsaye about which wd. bee the best jugement of the King in a dispute between Lords Macnare and Naulty. I scarce dare to speake out yet I will warn Him, for the boye is pale now as new parchment and trembles and cannot sleepe tho' wearey in extremis. He may yet fall into a fit. I shall warn this usage does abuse the truste put in me, which however they wd not allow my presense at the hearing prob. knowing of my likelie objexion.
>
> To-morrow we must pack all up for our transporte to Perth.

Apparently in a sort of code, which Dr Bond had transcribed using symbols, Newbolt recorded his dosing of the boy: "Today 6Ψ of Mastick w. one halfe χ of olium lavendulum, rubbed on the browe." "Twelve χ gingiver infusion w. 3ε ℘ swallowed at intervals thro day." At first glance I imagined these might be hermetic symbols, but they were nothing like, after all.

By the time I had finished reading the typed manuscript, I'd encountered only three incidents I had actually witnessed or known about through Newbolt, and read more than I needed to know about compounds and herbal mixes. I was longing to see the next batch of notes. They would cover the Falkland period, the lead-up to *The Blessing of Burntisland*.

CHAPTER TWENTY

"Isn't that a cheroot, Helena?" I asked, as she lit up a brown-papered cigarette. She had readily agreed to come before the others, to the little reunion at Stepan's place. I thought her knowledge of the seventeenth century might help with my current problem. Stepan had been delighted to host us, but I didn't want to impose on him too much.

"It's okay, I asked Stepan if I could smoke," she replied, shifting slightly. I guessed the horsehair, which in places had escaped the confining cover, was prickling through her natural-coloured linen trousers. Her long woven coat was draped over one dining chair, I sat on the other. The faded Persian rug between us was strewn with paper.

In the kitchen area, Stepan, dressed in a frilled turquoise apron, was labouring over his stove, with his tape-player close at hand thrumming out melodious middle-European folk-dance tunes. The way he tapped his feet occasionally made the whole floor jounce. It felt strangely normal, to be here in his cosy flat with Helena, to discuss the second batch of notes.

Helena scrutinized the page in her hand, which contained the coded passage, from 15th June 1633.

"Try to find the bits that you recognize from your waking dreams, closest to this one," she suggested.

Alison had sent me the rest of Newbolt's notes six weeks after the first. She'd enclosed a note, wondering if I could help with an undecipherable passage, which had stumped not only Bond but also an expert on code. It had stumped me too, so far.

I leaned forward and cast around for the relevant pages. Handling paper in such quantity was foreign to me. As we'd swooped and dipped, sampling here and there, during the past half hour, I'd tried in vain to maintain the chronological order of the photocopied sheets. Presently I found what I was searching for.

"Here, I think that's the last one I remember before the coded passage. Look: 10th June; he writes about the boy being feverish. You remember that, from Irma's account? The doctor used herbs for the boy, when he had a fever."

"Did the boy recover?"

"I think so. But," I hesitated, unsure where this came from, "I think it recurred. He might have been sick again when they embarked on *The Blessing of Burntisland*."

"That was later on. July wasn't it? Do you have any memories between this coded one and when they left?"

"Yes," I said, rustling around till I located 29th June. "Here's the bit where he tells of the boy running out of the castle so he had to chase after to recover him. This one is unusual, because there's nothing about Robbie being ill, or any words he said. Newbolt seems to have slipped from strictly observational notes to recording his own vexation at their treatment by the Soames clique. You remember, the other doctor, and that priest Cawley, the one he called the crow, they wanted Newbolt done down, thought he'd been gaining too much of the king's favour."

Something struck me suddenly as odd, something I had not noticed in my intense porings over these papers since Alison sent them to me a month ago. I asked Helena to hand that last page back to me. She saw my brows knit, I suppose, and asked what was the matter.

"See, he doesn't mention—well, this must be the time that Robbie threw the, you know, the trumpet." I cleared my throat, and glanced surreptitiously aside to check if Stepan was listening. Why, I don't know. One of my mental vows was to give up deception and secrecy. In any case, he was absorbed in his cooking and the music likely drowned out our voices. Soon, I was going to have to come clean and tell Stepan that I no longer had Sophia. "Threw it into the loch, or pool."

No mention of the trumpet, no mention of …

"Eureka!" I sprang to my feet.

Helena, startled, jumped up too. We stared at one another, her blue eyes wide with reflected excitement.

"He's got it!" she called.

Stepan dropped his spatula in the pan and joined us in a brief dance around the cramped space between the chairs, our arms on each others' shoulders.

"Stop! Stop!" I yelled, realizing we were churning up the papers. "Where's the coded bit? Helena, you were holding it."

"Here, on my chair," she said, laughing and breathless. She smoothed a lock of hennaed hair behind her ear.

Stepan had to attend to the stove. Helena and I returned to our scrutiny of the papers. I was anxious to pin down the meaning before the inspiration slipped out of my aching head.

The entry on 15th June began in ordinary writing, with Newbolt's description of the boy subsiding in a fit out on the moor, before switching to code.

"You see," I said, stabbing the page with my middle finger, "no mention of the trumpet there either."

"So?" said Helena.

"But I saw it, both times. I am sure these are episodes I saw in my waking dreams. Here: 'The severest fitte he yet had,' I remember that very well. That's when Robbie crushed the trumpet."

"Why doesn't your doctor talk about it then?"

I spoke hesitantly, feeling the ground. "It was a very precious gift from the king's music master, Lanier. Newbolt was always afraid spies might read his notes. Anything he wrote about Robbie's fits and the medication, that was legit. I think he reckoned the trumpet was in a totally different category. Robbie's business. Damaging it, throwing it, might get the boy into big trouble. So he didn't record it."

"Except in the code bit? Is that your breakthrough?" Helena looked less than thrilled.

"No, no, that's not it. Quick, grab some paper—yes, anything, that envelope will do—write while I speak, before I forget."

The absence of the trumpet in Newbolt's notes had held up my recognition of the scene. But the later episode, when Robbie cast it in the loch, had reminded me of the earlier one, when he had crushed it during his severe fit out on the moor. And that was where he'd uttered phrases that sounded to Newbolt like an ominous prophecy.

I slowly recited the words I had heard Robbie gasp out, in extremis as he lay on the moor clutching, crushing, the trumpet to his chest, as I or Newbolt knelt beside him, powerless.

An hour later, the others arrived, Irma looking bonny as if she'd been outdoors a lot, Zemon even more the gypsy king. Stepan was serving up his goulash when the doorbell rang again. I clattered down the three flights of stairs to answer. I knew it was Alison and I wanted a moment alone to greet her.

She stood in the little entry, dressed in her camel jacket, which I remembered from Edinburgh. Her hair was longer, drawn back in a dark velvet ribbon.

"How are you?" was all I could think of to say.

"Hi Joe, nice to see you again. Quite a surprise to get this summons. I thought only Zemon and Irma were going to be invited. Lucky I could get away."

We had communicated about the Newbolt papers, and I knew that was why she was here, but I could not help thinking of other reasons. "You come in your car?" I peeped past her into the street, searching for the familiar Vauxhall, scene of our times together.

"No, I came by Tube. Nobody goes to work by car in London."

"Come on up, supper's ready," I said.

Alison tapped the table, calling us to order after the meal. Helena had insisted that she take charge of the discussion; but I could still sense the authority radiating out of the older woman.

Alison picked up the envelope. "Okay everybody, sitting comfortably?" This was a tall order, as Stepan had borrowed a bench from the Barqas, and brought up two piano stools, to accommodate the influx of guests. Still, we'd managed throughout supper and everyone was relaxed now, the table cleared, the dishes piled up beside the sink for attention later. "Here goes then, the translation of the coded bit which we haven't been able to crack before. You are the first in the world to hear this. Verbatim as Joe told it to Helena, a couple of hours ago:

> His kingdom shall—or was it shall not?—come on earth as in heaven.
> Where his mother lost, so shall he.
> What his grandmother lost, so shall he.

Is that it, Joe?" Alison turned the envelope over, as if expecting more on the other side.

I knew what she meant. The coded section of Newbolt's notes seemed longer than the wording I'd given. I suggested that Newbolt may have written his own gloss on the prophecy; all I was sure about was that he had intended to write down, verbatim, what the boy had said in his fit on the moor, as soon as possible.

Zemon leaned forward, his usually pale face flushed. "Never mind all that, your code expert can crack it now Joe's given you some of the text. The point is, what does it mean?"

Alison shrugged her shoulders. She had, after all, only just encountered the words.

Helena answered. "It starts as though it's the Lord's Prayer, but we think it's referring to King Charles. The bit about the kingdom."

Zemon glanced sharply at me. "Was it 'shall', or 'shall not', Joe, about the kingdom coming on earth as in heaven?"

The exact words came back to me. "I've just remembered: 'shall come *undone* on earth as in heaven'."

Alison fiddled around in her jacket pocket, took out a smart biro, and amended the note on the envelope.

"A prophecy for Charles's kingdom, the civil war," proposed Helena.

Zemon still had me under the spotlight. "Well, that would figure, the kingdom coming undone. But why 'as in heaven'?"

"You don't need to take it literally. He starts with a notion of the wording of the Lord's Prayer, and applies it to the earthly kingdom."

Helena intervened again. "Or he could mean, there's been civil war in heaven already, with the Reformation, the dissolution of the monasteries, all that Henry VIII stuff."

"I doubt Robbie was aware of that much history," I said. Then I realized that was irrelevant. "Of course, he didn't need to be, just as he didn't need to know what was going to happen. It just came to him, in his fits."

Zemon had another question. "Charles's father was James I of England, VI of Scotland, we all know that after our visit to Falkland Castle, even if we didn't before; so who was his mother?"

I was only aware of the answer because the original wreck searchers, Healey and McKee and crew, had harped on about the coincidence. Why hadn't I thought of this before? "Anne of Denmark.

And you know what happened to her dowry when she came over to marry James VI?"

"James I of England," Zemon repeated.

Alison also knew about the dowry, because I'd filled her in, that time we were driving up to Newcastle. Still, I was surprised she remembered.

"It sank, I remember now, Joe told me, it sank in the Firth of Forth." For that moment, she sounded, and looked, like an eager schoolgirl.

"Yes, and do you know what I just realized? That first find I made, map dowsing for the treasure, was almost certainly Anne of Denmark's boat."

"Another treasure in the firth? Phew!" Alison's eyes lit up and I could almost see, not dollar signs—she was never mercenary—but the glitter of a queen's jewels and the popping of press photographers' flash bulbs. Then her face fell and I guessed she was thinking about the awkward Scots squad and their likely claim to first rights on this, and on *The Blessing of Burntisland*.

Zemon had another agenda. "What about the nuclear sub—the drawing you saw?"

I made an effort to visualize the plans I had seen in Anderson's folder. "It's not ruled out. I strongly suspect it's down there. Close by, if not on top of, the earlier boat."

"The *Blessing*, d'you mean?" asked Zemon.

"No, the Anne of Denmark one." I saw it now; that third diagram had not been a cruder version of *The Blessing of Burntisland*, as I'd thought at the time, but another boat altogether.

"A remarkable coincidence, surely, a new wreck on top of an old one?" said Zemon.

"Yes and no. You would be surprised how much tonnage litters that mile or two of sea bed. Firth bed, I should say." For it was mixed river outlet and tidal inlet, which added to the treachery of the waters.

"A dangerous stretch."

"Evidently. Wrecks from every century. That's why the seekers called on me in the first place. They'd get so many responses from other kinds of searches, and they'd heard rumours that specialist dowsers can tune in to specific targets. Roddy Pearce in Anderson's department asked around—probably sent one of those emails—and the East Anglia boffins who knew about my activities came after me, and that was the first I heard of *The Blessing of Burntisland*."

Irma asked, "Will they try for this other one first, the Denmark one, do you think?"

"No. They may not go for it at all. *The Blessing of Burntisland* is in deep enough water, but the other one's deeper still. The logistics would be a nightmare. Then again, the technology is developing all the time. They might eventually be able to salvage the treasure, if not the boat."

"Come to that, they might do the same with *The Blessing of Burntisland*," said Alison. "In fact, we've started—with the box—which brings me back to this coded text." She looked around expectantly.

"You mean, about this grandmother?" said Irma, more on the ball than me.

"Anne of Denmark's mum? Never heard of her. Gertrude of Denmark?" said Zemon, making Alison laugh.

"James's mum. Mary the Queen of Scots!" announced Stepan, triumphantly. I'd let him in on this little angle before the others arrived, as a reward for his wonderful hospitality. "And she lost—'What his grandmother lost so shall he'—she lost her head."

We all nodded ours, happy they were still joined to our bodies. I don't know about anyone else, but my neck tingled. What if someone had predicted something like that to me? Newbolt had considered the prophecy important enough to record, in special code. The boy had sealed the notes in a waterproof, airtight, hermetically-sealed box as if to ensure that the message would survive whatever happened. And Newbolt had colluded, even though it hadn't been his own plan. I suddenly felt sure that he had attempted to pass on the prophecy to King Charles, verbally, after the barge had gone down, but the king would not hear him out. That time on the king's boat, the *Dreadnought*, the look in Charles's eyes. He knew, didn't he? He knew it was bad, bad luck, losing the *Blessing*.

Zemon stared at his fingernails, and then his knuckles. I noticed the backs of his hands were smooth and pale beneath a pattern of fine dark hairs that ran along the tendon lines like a strange leaf or feather. They were not hands accustomed to digging, or any sort of manual labour. I wondered about his contribution to the collective, building their alternative dwellings in the Preseli Hills, raising their food on common land in the style of the Diggers back in Newbolt's last days. Winstanley, Newbolt's hero, had written amazing tracts, as I knew because I'd been reading up on the Diggers. But Winstanley had also got his hands dirty, digging with the rest. Not much point calling yourself a Digger if you didn't dig, was there?

"Okay guys, this is mind-blowing stuff," murmured Zemon. His tone belied his words, as if he was testing out a new kind of chewing-gum, rather than acknowledging one of the most amazing archaeological finds of the century. "Of course, we still need to check it out—see if Joe's words fit what's written there in code, yes?" Alison nodded at this, and he continued, "It's great, don't get me wrong. But people will ask, did anybody at the time take these prophecies on board? I mean, did the king get to hear about them, did it affect his actions? And, if young Robbie is into major epoch-making type prophecies, how come he's not more famous, a Caledonian Nostradamus? The bit about heaven coming undone. Blakeian." His eyes wandered to the window as if he expected a flash of illumination there. "And what about the fucking nuclear sub?"

"Zemon," whispered Irma, stretching across to take his hand, half chiding and half calming him.

"Good questions," I began. "The code suggests it was a secret at the time."

Alison chipped in, "And but for your waking dreams, Joe, a secret forever."

"Maybe. But I think they did try to tell Charles, only he would not listen. In any case, the prophecy didn't tell him how to avoid those things happening, did it?"

"Unless it's in the rest of the coded bit," said Irma.

I considered this a moment. Yes, Robbie could have added something on the way back to the castle, though I imagined he had to be in a trance state to make the prophecies. "About where Robbie gets to, I don't know, it's been puzzling me too. My best guess is that Newbolt found a cure for Robbie's fits, so the lad lost his prophetic abilities. Robbie might have stayed behind when the cavalcade went south—mind you, he'd never have been a Caledonian anything, he was a Geordie, remember?"

"All right, a Geordie Nostradamus," said Zemon.

"That's as maybe. About the sub, you've got a point. I think the Navy is fossicking about, all worried the thing may leak, in both senses. I thought in Edinburgh it was a Russian number, *Perseus* a code name, but since then I've come round to thinking it's one of ours, a test model maybe, from way back whenever. We'd know if we'd lost one, or at least your lot could find out, those anti-nuke lot. You'll need to dig back a bit in the records—it could be from the eighties."

"Why has this prophecy popped up now?" prompted Zemon.

"Because Joe located the wreck, then went back and sensed the box was there," said Alison.

For Zemon, this was a disappointment, I could tell. He wanted to read something apocalyptic into the discovery. As for me, I was delighted, and I beamed at Alison.

Just then, Stepan's bell sounded again. He nodded at Alison and this time, to my surprise, she went to answer the door.

I was returning from the loo, at the exact moment Alison walked in with the new guest, so I actually managed to bump into him.

"Kevin, Joe, you've met," Alison remarked unnecessarily.

I stared. It was and wasn't the same bloke I'd encountered on the Edinburgh to London train. His dandruff was magically gone, his hair was cut differently, so it looked sleeker yet thicker, he wore a heavy terracotta linen shirt and cream silk tie with a well-cut jacket and those expensive black jeans that fit. The hand he held out to me, though still nicotine-stained and knobbly, looked perfectly clean and acceptable. I grasped it, wondering at this transformation. Talk about frogs, who had kissed this one? Above all, his face, what was so different? The glasses—no, they were as thick as ever. Just his expression, keenly alert and alive and, well, *happy*. I felt a bit queasy.

"Hi, Kevin. Hope you weren't expecting an impromptu press conference?"

"No, though I'm happy to have advance notice, and I'll be in the front row when you guys break the news. Meanwhile Alison can fill me in on the latest. Whatever that is."

The others had gone, and I was washing up while Stepan dried and put away. He ducked down near my knees, and wriggled one baking tray under another. I liked his neat way of stowing his crockery and pans, so they all fitted into the limited cupboard space.

"Y'know, Joe, they would take you at their commune like a shot."

"It's going to be mid-January when they move." I remembered Kirsty up above Eden Valley, telling us how half the pioneers had left after the first winter. "And I'd never fit into a commune."

Perhaps it was odd that I didn't question the basic premise: that I needed a new direction, maybe a new home. It was what I'd been thinking for a while, but I had not confided in anyone.

"Helena had another idea." He reached out for a dripping wet sieve that I had just balanced on top of everything else on the dishrack. He wiped at it abstractedly.

"Go on then," I prompted him.

"You know she been talking to Alison."

I stiffened. Why was Stepan taking so long to say what he wanted to say? "So?"

"Well, thing is, Alison told her about your woodwork."

"My woodwork?" This was so far from anything I would have expected, I was flummoxed.

"She seen your work at home. A chessboard. You never told me about that. She mentioned to Helena. So Helena asked me, you want to get some help with the strings."

"Strings?" I was definitely losing track.

"Well, you could just try for bit, no obligation. Warm here in the winter."

"Try what, Stepan? Drop the code can you, please, and talk plain."

"There's a course up at Newark, if you take to it you could do that, but what I'm saying is, how about a bit of apprenticeship, I can show you all I know about mending them, violins and such, purfling even, then if you want to learn to make them, that's what Helena thought."

The viola da gamba. If I could make one of those, ever. Like he saw his Susan. In my perplexity I seized on the word in Stepan's sudden outburst that made absolutely no sense.

"Purfling?"

"Oh that, you'll soon find out. Think about it, anyway."

"Thanks Stepan, I will. Any chance of a slivovitz before I hit the Tube?"

Alison forwarded the transcript of the decoded passage just a week after our brief encounter at Stepan's. Sure enough, there was the prophecy, almost exactly as I had recalled. Part of the extra wording was Newbolt's notes about the unearthly appearance of the boy as he came out of the fit and made the prophecy: "as if he saw another realm". There was also a note on something I had not witnessed: Robbie had spoken to Newbolt, as the doctor half-carried the boy back to the castle. Newbolt reckoned he was still partly in another world. He'd said as if to the doctor himself: "The man in the mirror will seal your fate."

I shoved the balls of my thumbs into my eye sockets.

The man in the mirror will seal your fate.
Why on earth hadn't Newbolt let me in on that one, in amongst all the tantalizing glimpses into his head? Then perhaps I wouldn't have tried that dangerous ceremony with Sophia. But of course he had no control over my visions, no knowledge of my existence. It wasn't his fault. But it wasn't my fault, surely, either? I could not see where I had gone wrong.

I had saved a few items from my great house clearance. Alone in my stripped-down house that evening, I sat by a small fire and gazed at photos of myself as a small child, flanked by Jeannie, Mum and Dad. He hadn't always been rough; he'd had different facets that showed more or less, according to what he was going through. He'd taught me a lot. But he'd become increasingly frustrated with himself, with his limitations. Confronted by what I'd unwittingly done to a man from the far past, I faced memories of my own life that I had been pushing into the background.

I'd visited a burial mound up on Rushford Heath with Dad, one of the times he took me out treasure dowsing with him. It was a no-show, and although the heath was littered with mounds, Dad grew sceptical they had anything in them. He swore black and blue, took me home, and wandered off on his own, not returning till midnight. He developed a theory of his own, way off anything the rest of our tribe or any acquaintances believed, and spent more and more time hanging around the Sturston marshes north of Thetford, especially where there were signs up saying "Danger Area". He'd wander by foot, spending whole weekends away from home, fishing rod in one hand and dowsing rod in the other. He would come back Sunday night, the dank smell of marshes on his boots and clothes, truculent with disappointment and drink. Now and again, there'd be a glaucous light in his eyes as if they'd bathed in too much moonlight, and I felt a shudder of the supernatural on him. Mum said with all the tramping around he did, he may as well quit us altogether and become a regular tramp. That scared me, as if the walls of our house had turned from bricks and mortar into palings with gaps between that the wind came whistling through. What he was looking for, I didn't know in those days, what with his greatest triumph having been near Ixworth, with the Cross, well away from those swampy fens.

Looking back now, I realized he wanted to make one find that would be all for himself, not at someone else's beck and call.

Of course, that week when he never came home, Mum did think he had walked out on us, taking up her suggestion to spite her. I would have just as soon left it at that, but Jeannie nagged at me and I set to work with map and pendulum and—well, I was able to guide the police to him. That terrible, terrible moment, which I had tried so hard to forget. Even after all this time, the memory of his bloated, pale blue face, streaked with stinking mud, as they pulled him out of the ditch, was like an accusation.

CHAPTER TWENTY ONE

It was Helena's knowledge of the Digger movement that led us to fit the final piece of the jigsaw into place. Alison and I received a letter of permission to delve into the Guildhall Library archive, where unpublished Digger writings were preserved among others. On an October morning, the two of us sat in the dusty semi-basement room. We were under the beady eye of the curator, Dr Seuter, a middle-aged man with a wart on his nose, who wore a three-piece suit of pale brown tartan tweed. In any case I had no desire for a personal chat; it was enough to know that Alison was "seeing" Dooley. The consolation, I tried telling myself, was that any woman who could fancy the reporter could not possibly have been right for me. It was not a very convincing argument.

There was a special quality to the air that hung between the stacks of boxes and old volumes. It was fragrant with particles of the past, and although it was unmoving, I sensed a silent thrum, a potential humming of a thousand voices. It also tickled my nose.

After repressing the urge for what felt like ages, as we leafed through one box of manuscripts after another, I had to give way and sneezed mightily.

"Bless you," said Alison. Dr Seuter glanced at us with reproach.

The cataloguing was not minutely detailed. An hour and several bouts of sneezing later, we located Newbolt's writings, in a box with half a dozen other authors' works, marked "Misc. Levellers/ Diggers/Ranters IV". Judging by the thickness of the dust, this box had not been opened for years, possibly decades. In a buff file marked in pencil on the cover "MSS. L&D/IV/06 and 07", lay two sheets of yellowed, ancient paper, covered in fine angular writing which I recognized with a piercing pang, as if it had been my own, and me long dead. We asked permission to take a copy, but Dr Seuter told us such documents could not be exposed to the trauma of the photocopier. We were allowed to write out a copy, provided we used pencils and did not touch the manuscript pages except using cotton gloves, which he provided.

"You may have trouble making out the script," he added. I guessed he was about to offer a copying service at great expense and time.

"It's fine, I can read it, no problem," I assured him. His surprise was as obvious as his doubt.

Alison took on the role of pencil-sharpener and rubber-holder, while I laboriously copied out the first page in the file, which had a cover page of modern paper labelled: "06: Section of Digger tract?".

> This Cataclysm that has befallen our poor countrie, it is none of my doing; and if I along with many a soldier brother had my will, in years before, then we woulde have found another friendlyer waye, that avoyded the raising up of swords & letting of so much bloode (far more of it ye bloode of common men than of kinges). Yet it haveing come about, as it has, let us look to what of good we may garner from this bloode-bespatterd crop. Indeed we see times are such as never came before, and what was never thought may now be spoke; that the distinction between Master and Man is but of title, and if we allow *all* to be en-titled, all may eate together. And, saith Susan, what of Woman too, shall Man be Master still over her, Womb-man, who beareth all of our children the greatest Treasure of our now and future time?

I remembered as if through a haze, Thomas Newbolt pausing in his writing, wondering if "Cataclysm" was too difficult a word for his audience, and asking himself why he had slipped into rather biblical language near the end. It was not the end, of course. There would have been much more to come, had I not confronted the poor man with my ghastly image at his window, holding Robbie's trumpet.

There was only one other sheet in with the page of draft tract. A note laid on top said: "07: In hand of author of MS. L&D/IV/06; found together in family Bible of Veronica Smallclift, don. 13 Sept 1963." I set out to copy this sheet dispassionately, but by the end I was shaking.

> Dearest Susan, Since I wished you Godspeed I have devised my pamphlet and shall embark straitway after this on my writing of it. Wd. I were free to stand in the streets of London and witness the procession of you and yr. sisters, many hundreds who knows many moore? Wd. too, that Parlement will listen to yr call for ye voice of such to be heard. With yr efforts and the brethren, mine being one small contribution, we shall stir up such numbers of the people, Parlt. must and shall heare us all for our combyned voice shall be loud and clarion.
>
> As I mention clarion I bethink: do you remember my sweete, you asked what became of that boye Robbie who onlie besides me survived the dredfull sinking of ye Kinge's barge, whych latelie has haunted mee? Why think of him and clarion calls, you aske, and I replie: he once had a trumpet, delighting in its voice, tho' he cd not make as good or great a sound as he wd wish. Well here it is: after that disaster, he took afresh the fever, and tho' I nursed him in my arms, he dyed within two dayes. When ye King summoned me into his presense and was most distraut, with ye loss of his Treasure and the Boye perilously ill, I cd not well distinguish which smote him moste. But I beleeve he was less puffed up and suffered more, than on the Scaffold.
>
> Perhaps I shd have imparted Robbie's prophesie to him, then when he was tender, but I feared not to be beleeved and besides, was so distraut myself. It wd not have made a difference, wd it? Tell me so my Sweete, for my conscense troubleth me still a little, tho' I do not think one Man (be he King or doctor or humble Author) can effect that great a change in the course of all our affairs. Tho' Woman perhaps may. Yr loving and admiring, Thos.

A further note occupied the narrow margin. I had to don a glove, to turn the page around.

> I shd lyke you to compose a song about ye magical boye and his trumpet and his prophesy. Saye if we had onlie harkened to

him, ye Kinge might have his head stille tho not be Kinge, and alle be well. Ye boye standing for ye People.

Two months later, I left my new abode at Stepan's place early in the morning, dressed in my closest approximation to a smart suit, with an overcoat and scarf against the frost. Facing a press conference would be my biggest challenge yet, a lot harder than boiling rabbit skin to make glue for Stepan's violins and violas, or preparing the thin strip of ebony for the purfle, the beading around the edge. I ducked my chin into my collar. Helena's powers of persuasion, rather than Alison's curt summons, propelled my feet along the frigid pavements.

The Institute of Historical Research was harder to find than the Ritz or wherever they usually hold these things, being tucked away in a bottom layer of the vertical, rectilinear cake that is Senate House, the nerve centre of London University.

"Perfectly Stalinist building, isn't it?" I heard a thin young woman with pale, cropped hair and black-rimmed glasses saying out of the corner of her mouth to a drooping, heavily-mustachioed sack of a man. He snorted, and ran his fingers across his scalp to replace his disarranged quiff. My guess was that these hacks didn't so much object to the aesthetics, as to the violent wind which permanently rages at the base of Senate House, where three square archways pierce right through the monstrous white slab.

The Early Modern Room of the Institute was neutral ground chosen to suit the clashing demands of the Department of the Environment, Scottish Office, the wreck crew, Naval Archaeology and the historical researchers themselves. The press, initially, were most interested in the trumpet. They flocked around the glass case, where it was on temporary exhibition, cursing at the reflective qualities of the glass. A bouncer from Alison's department had to keep pushing back over-eager young men laden with phallic cameras, who seemed keen to prise the showcase open. Stepan, hovering in the background, was flapping like a frantic mother duck whose brood is being gobbled by foxes.

From my place on the dais, I looked forlornly over their shoulders as Alison and Farquhar from the Scottish Office filed in. The trumpet had been re-restored to its original shape, and the traces of fire-damage from my brush with death burnished off. It felt wrong, as if the squashed mouth was its preferred mode from so long in that state.

Farquhar rambled on about depth soundings, side-sonar images, display facilities in the Edinburgh National Museum. Scribes scribbled, questions were posed: muted, respectful. I was probably the most agitated listener, but even I had grown used to the notion that the silver plate and other treasures were to be salvaged from *The Blessing of Burntisland*—a long time in the future, when funds became available. Along with Irma, I was glad the bones—and the ship herself—were to be left below.

Now Alison was speaking, and an electric thrill ran around the room as she revealed that one item had already been raised and they were about to see it. (Though many, I think, were confused, having assumed the trumpet had been reclaimed from the wreck. The press release told otherwise but they tend not to read those till later.) The hacks craned forward, some forgetting to write for a moment; the be-corduroyed and be-tweeded academics, who were in the know, smirked with more than scholarly pleasure. We all, myself included, gasped when Alison opened her attaché case and lifted out the heavy box. The audience started to stand, those behind surging forward to see, pushing chairs aside; the ushers strained to keep them back. Alison looked uncertain, pale. I saw Kevin Dooley in the front row spreading his arms wide to try and curb those around him.

"Sit down!" I yelled, jumping to my feet. I slammed my open hand on the table, repeating the command, glowering at them all. As they faltered, and some obeyed, I sat down; all now followed my example. I can look fierce, with my beard and beetling brows, when I'm roused.

I knew where I'd gone wrong. It was in a bedroom of the Stag and Hounds in Falkland, when I chose the trumpet over Alison. I had betrayed the woman I'd come to be fond of—to love, even, given a chance—in favour of a chimera. An obsession. I had been supported and rescued by friends—Stepan, Zemon and Irma, Helena—and family. Dear Jeannie, dear Emma. All here, somewhere at the back. The whole while I'd been subject to those waking dreams, I had fought them, resented Thomas Newbolt, failed to realize what a fantastic insight they gave me into his time. Only when I shocked the man to death did I appreciate the contact—because I lost it. My dream of direct communion with Robbie was shattered. You cannot choose your companions from the past.

So, there was the second star, after the trumpet: the sealed box, now no longer sealed of course. Alison was explaining that the whole bunch of notes had already been transcribed into legible form, and a short summary, together with a gloss about the context, would be made available to any journalist who was interested. The actual papers, too fragile to display, were housed in a climate-controlled archive in the British Museum.

"But it's Mr Fairlie here who made the most spectacular breakthrough," she went on, telling them about the passage in code which had defied expert attempts at decipherment. She moved the microphone over so I could take my turn.

"I'm Joe Fairlie and I'm a dowser," I began. "Most of you know about dowsing for water, I expect, even if you don't believe in it. Well, I dowse for treasure instead. Loads of dowsers look for underground things, old ruins and the like, or telephone cables when BT have mislaid them." There was feeble laugh from a few. "This time, they called me in to dowse for this *Blessing of Burntisland*, which was deep under water. Didn't bother me, as I use a map for starters, then go out over the area and pinpoint it. Some might be sceptical but it turns out I was right."

Alison was beginning to twitch, pointing to the box; Joe get on with the translation business, was what she meant. I nodded, and pressed on.

"I had this feeling there was something bad down there, turns out I was right about that too. Before I found this one, I'd had vibes about another site in the firth, where there's another treasure boat sunk."

At that, a shout arose from the back. "The nuclear sub!" Heads turned towards the mop of black curls.

"I'm coming to that, Zemon. Yes, there's an earlier wreck, Anne of Denmark's boat. That's Charles I's mother; seems these royals were unlucky with their treasures in those waters. There is also a nuclear-powered sub, I think an early prototype, possibly leaking radioactive material, in about the same spot as the earlier boat. So I'd be awfully careful, Mr Farquhar, how you go about salvaging that one." Zemon's tousled topknot subsided; he was leaning sideways to whisper to Irma.

"Really, Joe," Alison began, but I raised my palm.

"Sorry for that digression. Now, as a dowser, I have—or had—other intuitive skills, so they brought these doctor's notes to me, and in a trance state I was able to visualize him writing them, and basically they were a prophecy from the magical boy Robbie, who was the subject of the notes."

They were all writing like mad, on notebooks and electronic pads, leaning forward to catch what I'd say next.

I recited the prophecy: *"His kingdom come undone on earth as it is in heaven. And where his mother lost, so shall he. And what his grandmother lost, so shall he."*

I told them what it meant, in terms of Charles I losing his treasure barge in the firth, as happened, and his head, as also happened, though a good few years later. Plus the "kingdom undone", the Civil War.

"Do you believe in these prophecies, Mr Fairlie?" asked the crop-haired woman.

"Believe? You tell me. Some people have an ability to see things no one else can see. Maybe it's a gift, maybe it's a curse. A prediction like that, it's pretty specific. Doesn't mean you can do a damn thing about it, mind you."

There were other hands up, a voice asked a question but I didn't hear. I was looking around the hall, seeing old and new friends and my sister and niece among the crowd. And I thought about the other prophecy. Not as it applied to Thomas Newbolt, not as a dire warning. The person in the mirror, that's me, or you.

ABOUT THE AUTHOR

Jenny Stanton grew up in Leicester, Portsmouth, and Birmingham. As a student at the School of Oriental and African Studies, she visited Ghana, and travelled to Timbuctu. She taught in Cape Town, London, and Oxford, then worked in the history of medicine at Oxford and the London School of Hygiene and Tropical Medicine, publishing academic articles and books. She moved on to writing fiction and poetry in 2001. Jenny Stanton lives in Oxford.